PERSISTENCE OF MEMORY

WINONA KENT

DIVERSIONBOOKS

Also by Winona Kent

In Loving Memory
Cold Play
Skywatcher
The Cilla Rose Affair

Diversion Books
A Division of Diversion Publishing Corp.
443 Park Avenue South, Suite 1008
New York, New York 10016
www.DiversionBooks.com

For more information, email info@diversionbooks.com

Second Diversion Books edition June 2016.
Print ISBN: 978-1-68230-043-5
eBook ISBN: 978-1-62681-885-9

CHAPTER 1

Charlotte Duran Lowe wheeled her bicycle out of the bright blue front door of her cottage and down the path of her untidy garden, to the cobbled street beyond.

The village of Stoneford, on England's southern coast, was as much as the passing centuries had organized it: a jumble of cottages gathered around a handful of cobbled lanes, leaded windows and front gardens filled with rockery and wildflowers. Some of the little houses still boasted thatched roofs. Others had surrendered to the necessity of waterproof tiles. But all retained their memories of the past, and if a restoration needed to be undertaken, the work required utmost care, inside and out.

Charlie's route to work took her along the village's main thoroughfare, past the storybook houses, and past The Dog's Watch, a venerable coaching inn that, centuries before, had serviced carriages, horses, drivers and passengers. Past St. Eligius Church, with its clock-faced steeple and tumblestoned graveyard. Past a row of shops: newsagent, bakery, hardware, Indian takeaway, greengrocer and chemist. And past the Village Green, with its massive 300-year-old oak shading early morning walkers from the misty seacoast sun.

She paused to study the tree from the road. Some of its branches were bare. Others still bravely held onto their greenery. But there was a fresh carpet of brown leaves scattered onto the grass below.

The Village Oak was the symbol of the village, the mainstay of the green. The Village Oak was Stoneford.

The Village Oak, Charlie thought sadly, was dying.

And Stoneford itself was under a threat of its own. Redevelopment loomed, spurred on by a consortium led by two brothers, Ron and Reg Ferryman. Though they'd grown up in the village, they seemed to have no sense of the past, and they certainly had no feelings for a historically sensitive future.

The Village Green was on its way to being turned into luxury flats with million-pound views of the sea. And nearby Poorhouse Lane was destined to become a driveway leading to 25 luxury homes with an underground car park. These events were not unconnected, in anybody's minds.

Charlie cycled on, unsettled and unhappy.

Stoneford Village Museum was housed in the building that had once been the St. Eligius vicarage. It was here that Charlie spent her days, immersed in her role as a Historical Guide and Interpreter, dressed in a Regency-era frock that would not have been out of place in a Jane Austen novel.

This morning she was explaining the museum's latest display to a group of seniors from a posh assisted living home in Bournemouth, just along the coast to the west.

The Travellers Room was housed in what had once been the front room of the vicarage, and it told the story of the Gypsies who'd once populated the nearby New Forest.

Charlie led the group to her favorite exhibit, a beautifully decorated and restored vardo painted in brilliant red and sunny yellow, sky blue and polished gold.

"How many of you know how the term 'Gypsy' came into existence?" she asked.

"Stevie Nicks, 1981," a dapper gentleman at the back piped up. "From the album, *Mirage*."

"Nigel!" admonished his wife, a little thing who looked as though she'd been embarrassed by her husband for most of her married life.

"Number 12 on the *Billboard Hot 100*," Nigel added.

"I'm terribly sorry," Mrs. Nigel said to Charlie. "He used to be on the radio."

"Not to worry," Charlie smiled. "It was the second single released from that album, wasn't it, and the second biggest hit after *Hold Me*."

"A woman who knows her music!" Nigel exclaimed, obviously delighted.

"My husband was the musician," Charlie said. "Knowledge acquired by default."

She led the little gathering around to the side of the vardo, where there was a mockup of an encampment, with a tent, the makings of a fire, and a collection of well-used cooking pots.

"The term 'Gypsy' comes from the word 'Egyptian'," Charlie continued, "as people once believed this was where Gypsies, or Romani people, originated. In fact, evidence suggests the Romani came from central India, landing in Europe around the 14th century."

"It's a lovely caravan," Mrs. Nigel ventured. "Is that what they lived in?"

"Yes and no," Charlie replied. "Yes…but only after about 1850. Before that, the Travellers walked on foot, and carts were used to carry their possessions. They slept outdoors in canvas tents, like this one, slung over bent hazel twigs."

"This is interesting," Nigel said, picking up a deck of Tarot cards lying on top of an upended pot.

"Yes," Charlie replied. "The Gypsies were well known for telling fortunes, usually for the benefit of the villagers at fetes and fairs. Among themselves, they tended to be less flamboyant. This deck is very old, but incomplete. It's missing The Fool."

"I imagine if you had The Fool, it would be worth a few quid," Nigel guessed.

"So we've been told," Charlie said. "But, not much chance of finding it, I'm afraid. It seems to have been misplaced in time…"

Charlie had discovered the deck of cards in Edwin Watts' antique shop. They'd been sitting on a table, wrapped in an old scarf, beside a very rusty knife and a dangerous-looking sword. The knife and the sword were of no interest to Charlie—and Mr. Watts wanted far too much for them, in any case. But the cards were going for a song, and had intrigued her. There were painted figures in period clothing, wearing robes of gold and silver and blue. Some of the figures had armor and crowns, while others held staffs and chalices and swords.

And so she'd bought the cards herself, and loaned them to the museum, with the proviso that if the deck ever turned out to be worth anything, she was going to have them back.

"Now if you'd like to come around here," Charlie continued, "Noah Roberts, our resident expert on Travellers—and a descendant of one of the New Forest Gypsy families—will give you a little talk about Romani ways."

Charlie left the pensioners in Noah Roberts' capable hands and went back to her office. The room had been created out of the vicarage's kitchen, and her desk was an ancient table salvaged from the vicar's dining room. She sat down. Next task: working out a budget for her proposed pet project, a village sightseeing tour.

At the back of the vicarage, in a ramshackle shed that had survived both World Wars, but not the ravages of sea air upon old wood, there was a very old wagon in dire need of restoration. One day soon, when the money could be found, Charlie was going to have the wagon repaired. And, with the help of Horace Inkersby, a local farmer who kept heavy horses, she was going to launch a sightseeing service that would take visitors around the historical sites of the village.

This was assuming there would be anything historical left in Stoneford to show off to anyone, if the Ferryman brothers got their way.

Some hours later, Charlie left for a walk. She did this every day, from one o'clock until two, combining her lunch break with an opportunity to stretch her legs, and a well-earned opportunity to think.

Charlie had lived in Stoneford all of her life. She knew its shaded lanes and its secret passages, its rolling, grassy fields and its wildflower meadows off by heart. She knew the village as well as she knew its history.

Plugging ear buds into her mobile and switching over to music, she let herself out through the wooden gate at the back of the Old Vicarage, and walked the short distance to the churchyard adjoining St. Eligius. She turned left onto a path that meandered between a collection of cottages, and emerged at the base of a rise that was just high enough to call itself a hill.

At the top of the hill, overlooking the village, sat a stately home which had seen finer days, but which still retained its classical dignity, in spite of its conversion to a three-star Bed and Breakfast.

There were historical documents in the Parish Council Office that identified the manor on the hill as having once belonged to Charlie's ancestral great grandfather, Louis Augustus Duran. There were also documents tracing the history of her cottage, which she'd inherited from her father, and he'd inherited from his father, all the way back to her ancestral great grandmother, Sarah Elizabeth Foster.

There was a marriage notice in the St. Eligius Church archives, confirming that on Saturday, the 30th of July, 1825, Sarah Elizabeth Foster had married Louis Augustus Duran.

But two years later, they'd sold the manor, for what was then a fairly substantial sum of money, to the family whose descendants had eventually turned it into the Bed and Breakfast.

Indeed, Sarah and Louis appeared never to have lived there as man and wife at all, and for some unfathomable reason, had chosen to begin their domestic life together in the little cottage at the bottom of the hill.

Charlie walked along the footpath at the base of Manor Rise, casting a glance up at what was now a graveled courtyard where the Bed and Breakfasters could leave their cars overnight. And that was only one of the enduring mysteries of her family's past.

The greatest mysteries of all were Louis Augustus Duran and Sarah Elizabeth Foster themselves. So far, in two years of spare-time searching, Charlie had been unable to come up with any kind of information at all about them, prior to their marriage.

The St. Eligius Parish records were extremely helpful when it came to descendants. The dusty volumes had given up details of christenings, marriages and burials of everyone who'd come after

9

Sarah's union with Louis.

But prior information about Sarah was another matter. Charlie suspected that Stoneford was not her birthplace, and that she'd arrived in the village at some point before 1825, from parts unknown.

Charlie had subscribed to an online ancestry site which was proving to be useful, but only in dribs and drabs, as information was only slowly being discovered and made searchable.

And since official records had only begun to be kept in 1837, they were of no use at all in trying to locate Sarah Foster's forebears, or even her date and place of birth.

But if Sarah's beginnings were difficult to pin down, her husband was even more of a puzzle.

Charlie turned off the footpath and trudged down the hill, doubling back to the main road that skirted the western edge of the Village Green. Here, there was a tiny bakery run by Clive and Rosa Parker that did a roaring trade over the summer, making up sandwiches and picnic baskets for visitors who planned on spending the day at the beach.

Charlie popped her head in through the open door—which was the signal for Rosa to create her special daily baguette. And while her lunch was in the process of being made, Charlie went into the newsagent's on the corner and bought a chilled fizzy water in an expensive bottle, and then a potted geranium from the hardware store.

Paddy McDonald was on the pavement outside his grocery, polishing apples.

"You seeing Emmy Cooper today?" he asked, spotting Charlie.

"After work," she said.

Paddy handed over an old-fashioned change purse, made of scuffled leather, with a well-worn kiss lock. "Left it in the lettuce," he provided.

Charlie checked inside. Two pounds, a few pence in coins, and an elastic band. "Thanks, Paddy. I'll make sure she has it back."

Baguette, bottled water, change purse and plant in hand, Charlie carried on to the last stop of her daily walk, the graveyard attached to St. Eligius Church.

The oldest part of the cemetery, in common with the churchyards of all of England's towns and villages, contained a collection of weathered tombstones in various stages of mossy topple and collapse. Sarah and Louis Augustus Duran were interred there, as were their children, Augustus and Emily, and their respective spouses. A few of their children were also there, but the rest had been caught up in the frenzy of relocation to cities during the urbanization of Queen Victoria's rule.

Charlie's great-grandparents were buried in a newer section of the graveyard, on the shady side of the church, where the polished granite markers had been civilized into orderly rows.

Charlie's husband was buried there, too.

Sitting on the damp grass beside Jeff Lowe's headstone, she removed a pink geranium that was outgrowing its little pot, and replaced it with the red one she had just bought. The back garden of her cottage was planted with many of these substitutions, a blazing riot of pungent color, celebrating Jeff's life as much as declaring his death in a traffic accident, five years earlier.

"Today," she said, unwrapping her baguette and screwing the lid off her fizzy water, "I was complimented on my knowledge of music. I blamed it all on you."

It was not as if Jeff ever replied, but she could easily imagine his half of the conversation. It was an eccentricity she maintained, unashamedly, the same way her grandmother had kept her grandfather's suits in a wardrobe in their bedroom, long after he'd died of cancer.

The interesting thing about sharing a village with a lot of one's ancestors was the prevalence of present-tense relations.

Most of the members of Charlie's family now lived elsewhere—including her parents, who had some years earlier retired to Portugal, and a sister and a brother who had long ago relocated to London. But there was still a smattering of uncles, aunts and cousins within the vicinity, and one of them was coming to see her now, limping through the churchyard with his cane, his bright Hawaiian shirt a brilliant splash against the shady grey stone walls of the church.

"Nick!" Charlie called, waving.

Nick Weller joined her, sitting on the grass. "How are you?"

"I'm all right. Chatting to Jeff. It's been five years."

Nick contemplated Jeff's date of death. Five years to the day. He didn't need reminding.

"How's you?"

"I'm good. Been playing with sprites and tachyons."

Nick lectured at a university in London for most of the year, but spent his summers in Stoneford. He had a wife and children somewhere—Charlie had met them. But they seemed not to like the English countryside much, and were always staying at their villa in Spain, or on their way to New York for shopping, whenever anyone asked after them.

"Sprites and tachyons," Charlie mused. "Go on then, give me a few more clues."

Nick showed her his mobile. On the little screen was a photo of something resembling a fountain of red particles, streaming up into a black sky from the top of an immense thundercloud.

"A sprite," he announced, with obscure delight. "A massive electrical discharge that occurs during thunderstorms. It only lasts a nanosecond. And it's exceedingly rare."

Fiona, Nick's wife, would not have been impressed. But Charlie was amused by her cousin's obsession with electrical discharges and subatomic particles.

Nick changed the picture.

"And that's an outer space sprite, shooting up from earth. They took that fantastic shot from the Space Station."

Charlie peered at the little screen.

"Where's the tachyon?"

"It's hypothetical. You can't see it. We don't even know whether it exists."

"If it did exist, what would it do?"

Nick put on the face and the voice he reserved for his first year physics students.

"Simply put, when matter approaches the speed of light, time slows down. As it reaches the speed of light, time stands still. Below the speed of light, we travel in space. Above the speed of light, we travel in time. Tachyons are particles that allow us to accomplish this."

Charlie turned Nick's mobile towards Jeff's gravestone.

"Look, Jeff—Nick's writing the next *Doctor Who.*"

Nick regained control of his phone.

"Under the right conditions, a tachyon event and a sprite event could combine to create an energy field that would be extremely conducive for time travel."

"Wouldn't that be interesting," Charlie said. "What are the 'right conditions'?"

Nick shrugged. "The most accepted theory seems to be a massive electrical discharge."

"Wouldn't it be fantastic if we could go back, Nick. Visit our ancestors…solve all those little niggling mysteries…"

"You want to be careful with that thought," her cousin said. "What would happen if you changed something—and ended up not being born, for instance."

"Then I wouldn't be around to worry about it, would I?" Charlie answered, cleverly. "Perhaps I'd end up being you."

"Now you're really frightening me," Nick said.

"There's that theory that you carry, in your genes, memories passed down from your ancestors. Your DNA remembers. Jeff used to joke that he'd descended from the same line as Hank Marvin. There's a Rankin somewhere in his ancestry. He couldn't explain his obsession with The Shadows any other way. A bit unlikely though, as I think all Hank Marvin's people came from up north. Newcastle."

"Rankin?" Nick inquired.

"Yes, it was Hank Marvin's name before he changed it. Brian Rankin."

Charlie remembered why she'd asked Nick to meet her.

"I'm still having problems with my family tree program," she said. "Can you fix it?"

As well as being a whiz at quantum physics, Nick was also Charlie's computer guru.

"I think it must have some kind of virus," she said. "It won't save anything properly. And it keeps linking up all the wrong people."

"I'll download a new release," Nick said. "I'll pop in after dinner and do a clean install. And I'll check for viruses. That should solve it."

"I thank you. Our ancestors thank you."

Nick got to his feet, slowly, using his cane for leverage.

Charlie picked a dead leaf off the new geranium plant, and leaned her head against Jeff's grave marker as Nick limped away.

"There you are, love," she said, wistfully. "Sprites and tachyons. That's all that's needed to turn back the hands of time."

CHAPTER 2

At the end of the afternoon, after work, Charlie rode her bike towards the old wooden bench at the top end of the Village Green. There was old Emmy Cooper, in her usual spot beside the stone birdbath, feeding the pigeons crumbs from a brown paper bag.

"Hello," she said, leaning her bike against the back of the bench. "Pigeons all right today?"

"That one's got the mange," Emmy said, pointing to a rather threadbare individual pecking at a bit of crust.

Charlie joined her on the long wooden seat.

"Toast from your breakfast?" she asked, conversationally.

Emmy lived alone in Poorhouse Lane, renting a tiny flat in one of the listed buildings the Ferryman brothers owned. She was 89 years old and her memory was not what it once had been.

"Yesterday's," Emmy said. "It was boiled eggs this morning."

Because she deliberately kept to herself, it was really only Charlie who ever bothered to stop and say hello, to sit with her for a few minutes, ask how things were and whether or not she was eating properly.

"And you remembered to switch off the stove, didn't you?"

Emmy stopped to think.

"Yes. Because I was tidying my cupboards and I put Kenneth's picture on the counter. I remember switching it off."

Emmy had loved a flier who was shot down in World War Two, and had never, because of this, married. She did not, as far as anyone knew, have any living relatives anywhere in all of the United Kingdom.

Charlie took the change purse out of her bag, and gave it to Emmy.

"Mr. McDonald said you left this in the lettuce."

"Dear me," Emmy replied. "What will it be next?"

Last week it was her keys on the counter in the fish shop. Emmy muddled the hours of the day, and the days of the week. And forgot to wash. And change her clothes.

"I've been in touch with the Parish Council again," Charlie said, carefully. She needed to tiptoe up to this conversation.

But Emmy knew what was coming.

"Not interested. I can manage on my own. Thank you."

"You can't, though. Not really."

Only Charlie could say that to her without having her head bitten off. Emmy had no money, and she'd had an increase in her rent which she obviously couldn't afford. She was going to be evicted by the Ferryman Brothers. She knew what Charlie was telling her was true. The Parish Council desperately needed to be involved.

"I've written down a telephone number, and a name. She's lovely, this lady. Josie Griggs. So helpful."

"Griggs," Emmy sniffed. "Gypsy name. Wouldn't trust her."

Charlie studied the plaque on the stand beneath the birdbath, memorializing Mrs. Tamworth, an early women's rights campaigner. At the age of 35 she'd donned a pair of her husband's knickerbockers and turned cartwheels on the green, observed by all of her children and most of the villagers.

Even Mrs. Tamworth wouldn't have had the patience required to deal with Emmy Cooper.

Back to the drawing board. She'd find another counselor who didn't have a last name Emmy would consider suspicious.

It was, she thought, as she cycled on to the middle of the grassy triangle, where some members of the Committee to Save the Village Green and Poorhouse Lane were unfurling a large banner, almost ironic. At the beginning of the 19th century, the Village Poorhouse had looked after its inhabitants. There had been a matron to ensure everyone had proper clothing and regular meals. And the children had been apprenticed to local tradespeople, so that later in life, they would be able to earn a decent and honest living.

Until 1834, anyway, when the Poor Law changed and the poorhouses became workhouses and poverty was seen as a dishonorable state, requiring corrective servitude.

Ron and Reg Ferryman, Charlie thought, would have made excellent workhouse guardians.

She stopped her bike at the large banner, which was now unfurled and fastened to the low stone wall that ran the length of the west side of the green, facing the road.

SAVE STONEFORD VILLAGE GREEN AND POORHOUSE LANE FROM UNSCRUPULOUS DEVELOPERS, it proclaimed, in large red hand-painted letters.

The issue was not the Georgian houses that lined the tiny cobbled lane, eight on one side, six on the other, all constructed in the 1790's, all Grade II listed. They were untouchable. The issue was Poorhouse Lane itself, a mere eight feet wide and 100 feet long, and the only way in to the vacant plot of land slated for development. It was the Ferryman brothers' intention to turn the road into a truck route—a decision which would mean eight heavy vehicles an hour for at least four years.

That was the other thing that occupied a great deal of Charlie's time, when she wasn't at work. And in a way, it was all connected; because, interestingly, she'd recently discovered that the Village Green, together with that vacant plot of land, might once have been owned by her family.

In a dusty box in the Parish Council Office, she'd discovered a letter. It had been written by a woman named Catherine Collins to Sarah Elizabeth Foster in 1823, and Sarah's ownership, and subsequent loss, of both plots of land was mentioned. But there were no further details and there was no singular piece of paper that actually proved it. The document which would have confirmed the chain of ownership—a deed to the properties—had apparently gone up in smoke at about the same time that Sarah Elizabeth Foster had taken Louis Augustus Duran's hand in marriage.

For centuries it was believed that both the green and the vacant land at the end of Poorhouse Lane were under the protection of the village. That was until Ron Ferryman had come up with his grand designs for seaview flats and luxury houses.

Never mind fetes, carnivals and May Days, dog walkings and informal footie matches. Ron knew someone at the Land Registry Office, and had done his research. The horrible truth was out. In spite of there being no piece of paper to confirm it, the Village Green and the empty field had reverted to ownership, in 1825, by one Lemuel Ferryman. He was proprietor of The Dog's Watch Inn and ancestor of Ron and Reg, who now comprised Ferryman Bros. (Property) Ltd. And the Ferryman Bros. were in no mood for historical conservation. They were planning a prosperous retirement somewhere warm, preferably in a country where English was understood, but was not necessarily the language of everyday life.

Charlie wheeled her bike across to the Village Oak, where Mike Tidman, an almost-retired arborist from Southampton, was on his knees on the ground beneath the spreading branches, collecting samples of earth from between and under the tree's gnarled and massive roots.

"It's definitely a poison," he said, acknowledging Charlie's presence. "Some kind of liquid suspension, poured directly into the soil here. Likely over a period of time, to counteract the tree's ability to produce a new set of leaves as the old ones died. I suspect it was probably a herbicide designed to kill trees, and it was probably applied in a much higher dosage than would be required to do the job."

"That's deplorable," Charlie said. "Can you save it?"

Mike pocketed the little plastic bags that held his collected samples.

"I'll do my best," he promised. "It's criminal, what's been done to this lovely old thing. And if it's what I suspect it is, we're going to have a fight on our hands. Whoever's responsible ought to be hanged. Preferably from one of the higher branches."

He stood up.

"Sorry. I'm letting my emotions get the better of me. I'm too sentimental, especially about trees."

"We all are," Charlie replied. "Especially this one."

She glared at Ron Ferryman, with his Savile Row suit and his London haircut, standing at the eastern edge of the green, texting into his mobile.

"And you're right. The person responsible for this ought to be charged with vandalism. At the very least."

Charlie unlocked the front door of her cottage, and wheeled her bike inside.

Normally, she'd have left it in the garden, propped against the wall. But the sky was smudging over with ink-bottomed clouds, and Natalie at the museum had mentioned thundery showers along the coast. And so, it was best brought indoors, to preserve its rather ancient parts from the possibility of further rust.

Parking her bike at its rainy-day post beside an old dairy can that had been converted into an umbrella stand, Charlie pulled off her helmet. She kicked off her shoes, then collected the letters that had been dropped in through the mail slot halfway up the door.

The latest leaflet from the local wildlife charity, imploring her to Save the Hedgehogs by growing shrubbery borders in her garden, and minutes from the most recent meeting of the Committee to Save the Village Green and Poorhouse Lane. The monthly newsletter from Jeff's guitar club.

Charlie threw them all on the stove, an ancient cast-iron AGA that her mother had bought at an auction when Charlie was two. After Jeff had died, she'd given up cooking—real cooking, anyway, with gas rings and pots and pans. If anything had to be heated, there was a microwave on the table under the window, and a small convection oven beside it for baking or broiling or browning. The abandoned AGA was piled high with books, papers, old magazines, even older newspapers, and a stack of Jeff's favorite CDs that were perpetually in the process of being converted to mp3 and then put somewhere else.

She went through to the sitting room.

Embedded in the back wall was a huge open fireplace, where she could easily imagine her forebears sitting on chilly winter evenings, faces lit by the crackling flames, rain-damped shawls and stockings draped over chair backs to dry. It was a grand but necessary cousin to the much smaller fireplace in the kitchen, which had long ago been converted into the alcove where the AGA lived.

In the sitting room, too, was an old second-hand upright piano. Jeff had bought it for Charlie not long after they'd married. She'd played it often when Jeff was alive, but since his death, it had slowly reverted to the same fate as the AGA, an unused appliance littered with CDs, random sheet music, bits of notepaper scribbled with song titles and singers' names.

Facing the big open fireplace was a venerable wooden desk that had always been there. Its drawers squeaked in protest when they were opened, and stubbornly stuck fast when she tried to shut them again. But it was solidly constructed, and it was immense. One did not merely sit at this desk, one occupied it.

Antique though it was, the desk was entirely up-to-date when it came to technology. There was Charlie's laptop. And things attached to it which charged her mobile and an iPod. There was a hub that routed a Wi-Fi signal, a printer, a scanner and a wireless mouse.

And there was a timepiece. It was clever—it looked like one of the melting clocks in Salvador Dali's famous painting *The Persistence of Memory*. Charlie'd bought it on a whim from an online shop. She wasn't a particular fan of Dali. Her imagination had been captured more by the whimsical idea that time was something that could bend and drip, instead of being fixed to rigid hands and perfunctory tick-tocks.

Charlie didn't bother to change out of her Regency frock. It was actually quite comfortable, with no confining waistbands and a low-cut neckline that was pleasant in the heat of a summer's afternoon. She plugged her mobile into its recharger, set it to play music and switched on her laptop.

Its default page was *Stoneford Village Online*, which had the Village Oak as its welcoming photo. It was a glorious picture, taken two summers earlier, when the tree was in full leaf, branches still spreading and healthy.

Charlie was shocked at the difference between then, and now. What was happening now was devastating.

Anger was something she rarely felt. She'd wanted to be angry five years earlier, when Jeff was speeding home with Nick after a get together of pals to celebrate a pending nuptial. On the other side of the road, an irresponsible git who'd been drinking all night had lost control of his Porsche. He'd slithered over a patch of wet leaves and smashed headlong into Jeff's old Nissan, killing him and seriously injuring Nick.

She'd wanted to be angry then. But nothing had come, defying all of the rules of grief, completely skipping over Step Three of the agreed-upon stages. Completely skipping over all of the steps, really, except shock, and loneliness.

And then, after about two years, Charlie discovered she'd reached Step Seven, and that she'd ended up in a kind of mute acceptance, as if all of her emotions had been put on hold. She would not be sad. She would not be happy. She would not love. Or hate. She would not be anything, except what her job at the museum required her to be. And it was an incomplete Step Seven, because the rest of it was supposed to include an element of hope.

And there was no hope.

But now, there seemed to be an emotion. A strange kind of sense, struggling to beat its way out into the open. Something she'd not experienced since she was a child, hurling herself to the floor over a perceived personal injustice, kicking her legs in the air and shrieking at the top of her little lungs.

It was anger. No, it was rage.

Pure, unadulterated, focused, rage.

Charlie stood up.

Her rage was directed squarely at the Ferryman brothers, for daring to impose their selfish wills on her, and on the other villagers of Stoneford. For daring to evict an elderly woman whose family had lived in the village for as long as anyone could remember.

She stormed through the kitchen, her anger rising.

For threatening to wreck a small road and make life dangerously miserable for all of its inhabitants.

For daring to destroy the enduring symbol of Stoneford's history, the Village Oak.

Charlie slammed the kitchen door of her cottage, and with her head down, fists balled, walked purposefully down her cobbled lane. She crossed the main road and cut through the Village Green, then turned towards the row of establishments on the eastern side of the grassy triangle.

There were two solicitors' offices, the office of the *Stoneford Village Post*, a hairdresser's, Oldbutter and Ballcock Funeral Directors. And the little place that had once been Patrick's Coffee Shop, but which had since been taken over by Ron Ferryman as his planning office.

It was past six and the office was shut. But Charlie knew the layout of Patrick's well, having spent a summer when she was at school behind the counter, dishing out doughnuts and slices of cake, frothy coffees and hybrid teas.

She knew that there was a back door to Patrick's and that there had once been a spare key to that back door hidden under a flowerpot. It was still there now, eight months and one superficial renovation later.

And it still fit into the lock, which Ron Ferryman had evidently never thought to have changed.

The rage was still burning as she let herself inside. She saw the desk upon which Ron Ferryman's laptop sat. She saw the rolled up plans, his telephone, his nameplate. A certificate, presented to Ron by the Parish Council, for a donation that had helped fund activities at the Stoneford Youth Club. A photo, in a heavily embellished silver frame, of Ron and Reg, turning over a symbolic shovelful of sod at what had become a garish pink block of flats along the coastal road. And his nameplate.

That picture was the first to go, flung to the slate tile floor and smashed into pieces.

There.

Serves you right, you bastards.

Charlie fought back sobs as she seized the cardboard tubes and slammed them into the edge of the desk, over and over, fracturing their protective shells and tearing to bits the paper blueprints inside.

Her ragged tears would not be contained. And neither would her anger, exploding into a maelstrom of indignant fury.

She picked up the laptop and hurled it to the floor. Not once.

Not twice. Six times in total, until its lid was bent and its screen was shattered and its keyboard was in three pieces, keys scattered everywhere like a boxer's teeth.

"And this," she cried, giving the screen an extra few smashes with what was left of the silver picture frame, "is for Emmy Cooper, you greedy pig."

Charlie was kneeling on the floor, in full mid-smash, when Ron Ferryman unlocked the front door and let himself into the office.

Charlie froze.

If she had been thinking rationally, she would not have stood up at that precise moment and exited through the back door, giving Ron Ferryman a perfectly good view of her retreating back.

If she had been thinking rationally, she'd have crawled away, quickly and quietly, before Ron Ferryman had a chance to switch on the lights and discover his laptop and picture in pieces on the floor.

But Charlie was not thinking rationally. She was driven by fear and the overwhelming need to flee. And she was determined to put enough distance between herself and Ron Ferryman that he wouldn't be able to follow her, or even determine which way she'd gone, once she'd disappeared into the early evening.

Heart pounding, her breath ragged, Charlie retreated into the jumble of little streets on the eastern edge of the village, purposely complicating her retreat. She was aware, as logic displaced rage and panic, that she had been seen. And she would likely now be arrested for vandalism. Charged, found guilty, and sent to prison.

Disgraced. She'd lose her position on the Committee. Lose her job, her cottage, her self-respect…

Gentle Charlie, who had never lifted a finger against anyone.

Placid Charlie, who'd fallen all over herself apologizing with mortification when she'd accidentally walked out of Asda with a packet of crisps that she hadn't paid for.

Quiet Charlie, who spent her lunch hour talking to her poor dead husband in the churchyard…

It was a nightmare. It was worse than a nightmare. It was real.

What, oh what, had she done?

CHAPTER 3

The Dali clock was dripping round to seven. Charlie's mobile was playing one of Jeff's favorites—*Atlantis*—a quiet instrumental by The Shadows that he'd been in the process of mastering when that imbecile had smashed headlong into his car.

Charlie sat at her desk, heart pounding, waiting.

At any moment, there would be a knock at the kitchen door. At any moment, Ron Ferryman would arrive on her doorstep, accompanied by the Stoneford Constabulary, to arrest her and take her away in handcuffs.

Her brain racing, Charlie tapped the screen on her mobile to bring up Nick's number. She had to warn him. He'd expect her to be here. He'd promised to come over after dinner to sort out her family tree program. He'd very likely already left his house.

But her mobile was not cooperating. Instead of Nick's number, a photo popped up: a perfect white wax candle in an old-fashioned brass holder.

"Go away," Charlie said urgently, tapping the screen again.

But instead of vanishing, the clever picture lit the candle's wick. It flickered momentarily, and then burned with a strong, bright flame.

"Bugger off!" Charlie said. "Go!"

She tried again.

There. But it was only Nick's voicemail. He wasn't picking up.

"Nick," she said. "In case you can't find me when you get here, check with the Stoneford Constabulary. I've done something awful. Hurry."

• • •

Nick was in the process of arriving.

The accident had left him with permanent damage to his right leg. He'd almost become an amputee as he'd been cut from the wreckage. But the mangled mess had been pieced back together by surgeons in an operating theater. He'd been pinned and grafted, and after months of physiotherapy, his leg had been restored to a workable facsimile.

But what he'd gained in stability, he'd lost in velocity, and even with his cane, progress was, these days, frustratingly slow.

If Charlie had lived further away, he'd have driven.

But it was only a few hundred yards.

And so, Nick had walked.

He stopped at the corner of Charlie's road to check his mobile. And realized that, annoyingly, he'd left it at home, sitting on the little table beside the door.

And it was starting to rain.

And he'd come out without his umbrella.

It was no good. He'd have to go back. He had important information stored on his mobile, data that he needed to resolve Charlie's computer problems.

Nick turned around, and began the quarter of a mile walk back to his house, passing, in the process, PC Kevin Smith, arriving at the Stoneford Police Station, no doubt intent upon solving some beach hut transgression down on the seashore.

A brief flash of lightning flickered in Charlie's sitting room window, and a distant roll of thunder echoed off the walls of the Manor Bed and Breakfast, at the top of the hill.

She wasn't bothered by the lightning and thunder, though Jeff had been petrified. When he was six, a storm had boiled up and rain had poured down in sheets until the drains were full and the roadways flooded. And lightning had struck a small boy, his own age, stone dead on a playing field as he ran for shelter. Jeff had seen it all from his upstairs bedroom window.

Impatiently, Charlie tapped the keys on her laptop.

If Nick was going to be late—and he was, by some twenty minutes now—and if Ron Ferryman was going to take his time reporting her to the Stoneford Constabulary—she was going to get some proper work done. If nothing else, it would distract her from the greatest sin she'd ever committed. Ever. If nothing else, she could bury herself in her passion, like a child who's been very very naughty, and who's crawled under the duvet in her parents' bedroom in a hopeless attempt to escape punishment.

Obediently, her family tree program opened. The little squares representing Charlie's ancestors appeared in the right order, all the lines connecting in the proper places. There was Louis Augustus Duran, and there was Sarah Elizabeth Foster and there was their date of marriage: July 30, 1825.

In the program, if you clicked on one of the squares, you were taken to an information page that contained all of the things you'd collected about that person. It had photographs, census records, scans of certificates, all the bits and pieces of details from online excursions into registries and databases.

Charlie thought she might review, yet again, the hodge-podge of facts, just to see, yet again, whether there was something she could possibly have missed. She clicked on the square belonging to Sarah Elizabeth Foster.

The square responded with quiet compliance, changing colour as it ought to. But then…nothing.

Charlie clicked again. The screen froze.

"Bastard," Charlie said, under her breath—for her laptop was, without a doubt, a male.

Undaunted, she restarted the laptop, wishing Nick would hurry up and get there with his fixing skills.

The program opened as before, but she wasn't going to tempt fate a second time by visiting Sarah Foster's square. Instead, she chose the square belonging to Lucas Adams, an ancestor of her distant cousin, Morris Adams.

Lucas had distinguished himself by joining the Royal Navy on his 19th birthday, then subsequently spending the next seven years either drunk or AWOL. He'd finally married, at age twenty-six, on shore leave in Portsmouth, listing his home as "The Sailor's Rest."

And then he'd promptly shipped out again, leaving poor Fanny on her own and, not surprisingly, with child.

His history following his discharge from the Navy was murky, but Charlie suspected he'd taken up smuggling in Christchurch. And also, quite possibly, he'd become a member of the King's Press Gang.

So intent was Charlie in tracking Lucas Adams' less-than-stellar career at sea, followed by his even less-than-stellar career ashore, that she was completely unaware of the brilliant flash of lightning just outside her window. But she couldn't ignore the ensuing explosion of thunder, as loud as an avalanche of boulders crashing down a mountain of mythical proportions.

Startled, she couldn't know at all about the red sprite that which, at that instance, was leaping up from the vortex of thunderheads gathered over Stoneford, shooting a sparkling spray of particles into the universe.

She did, however, see the second blaze of lightning that forked down to the ancient oak in the center of the Village Green, sending a jet of charged particles showering across the roof of her cottage.

The sitting room went black. Her laptop, plugged into the wall, blinked off, then flickered back to life as its battery cut in.

Stunned, sitting in the dark, Charlie waited for the roll of thunder to fade, and for her heart to stop racing, and for the blood to stop pounding in her ears.

That had been uncomfortably close.

Seconds later, the lights came on again. On her laptop, the family tree program recovered. Lucas Adams' page reopened. So did Sarah Foster's page, changing into quite a lovely shade of lilac that Charlie wasn't certain she'd ever seen before.

But beyond the laptop—beyond the desk—something else was going on.

The walls, windows, floorboards and fireplace in the sitting room were unchanged. But, as Charlie stared, the furniture, carpets and curtains began to dissolve...and then, resolve...into items more familiar to a household from the 19th century.

Charlie stood up.

This wasn't real.

It couldn't be.

But it was.

She stretched her arm out, so that her fingers touched the threshold between Now and Then.

And as her fingertips dimpled the quivering transparency, it rippled, like the surface of a vertical pool of water.

On the pavement beyond the cottage gate, in the driving rain, Nick had, at last, arrived.

So had PC Kevin Smith.

And so, it seemed, had Ron Ferryman, in his black BMW.

"Good evening, gentlemen," Nick said pleasantly, raising his umbrella to accommodate the three of them. "Quite a light show tonight!"

"I'm afraid I shall have to ask you to wait outside," PC Smith replied, in his best policeman's voice.

"I'm in a bit of a hurry," Nick replied, good-naturedly. He'd been at school with Kevin. The two of them had been quite good friends for a time, especially after Kevin had been prescribed spectacles, which made him an easy target for non-spectacled bullies.

"Out of the way, Weller," Ron Ferryman said, reverting to Nick's last name, as he often had during their youth.

Nick had been at school with Ron and Reg Ferryman, too. He'd never particularly liked either of them, especially after they'd attempted to set up a junior extortion ring that involved pocket money and lunches, and occasionally Kevin's stolen spectacles.

"And what business do you have with Charlie?" Nick inquired.

"I'm here to witness the arrest your cousin, Weller. Stand aside."

"For what?" Nick asked, flabbergasted.

"Break and enter, for a start. Malicious damage."

"We are talking about Charlie...?" Nick checked.

"Apparently so," Kevin said, looking distinctly unhappy.

"I'm sure it's all a misunderstanding," Nick said. "Let's see what Charlie has to say."

And before Ron Ferryman could object, and while Kevin was thinking of a reason why this should not be so, Nick unlatched the little wooden gate, and walked up the garden path to the blue painted front door.

Inside the cottage, Charlie had abandoned her laptop and was desperately trying to ring her cousin on her mobile.

"Nick! Nick!" she said, frantically tapping the little screen, as the transparent, vertical wall of ripples raced towards her. "Help!"

Outside the cottage, oblivious to the transformation going on inside, Nick knocked on the blue-painted door with the handle of his cane.

Inside the cottage, hearing Nick's knock, Charlie tried to run to the kitchen to let him in.

But her progress was prevented by the transparent wall of ripples, washing over and around her, like a bath of warm, liquid jelly. She was trapped—suspended—like an insect caught in liquid amber.

Outside the cottage, Ron Ferryman shoved Nick aside and tried the door handle. It was unlocked.

Kevin interjected himself between the door and Ron.

"I believe Nick should go in first," he suggested. "A friendly face."

"We don't want a friendly face," Ron fumed. "We want an arrest. Followed by a prosecution. Followed by a swift execution."

Nick ducked between the two of them, and went inside.

"Only me!" he announced, walking through the kitchen.

"PC Kevin Smith!" Kevin added, from the doorstep. "Stoneford Constabulary! I'd like to ask you a few questions, Mrs. Lowe, if you wouldn't mind!"

"And don't think you can run away this time," Ron added, sourly.

Trapped in the undulating transparency, unable to move, Charlie saw Nick enter from the kitchen. She saw the expression on his face and noted that he dropped both his cane and his umbrella as he tried to grab her.

She experienced the oddity of his hand passing right through her arm, as if she really wasn't there at all.

And then…he wasn't really there at all either.

And the warm, liquid jelly was thinning, dissipating, melting away…

Gone.

Suddenly unsuspended, Charlie grabbed the edge of the desk to prevent herself toppling to the floor.

It was the same desk as before. However, it no longer held the accoutrements of her life.

And the sitting room—which was still her sitting room, with its familiar fireplace, and windows, and broad wooden planked floor— was suddenly plain. It was bereft of the little rugs she'd scattered here and there, the curtains, and the put-together-yourself IKEA furniture she and Jeff had slaved over.

In its place was furniture that was unfamiliar, yet not strange, because it was similar to the furnishings she'd seen in historical photographs and museum displays.

The last of the day was disappearing beyond the window where, before, the spider plant had lived. Charlie stood in the dimming light, not quite able to accept what had just happened as fact, yet unable to summon anything from her cache of life's experiences to account for any of it.

She was no longer in 21st century Stoneford.

She had arrived somewhere in its past.

CHAPTER 4

Charlie took a tentative step forward.

The desk—her desk—was missing all of its familiar bits and pieces. Melting clock and laptop, scribbled notes on scraps of paper. Nubbed down pencils and pens permanently running out of ink. Pamphlets and newsletters.

In their place was a brass candlestick, set with a tallow candle that had burned halfway down, its solidified drippings puddled on the lip of the holder. And beside it, an open book, bound beautifully. Next to that, a bare wood pencil, knife-sharpened to a writing point, and a square of rubber, worn down at one corner from use.

Charlie took another step, terrified of what might happen next.

She glanced behind her.

No surging ripples. No quivering transparencies.

The sitting room was extraordinarily quiet.

And silent.

The floorboard creaked, making her jump.

What had just happened?

And where was Nick?

Where, for that matter, was she?

Charlie risked a third step, and peeked at the book lying open on the desk.

It was a journal...a diary. Filled with neat rows of pencilled handwriting. And at the top of the page...a date. The 30th of June, 1825.

She caught her breath.

1825.

She swallowed.

This wasn't possible. It couldn't have happened. She'd read

about it in novels, seen it in films and on television. Speculated about it with Natalie, over tea and mid-morning biscuits.

Joked about it with Nick, over geraniums and fizzy water.

Sprites and tachyons. Electrical discharges. Subatomic particles.

"Nick," she said, very quietly. "I don't think we're talking about hypothetical events any more."

Cautiously, Charlie walked through the doorway that led to the kitchen.

It was familiar, but not familiar. Her plastered walls and stone floor and deep-set windows were the same. There was a sideboard. And a table and chairs.

It was her table, solid and made from hand-hewn wood.

She paused to touch it, lovingly.

Jeff had been a stickler for formal eating: knives, forks, spoons and plates, cloth napkins and drinking glasses. Everything had to be properly laid out, an adjunct to his edict for balanced nutrition. Always, there would be the prescribed portions of carbohydrates and proteins, a green salad, fruit or cheese for dessert.

They'd always sat at that table, discussing their days over soup. What had gone wrong, and right, and what their plans were for tomorrow, and next week, and next year.

Without Jeff, Charlie had reverted to tins and jars, boxes taken out of the freezer, things heated up in glass bowls in the microwave.

Poor table.

She'd moved it out of the kitchen and into the back garden. It had been there ever since. With each changing season it had become more and more weatherbeaten, a repository for broken bits of flowerpots and empty nutshells from the squirrels.

And here it was, newly built, barely scratched.

Charlie glanced at the place where the AGA should have been. It wasn't there, of course. Its alcove had reverted to its original function—a fireplace.

And the fireplace was actually in use, in spite of it being July.

There was no visible fire, but there were banked embers glowing hot underneath a hole-studded brass dome. A curfew—

she remembered that from her historical research. From the French phrase *couvre-feu*, which meant, literally, "cover the fire". The time for blowing out all lamps and candles.

A lidded pot, simmering something that smelled like stew, hung from an iron crane above the curfew.

Charlie crept towards the kitchen door, wondering, with a good deal of trepidation, what she was going to find when she opened it.

As she approached the door, she realized that something else— besides herself—had survived the journey from there to here.

Her phone.

She'd been holding onto it as the warm jelly had swallowed her.

And its little screen was still on, and displaying Nick's number.

Worth a try. Why not.

She gave it a tap.

The screen seemed to be thinking for a moment, as if it, too, had been confused by what had just happened.

No signal.

Of course.

What was she thinking? This was 1825.

Charlie switched her phone off.

And then very cautiously, she opened the kitchen door, and looked outside.

Her front garden seemed not to have changed at all. A path led down to the wooden gate in the stone wall. Brilliant wildflowers nodded red, orange, blue and pink, fragrant in the evening air.

Charlie followed the path to the gate.

On the other side of the garden wall she could see cobbled roads, whitewashed cottages, bow-windowed shop fronts, and in the distance, the familiar steeple of St. Eligius Church, with its clock.

Over the way was the Village Green with its spreading oak, two hundred years younger, comfortably familiar, and in excellent health.

There were villagers. The women were all wearing the same sort of frock that she was dressed in. The men were in clothing that she'd last seen on TV during a Jane Austen week.

There were horses. And carts.

This is, Charlie thought, most interestingly, most excitingly, most enticingly, and most wonderfully, peculiar.

But someone was coming. Four people, in fact: a woman and three children—two boys and a little girl.

Charlie ran back into the cottage. She closed the kitchen door behind her and fled to the relative safety of the sitting room.

Had they seen her?

The door was opening.

Charlie froze as the woman and her three children entered the kitchen.

Was this their home?

"I still do not understand," one of the children was saying, "why we must learn how to sew buttons on things. Is it not an occupation more suited to Mary?"

"I believe in a well-rounded education for boys and for girls, Jack," the woman replied, "and that is why Mary is learning Algebra and History."

"I fail to see the point of it," said the other boy. "No man in his right mind wants a wife who knows more than he does."

"I am not going to be a wife," the little girl reminded him.

"Yes you are," said her brother. "What else can you be?"

"An old maid!" the other brother shouted, and the two boys laughed uproariously at his joke.

"I know as fact that the vicar's sons have no desire to learn about buttons," the first boy argued, as the little girl, unamused, ran into the sitting room and then stopped, abruptly.

"Who are you?" she said, curiously.

Charlie stuffed her mobile down the bosom of her frock. "I was about to ask you the same thing," she replied, sensibly.

And she was still trying to formulate a reasonable, feasible, and perfectly logical explanation for her presence in their sitting room, when the woman walked through from the kitchen, and solved it all.

"My dear!" she exclaimed. "Children—I promised you a wonderful surprise this morning—and here she is! It is our cousin, Catherine Collins. She has come all the way from London to stay for a fortnight!"

It was not the optimal time for hunches. But Charlie now had a very good idea who this woman was, her face wreathed in smiles.

"Sarah?" she guessed.

"My dearest fondest cousin," the woman replied, taking Charlie by the arm, leading her to a chair beside the fire. "It has been many years, I know—and you have changed much—as, indeed, have I! But how wonderful it is to see you again!"

Charlie couldn't help herself. She was staring.

It was peculiar, reading about someone for ages and ages, researching them, digging up morsels of their history, and then suddenly being presented with the most unlikely opportunity of meeting them. In the flesh. And then stitching together the imagined person with the real.

Sarah Elizabeth Foster. Origins unknown. Died, aged 80, in 1873. Charlie had a colour photocopy of her death certificate. Married Louis Augustus Duran on July 30, 1825, which made her, on this day, thirty-two years old. A bit of an old maid, Charlie had always thought, since most women were spoken for by eighteen.

But this woman was, beyond any shadow of a doubt, her ancestor. She had Charlie's nose and eyes. Unmistakably.

And Catherine Collins. The woman who had written the letter in the box in the Parish Council Office. A cousin? There was nobody named Collins in the documents she'd carefully researched and just as carefully noted down in the family history. How had she missed this?

And who did these three children belong to? Sarah? It was a month before she was due to marry. And years before Emily and Augustus would be born.

"Children," Sarah said. "Come and be introduced to your cousin!"

The eldest boy stepped forward, and in a remarkably grown-up manner, said, "I am Tom, Mrs. Collins, and I am very pleased to make your acquaintance. Although I was very sorry to hear that your husband had died."

"Thank you," Charlie replied. Catherine was a widow, then. Piece of cake.

"And I am Jack," said the middle one.

It was obvious all three belonged to Sarah. But why hadn't they shown up somewhere in the family's history? Charlie knew nothing about them. She had no point of reference from which to start. Census records only began in 1841, and by then, all three would have been grown up and married and had likely gone to live elsewhere.

"Pleased to meet you, Jack."

"And this is Mary," Sarah said. "My youngest."

"Hello," Charlie said, with a small wave.

"Have you got any children?" Mary asked.

"Mary," Sarah said, "I've told you. Cousin Catherine has, alas, not been so blessed. Although..." And here, she turned slightly, to acknowledge Charlie. "That is not to say it may not yet happen, should circumstance avail itself of opportunity. Your period of mourning has passed, my dear cousin. A matrimonially-minded gentleman is not as difficult to locate as you may have convinced yourself."

"But I don't wish to be married again," Charlie protested, truthfully.

"Nonsense," Sarah replied, dismissing the very thought. "The last time you and I set eyes upon one another was at your wedding to Mr. Collins, in London. I do believe it was the most joyful and fulfilling moment of your life. His loss was tragic and premature. There will be another to make you whole again, I am certain."

She turned back to Tom.

"Please take Cousin Catherine's bags up to Mary's room."

Tom located two travelling cases Charlie had not noticed before, grasped their handles and dragged them to the stairs. He bumped them up to the cottage's second floor, one at a time.

"Mary and Jack," Sarah said. "Faces and hands. I should like them scrubbed, if you please."

The two younger children disappeared into the kitchen.

"I must see to our supper," Sarah said, over her shoulder, following them through the doorway, leaving Charlie alone in the sitting room to contemplate her ancestry.

If Jack, Tom and Mary belonged to Sarah...then where was their father? *Who* was their father? Louis Augustus Duran?

Charlie didn't think it likely. Two centuries from now, having three children without benefit of marriage was commonplace. But in Sarah's time? There were different social norms, and very specific rules of decorum and etiquette. Having a child on the way before marriage did happen, but the unmarried state of the couple was usually remedied before the infant's birth.

Charlie glanced again at the open diary. The writing was plain but educated, the words carefully chosen, the script nearly perfect. It was clearly Sarah's journal, and in it, she had been noting her thoughts.

It has been five years, she had written, *since my beloved Aiden was cruelly taken from us. I am meant to have recovered from this dreadful misfortune. I am certain I have done so, in many ways, however there will always be an emptiness in my heart...*

Mr. Foster.

Of course.

Sarah was a widow, too.

Her marriage banns, published on the three Sundays before her wedding to Louis Duran, had said nothing about her status. Nor his, for that matter. They could have been a Spinster and a Bachelor of This Parish. Or, just as easily, a Widow and Widower. It was usual for such things to be stated. But it was just as usual for the information to be missing.

And their actual certificate of marriage had been just as vague.

No wonder Charlie had been unable to discover anything about Sarah prior to her marriage to Mr. Duran. She'd been looking for the wrong surname. Sarah had been called something else at birth.

Mary came back, her face shiny from washing.

"Mary," Charlie said. "Show me how clever you are. What is the name of your grandfather?"

Mary frowned. "Grandfather," she replied, with utmost seriousness.

"Excellent," Charlie said.

There would be other opportunities.

"And can you tell me what happened to your own father?"

Mary's face fell. "Father is not here anymore. He has gone to his great reward."

Jack came through the doorway from the kitchen.

"She was a baby. And I cannot recall any of the circumstances. You must ask Tom."

Tom clattered down the narrow little staircase. "Surely mother wrote to tell you? He was swept out to sea."

Missing, then, and presumed dead. A widow by circumstance, if not by law.

"Thank you," Charlie replied. "Of course she did. But I'm afraid the shock of losing my own husband has done some very peculiar things to my memory."

"Come and sit down!" Sarah called, through the doorway.

Charlie followed the three Foster children—the siblings of their yet-to-be-born half-brother, Augustus, who was Charlie's ancestor—into the kitchen for supper.

CHAPTER 5

Nick's pragmatic mind was not altogether accepting of what he had just witnessed. He had seen it with his own eyes, so it was not imagined. His fingers had plunged through a gelatinous substance. He had touched it, felt it. It did exist.

And it seemed to him that in that moment when the substance had surged forward, sucking his fingers in, Charlie had disappeared. Gone...dissolved, like a frame in a film, transitioning from one scene to another. And then, in the next moment, undissolved. Back...but with a very confused look on her face.

"Charlie!" Nick said. "Are you all right?"

Behind him, Kevin had beaten Ron Ferryman through the doorway from the kitchen. "Mrs. Lowe," he said. "PC Smith."

"And we're here to make damned sure you pay for every bit of damage you caused," Ron added, entering the room at last.

"I beg your forgiveness," said the woman standing before them, "but I am not acquainted with Charlie. Who might he be?"

"Very clever," Ron laughed. "Feigned amnesia. I think not."

Kevin cleared his throat importantly. "Mrs. Lowe. Where were you at approximately six o'clock this evening?"

"You are much mistaken, sir. I am not Mrs. Lowe. I am Mrs. Collins, and I have this afternoon arrived by coach from London to visit my cousin, Mrs. Foster. She will be here at any moment."

Nick decided to play along.

"Mrs. Sarah Foster?" he inquired.

"Indeed, the same. This is her cottage. But surely this must be common knowledge...?"

"Can't you just arrest her?" Ron said. "I'm late for dinner."

"My name," said Nick, "is Nicholas Weller. I am, in fact, a distant cousin of Mrs. Foster's, and because of this, you and I must also be related. Though it would take me some time to work out the lineage. Pleased to meet you."

"As am I," Mrs. Collins replied. "Although the circumstances are undeniably odd. Perhaps it is just my mind, fatigued from the journey, which was lengthy and hot, and very much delayed."

"I think," Nick said, turning to Ron and Kevin, "that your questions might have to wait a day or two. She's clearly not altogether there. Or here. Tell you what. I'll make sure she doesn't skip the country if you'll agree to putting your interrogation on hold until she's in a more…lucid state."

Ron was showing every sign of imminent internal combustion, but Kevin seemed relieved. "It's all right with me," he said. "As luck would have it, I've got a very nice dinner date waiting as well. After you, Ferryman."

"Bollocks," Ron replied, bad-temperedly, but Kevin gave him a poke with his baton, and he departed, with very bad grace.

Which left Nick alone with Mrs. Collins, who was attempting to apply logic to what she had just experienced.

"At one instance," she said, her brow furrowing, "I was standing in my dear cousin's sitting room, awaiting her arrival from the vicarage. And at the next, something altogether unexpected occurred…a not unpleasant sensation, somewhat similar to being showered by warm water and then wrapped in a cosy towel heated by the fire. A fleeting embrace. And then…"

She looked up at Nick.

"Gone."

"And here you are," Nick replied.

"And here I am," Mrs. Collins echoed, looking around. "Although I am certain I am still standing in my dear cousin's sitting room, it seems, somehow, altered. Indeed, it is altered. Very much so."

She returned her attention to Nick, and his bold Hawaiian shirt.

"And what a curious costume you are wearing."

Nick had his mobile out. He dialed a number.

"Sam!" he said, into the handset. "Can you come over to Charlie's cottage? Yes, now…very much now, if you can manage it. I think we've got a bit of a problem."

By the time Samantha Palmer arrived, Charlie's demeanor had descended into something verging on distraught. Accepting Nick's ministrations of comfort, including a cup of warm milky tea and a cold flannel compress, she had sought refuge in a large overstuffed armchair. She was sitting there now, with a look of befuddlement on her face that reminded Nick of old Emmy Cooper after she'd been found wandering across the Village Green at three o'clock one morning, wearing only a cotton nightgown, a straw sunhat and green Wellington boots.

Nick went through to the kitchen to answer Sam's knock on the door.

"You've dragged me away from a mess that had every intention of becoming Fettuccine Alfredo," Sam said. "What's up?"

"Come and see," Nick suggested. "And keep an open mind."

Sam followed him into the sitting room. "Hello, Charlie."

"I am not Charlie," Mrs. Collins replied. "I am Mrs. Collins. I have come from London. And I wish only to see my cousin, Mrs. Foster. What can be keeping her?"

Sam took a moment to organize her thoughts.

"Mrs. Collins," she repeated.

"The same."

"And you don't recognize me?"

"How might I recognize you?" Mrs. Collins said. "I have only just arrived."

"Dissociative disorder," Sam said, quickly, to Nick. "Some sort of trauma. She hasn't hit her head, has she?"

"Not as far as I know," Nick replied.

"Have you fallen down?" Sam inquired, using the same tone of voice she usually reserved for the elderly and hard of hearing.

41

"I have not," Mrs. Collins replied, pulling away as Sam attempted to conduct a quick physical examination of her head. "What are you doing?"

"I'm a District Nurse," Sam said. "I'm looking for bumps. Signs of bruising. I'd like to take you to the hospital so they can check you over. Just to make sure everything's all right in there."

"The hospital?" Mrs. Collins answered, haltingly. "But I am not ill…"

"Just to make sure," Sam coaxed. "Would you like to change out of your museum frock and into something more comfortable?"

Mrs. Collins considered her gown, and then the place where she had been standing when Nick had discovered her.

"I am quite comfortable, thank you. I had my bags brought to the cottage by a boy from the inn…but I do not see them now."

Again, she looked befuddled.

"Where have they gone?"

"Let me take you upstairs," Sam suggested. "We'll have a peek in your—Charlie's—cupboard. I'm sure there's something there that'll fit you."

Nick was waiting on the pavement beside Sam's Honda Civic. He'd resisted the impulse to sit on the hood, lounging instead against the passenger door, arms folded, as Sam and Mrs. Collins, still wearing her museum frock, emerged from the cottage.

"I do not understand why you wish me to be disguised as a boy," Mrs. Collins complained, as Sam threw an unimpressed look at Nick. "And as for the unnatural apparel you have suggested I should put on underneath…"

She stopped as she caught sight of Sam's little Civic.

"What monstrous contraption is this?"

"This," Sam replied, moving Nick aside and opening the passenger door, "will take us to the hospital."

Mrs. Collins considered the car with a great deal of doubt.

"We shall walk," she decided, gathering her shawl about her shoulders. "It is a pleasant enough evening. Although the air has an odour to it which I find both unfamiliar and an insult to my eyes and nose. I wish I had brought my lavender water. Mr. Weller, will you accompany us...?"

"We shall not walk," Sam replied, taking Mrs. Collins by the arm and bundling her into the Civic's back seat. "It's six and a half miles. Get in, Nick."

Mrs. Collins had spent the first part of the journey cowering in the back seat of Sam's Civic, overwhelmed by the onslaught of 21st century life, most of which had come hurtling towards her as they'd sped along the main coastal road on their way to the hospital.

However, Nick observed, after having recovered her composure enough to recognize that neither he, nor Sam, were the least bit concerned, Mrs. Collins had concluded she was in no danger. And she was now offering a wide-eyed and nonstop commentary which reminded Nick, rather humorously, of his daughter Naomi, when she was four and a half.

"What is that?"

"A bus," Nick provided.

"And that?"

"A lorry."

"Goodness. How foul it smells. And those square boxes with windows?"

"Dwelling places. Quite expensive. With excellent views of the sea."

"I should not like to live in one," Mrs. Collins decided. "There are no chimneys. They must be exceptionally cold in the winter. And those tall posts with the glass globes?"

"Street lights."

"How peculiar. You must have an unfathomable number of candles at your disposal. Do you employ a man to light them each night?"

"They're electric. They're switched on."

"What is electric?"

"It's like a wick," Nick said, "that never burns down."

"Most odd," Mrs. Collins remarked. "I am quite convinced now that I am asleep and must be dreaming. When do you propose I should awaken?"

"Just stay asleep," Sam suggested. "It'll be easier on all of us."

She drove into the parking lot adjacent to the Royal Memorial Hospital, and manoeuvred the Civic into one of the places reserved for doctors and nurses.

"Are we here?" Mrs. Collins inquired, staring through the window at the very modern hospital, which had been opened by the Queen in the Millennium Year and which provided excellent—if slightly chaotic—emergency care to the village of Stoneford and its surrounding communities.

"We are here," Nick replied, humorously, opening the passenger door.

"Will there be bloodletting?"

"No doubt," Sam replied, unbuckling Mrs. Collins' seatbelt and bundling her out of the car.

"Then I must prepare myself. I have endured this procedure upon two previous occasions. During the first, I became faint, and was overcome."

"What about the second?" Nick asked as Sam led the way towards the A&E entrance.

"I was suffering from a fever which rendered me insensible for some days," Mrs. Collins replied. "Thankfully, I recovered, with no lasting ill effects."

Nick pretended he didn't see Sam's rolling eyes as she opened the door to the hospital, and they went inside.

CHAPTER 6

"I must apologize for the hurriedness," Sarah said, as she ladled out bowlfuls of thick, meaty soup from the iron pot which had been hanging over the carefully banked embers in the fireplace. "If I had been able, I would have finished lessons early and prepared more of a welcoming meal. But the Vicar's wife was behaving with particular petulance today, and so I felt it best to avoid her discomposure."

"It's quite all right," Charlie assured her. "I don't usually eat much, really."

There was bread on the table, freshly baked and crusty and brown, and butter, which Sarah had brought out from a cold cupboard, and tea with sugar and milk.

"So you don't stay at home during the day to look after the children?" Charlie asked.

"Indeed I do not," Sarah replied, "or we would have no food on the table. Mr. Foster left me the cottage, but little else to provide for our welfare. The Vicar and his wife employ me as their governess."

It seemed odd to Charlie that Sarah worked for a living. Many women did, of course, most out of necessity. But they were usually menial jobs, taking in laundry or braiding straw for hats.

And there were also many things which required daily attention in the cottage, the most important being the kitchen fire, which needed to be kept burning at all times. It was their source of light as well as their heat for cooking. In the winter, it was what kept them warm. And all of the candles in the evening would be lit from the kitchen fire's flames. Who ensured all of this, if the housewife was not in daily attendance?

"And what would happen," Mary piped up, "if the Vicar and

his wife had not been so generous?"

She's heard this story before, Charlie thought.

"Then I should have to take in washing and you would be sleeping in a hayloft."

"Like our Great Uncle Hamish!" Jack and Tom finished, in unison, much to Mary's delight.

Or living in the Poorhouse, Charlie thought, remembering Emmy Cooper's little flat at the end of the cobbled lane near the Village Green.

"I think sleeping in a hayloft would be interesting," Jack said.

"Not all year long, though, Jack. It would be very draughty in the winter."

Sarah passed Charlie a bowl of the hot soup, which she had smelled earlier, simmering in the pot. It was made, from what she could see, of all manner of chopped up root vegetables, and a little barley, and meat she was sure she'd have turned her nose up at, two centuries on.

But, she was hungry. And someone else had prepared the meal. And that made it all the more palatable. She tasted it, cautiously—and then tucked in.

Delicious.

"Now, my dearest cousin," Sarah said. "Do tell us all about your journey from London."

"Were you waylaid by highwaymen on the turnpike to Winchester?" Jack added, hopefully.

It was not as if being chucked back to 1825 was something that happened every day. Like taking off in a plane in a winter snowstorm, flying halfway around the world and landing in a place where it was hot and sunny and the beaches were sandy white and populated by tanned bodies smelling of coconut oil and bananas.

Once she'd got over the initial shock, and assured herself that there was nothing, at the moment, anyway, to fear, Charlie was surprised at her calmness. She ought to have been panicking. She ought to have been worried about getting back to the present as quickly as possible. She should have been fretting over bills that needed to be paid. Things at the museum that required her immediate and constant attention, if not her physical presence. She should have been agonizing over what she'd left behind.

Nick.

And Ron Ferryman.

It was, in fact, an utter relief to be here, and not in her own time, where she'd been about to be arrested for vandalism.

And she was sure Nick had probably worked out exactly what had happened, and was busily trying to find a way to reverse it.

If reversal was possible.

The thing was, after the initial shock had passed, and she'd got used to the idea, Charlie had found that she quite liked it here.

And she was entertaining a very daring thought.

This is my time. This is where I ought to be.

It was, at once, both frightening and exciting. It was as if her life two hundred years in the future, working at the museum, had been a prelude to now. She'd been given a new opportunity to use all that knowledge. She'd been able to slide gracefully and smoothly into someone else's time. And someone else's identity.

Supper was finished.

It was Tom's job to light the candles. The main ones were made from tallow, not the more expensive beeswax that Charlie was familiar with.

"Perhaps, on Sunday, we will make an exception," Sarah said, showing Charlie her special cupboard in the kitchen.

Inside were two lovely cream-coloured, honey-scented candles.

"A gift from the Vicar. Who can well afford the extravagance."

"And what are those?" Charlie asked, indicating what looked like reeds, bunched in the corner.

"Do you not have rushlights in London? I confess, I am not overly fond of them. See here—they are picked and prepared and dried, then dipped in animal fat. But they only burn for twenty minutes. Ten if you light both ends at once. And their drip is foul-smelling and their output meagre."

She closed the cupboard door.

"We only use them if Tom has forgotten to buy candles from Mr. Rigby. I have socks to darn, if you will keep me company for a little while in the sitting room."

The day's mending was completed by candlelight, and as the evening's conversations dwindled into yawns, Mary and Jack climbed the stairs to bed.

Charlie wondered what the best way was to inquire about the toilet.

Two hundred years on, her cottage had a perfectly lovely bathroom that had been fitted sometime in the mid-20th century. It was upstairs, and had all the requisite fixtures; everything was plumbed and piped with constant hot water.

Sarah's version of the cottage had no such convenience. Water had to be fetched every day in buckets from a common pump near the Village Green. And a flushing lavatory had yet to be properly invented.

"Where might I be able to relieve myself?" Charlie asked, deciding that it would be best to just ask.

"Goodness," Sarah said. "Forgive me for not showing you earlier. Come with me."

The household convenience was a little brick hut at the bottom of the back garden. It had a thatched roof and a wooden bench with a hole in it, and a cesspit underneath that collected what you left.

Sarah handed Charlie one of the two small candles she was carrying.

"If you would rather not," she said, "there is a pot underneath your bed. The spiders come out at night, and Mary is quite terrified of them."

"I'm not afraid," Charlie assured her.

Sarah returned to the cottage, and Charlie went into the hut.

It was, she thought, a trifle whiffy. But, like chamberpots and lights that were made from beef drippings, it was something the people who lived in this time were used to. They knew nothing else.

Shielding the dancing candle flame with her hand, Charlie

trudged back to the cottage, and bed.

"This is where I sleep," Sarah said, introducing her to the upstairs arrangements.

It was the largest of the three bedrooms. The same bedroom that Charlie had occupied with Jeff. And then occupied alone, after Jeff.

Mary was tucked up under the eiderdown in the double-sized wooden bed.

The next smaller room, where Charlie and Jeff had put all of their books and magazines and where Jeff had kept his guitars and his collection of CDs, was where Tom and Jack now slept.

"And this," said Sarah, indicating the tiny third room, "is Mary's. Which will be yours for the fortnight."

Charlie smiled. It was her future bathroom.

Moonlight streamed in through the little window high on the wall, painting the room with a silvery wash.

Alone, she sat on the edge of Mary's bed and switched on her mobile. She had no reasonable explanation for this act. It couldn't possibly function in 1825 Stoneford. It was more habit than anything else. The last thing she did, every night, was check for messages.

Not that anybody ever really called. But there was always the possibility that Nick had thought of a joke he knew would make her laugh, or Sam was having one of her regular rants about Roger. And the night Jeff had died, he'd texted her just before he'd left, and was getting into his car. She'd been in bed, asleep, when the police had rung to tell her about the accident. Jeff had been dead for two hours when she'd finally read his message, unable to convince herself that he wasn't still alive and vital at the other end of it. She hadn't deleted it. She'd saved it in a document that was stored in her phone's memory. She still opened and read it, every night.

The tiny screen searched for a signal.

Nothing.

It was ridiculous to suppose otherwise.

And she'd used up 2% of the phone's battery looking. More than 2%. It seemed to have lost some of its charge in the leap from there to here.

Still…what was that?

It was, in fact, a faint image…a flickering candle.

The flickering candle. The one that had been onscreen just before the warm oozing jelly had swallowed her.

Charlie's heart skipped a beat.

It wasn't a graphic that was resident in her phone's memory, like Jeff's last message. It was an animated picture someone had linked to on Twitter, that she'd clicked on to look at, a few days earlier.

She hadn't downloaded it. It was still out in there, in the universe.

And the flickering candle was growing stronger, the flame burning steadily and brightly.

This was completely impossible.

But so was sitting on Mary Foster's bed in 1825, in what was to become the bathroom in her cottage two centuries later.

Charlie stood up, and walked quietly around the room, holding out her phone, searching for…what?

A signal…?

A signal.

Couldn't be.

It was.

In the dark, Charlie tiptoed out of the bedroom, following the little indicator at the top of her phone's screen. Down the narrow stairs. Through the sitting room and the kitchen. Out through the kitchen door.

She walked down the garden path, phone held aloft.

This defied logic, physics and everything she knew about the transmission of whatever waves were responsible for mobile telephone calls, text messages and commerce on the internet.

This defied common sense.

She was most definitely picking up a signal.

CHAPTER 7

It was quite peculiar, wandering along the cobbled road in the dark, the only light coming from the moon and Charlie's faintly glowing mobile, with its dancing artificial flame.

There was a mist drifting in from the sea, and she could smell kelp and fish and salt water, mingling with the chimney smoke from several hundred kitchen fires.

The village was so quiet. She could hear the waves rushing onto the beach, which was well down the road and over a small cliff. Unheard of in her own time, even at four o'clock in the morning, with all of Stoneford asleep.

The narrow meandering streets and secret lanes of the village were exactly as she knew them. Because the historical heart of Stoneford, like the historical hearts of many little towns and villages along the south coast, had been allowed to stay virtually untouched over the centuries, unimproved and untinkered-with.

And so the old Cliff Road, which took you down to the pebble-strewn beach in one direction, and up to the Village Green in the other, was as it always had been. Except that it was more a cart track than an actual roadway. And the dwellings on either side of it were tiny and ramshackle. They looked as if they'd have no trouble housing the smugglers that the Parish Council in the 21st century liked to play up when they enticed visitors to come and walk in the footsteps of history.

And where Cliff Road became the High Street, Charlie could see that all of the buildings she was used to passing on her daily bike ride to work were exactly the same. Except that their roofs were made of thatch, and instead of being a newsagent, a bakery, a hardware shop, an Indian takeaway, a grocery and a chemist, they were a blacksmith, a butcher, a fishmonger, a tailor, and a shoemaker. Only the greengrocer had survived the centuries.

And there, where the High Street met Church Road to form the top of the Village Green triangle, was The Dog's Watch Inn, virtually unchanged.

And if Charlie were to follow Church Road along, she knew she would find St. Eligius, its old cemetery not so ancient, its tumbledown granite and marble markers standing alert and new in the moonlight. And the vicarage being used for what it was intended—a home for the Vicar and his family.

Charlie wandered across the road, aware that she was the only person about at that hour. She could see the clock in the church tower. It wasn't late—only about ten. And she could hear loud laughter coming from inside The Dog's Watch. Just as she could smell its ale, wafting towards her on the gentle, misty breeze.

As she watched, a large, greasy looking man walked out of the inn, stopped to breathe in the night air, yawned, and then paused, as if he was waiting for someone. Charlie recognized him instantly. It was Lemuel Ferryman, ancestor to Reg and Ron. His portrait hung on the wall of the contemporary Dog's Watch, behind the bar. It was just above the rack where the packets of crisps and peanuts were kept, and beside the two dozen awards from pub guides that Reg Ferryman, the current owner, had proudly displayed in three tidy rows.

"In the flesh," she said to herself, as the publican was approached by another fellow, very dodgy-looking and wearing an eye patch. The two exchanged brief pleasantries, and then a quick word about something, which Charlie couldn't quite make out.

The dodgy-looking man removed something from inside his shirt—a piece of white paper. He unfolded it, and allowed Lemuel Ferryman to look at it—but not to touch.

Indeed, when Lemuel reached across to grasp the paper, the better to see it in the dim light shining through one of the inn's windows, the other fellow snatched it away, and tucked it back inside his shirt.

Lemuel Ferryman then offered him a handful of coins.

The man with the eye patch laughed derisively, and shook his head.

Lemuel Ferryman was not happy. "You, sir, are a maggot. More than a maggot. A cheat and a crook."

The man with the eye patch laughed again. "You may call me what you wish. It will gain you no favours."

He departed with his piece of paper, and Lemuel Ferryman went back inside the inn, foul-tempered and quite red in the face.

Charlie continued to follow her mobile's signal, like a water-seeker with a dowsing twig. She wandered down Church Road, away from St. Eligius and The Dog's Watch, along the eastern boundary of the green...and then...

There.

There it was, standing dark and silent in the night-dewed grass: the Village Oak.

Of course.

She ought to have known.

It had always been there. And it always would be there, in spite of the efforts of those in the future who were trying to drain away its life.

Charlie held her breath as she stared at her mobile's little screen.

The signal was strong.

And completely impossible.

But—if Alice could tumble down a rabbit hole, and discover keys and cakes and Cheshire cats...

Quickly, Charlie typed in some text. Nothing of major importance. Nothing too shocking. Just that she seemed to have been deposited in 1825, the Village Oak appeared to have peculiar properties hitherto undocumented in the English *Quercus robur*, and...

She paused.

Do you or Sam know anything about a cousin, Catherine Collins? Married to someone who died before 1825. Need to find out more.

She selected Nick's number...and touched Send.

And she was absurdly pleased to see the brief, completely impossible, absolutely ridiculous response: Message Sent.

She waited. Nick had to still be awake. It wasn't even eleven o'clock.

Nothing.

He'd either switched his phone off...or he hadn't received her message.

She really shouldn't have expected anything else. What was amazing was that there'd been a signal at all.

The signal was still there, though, as strong as ever.

"So you may send," she mused aloud, to herself. "But it does not, apparently, follow that what you send will be received...?"

"Have you lost something?"

Startled, Charlie looked up.

It was not a White Rabbit with a pocket watch, but a rather handsome fellow in a white shirt and dark waistcoat, with a bright red handkerchief knotted around his neck. He had long thick dark hair, and seemed to be about her age.

For a moment, Charlie thought it was a trick of the moonlight, and she was looking at Ron Ferryman. For a moment, she panicked.

But it was only a trick of the moonlight. And her own sense of guilt.

"Yes," she said, quickly clasping her mobile behind her back. "I'm looking for..." She racked her brain. Shrubby borders. "Hedgehogs!"

Daft thing to say. Utterly ridiculous. But the gentleman was amused.

"Not too difficult a task," he said. He strolled across to a thickety hedge on the edge of the green.

"Here we are," he said, quietly, beckoning to her. "Having a little meal."

Charlie peered into the bushes. Caught in the sudden silvery moonlight was a family of hedgehogs, feasting on snails.

"Where I come from," she said, "people are obsessed with turning their traditional English gardens into neatly manicured Outdoor Living Spaces. The hedgehogs have nowhere to go, poor things."

The gentleman seemed surprised.

"We have dozens up at the manor. Mrs. Dobbs likes them as they keep the slugs and caterpillars away from the vegetables."

He paused.

"Although I have heard that the Gypsies in the New Forest catch them and roast them for their supper."

Charlie looked grim. "Yes, I know."

"I presume to be bold," the gentleman said, "and you must forgive my curiosity as well as my manners. But I have not seen you here before this night, and it is not wise for a lady to be discovered, at this late hour, unaccompanied on the Village Green."

He paused, with a nod in the direction of The Dog's Watch.

"There are smugglers afoot. It is best you were indoors."

"Oh," Charlie said. "Yes. Thank you."

"You are most welcome," the gentleman replied, though, having warned her of the danger, he now seemed a trifle aloof.

"Is anything the matter?"

"Nothing at all," he assured her. "It is only my discomfort, engaging you in the dark and in the absence of a chaperone. I do not wish to compromise your integrity and reputation…"

Charlie smiled. Of course. Those damned rules of etiquette, which were as rigid as the class standards which implemented them.

"You have not compromised my integrity," she assured him. "I am a widow, and so, I am exempt from the customs and courtesies which are in place to protect those who have yet to entertain thoughts of marriage."

What nonsense. She had no idea if that was true. The subject had never come up at the museum. She knew about Regency-era women who were already married and producing children as quickly as the calendar would allow. And she knew about women who had yet to be married, who were forced to follow the strictest of measures in order to protect not only their reputations, but those of the gentlemen who sought to become their suitors.

But she knew nothing about widows. Which was odd, considering she'd been one herself for half a decade.

"May I then have the honour of introducing myself? I am Mr. Deeley, head groom to Monsieur Louis Augustus Duran."

Charlie's heart leaped for a second time that evening. Louis Augustus Duran, her great grandfather six times into the past! And he was French!

"And I am—"

She caught herself. Who was she? Charlotte Duran? Married name Lowe? That would not do at all. Sarah's family believed she was their cousin from London.

"I am Mrs. Collins. Cousin to Mrs. Foster, who is governess to the Vicar."

Mr. Deeley bowed, and, boldly, took her hand.

"I am delighted to make your acquaintance, Mrs. Collins. What good fortune! I presume Mrs. Foster has spoken to you about my employer?"

"Not," Charlie said, "in so many words."

In fact, she realized, for someone about to be married in less than a month's time, Mrs. Foster had been uncommonly silent on the matter of her future husband.

Mr. Deeley released her hand. He had already held it for ten seconds too long, and Charlie was certain he would regret it immediately, if she did not offer him reassurance.

"Will you walk with me?"

"I would be most grateful for the opportunity," Mr. Deeley replied, his face brightening.

"I am staying with Mrs. Foster while I visit from London," Charlie said. "Are you familiar with her cottage?"

"I am," Mr. Deeley replied. "A young gentleman lives there, by the name of Tom, who has shown great interest in becoming apprenticed to the stable as soon as he finishes his studies."

"I gather," Charlie said, with great care, as they walked towards the long, low stone wall that separated the west side of the Village Green from cobbled road beyond, "that Monsieur Duran has proposed marriage to my cousin…?"

"Oh, indeed," Mr. Deeley answered, easily. "He has, in fact, been quite persistent in his overtures. But Mrs. Foster has been reluctant."

"How so?"

"She despises him."

Mr. Deeley's revelation stopped Charlie cold.

She despised him? The man she was destined to marry in a month's time? Despised him?

"In confidence," Mr. Deeley continued, as they crossed the road, "I do not blame her in the least for refusing to entertain his affections."

Worse and worse.

"Why?" Charlie asked.

Mr. Deeley consulted the moon before he spoke.

"Monsieur Duran is my employer," he said, after a moment, "and he is a nobleman—the son of a *comte* with a chateau in France. But as God is my witness, I cannot recommend him as a gentleman. He is mean with his money. He is bad-tempered and disagreeable. He has no respect for man or beast. And there are not many in this village who would volunteer a kind word for him—except perhaps those who wish to remain in his favor."

Charlie's heart sank. The man from whom she had descended was despicable. No wonder there had been no mention of him by Sarah.

They continued together along the High Street.

"And he is a count?" Charlie ventured. "From France?"

"He is," Mr. Deeley confirmed. "And it is a title that was earned, not merely assumed by an ambitious family. His father possesses as much decency and kindness as his offspring lacks. I have met him, many times, as he visits often. In fact, he is expected to arrive from France tomorrow. The lesser Monsieur Duran has arranged his customary Grand Summer Ball to welcome him."

They had reached the cottage, with its scented wildflowers, nodding in the night.

And here Charlie paused, to try and arrange her thoughts. She existed in the future. She had come to be, through all of the lines of genealogy, from marriages and births and more marriages and more births. The entries written in parish books, on official certificates and census records, were indisputable.

Sarah Elizabeth Foster and Louis Augustus Duran had become man and wife.

But Charlie was struck with a dreadful thought.

Perhaps, in this time—the time past, the current present—the facts, as she knew them, had been altered.

Perhaps, in this current present, Sarah Elizabeth Foster and Louis Augustus Duran did not become husband and wife.

And then what? Who was she destined to be—if she was not Charlie Duran?

Perhaps Sarah wouldn't remarry at all, and there would be no Augustus and no Emily, and therefore no ancestors and parish entries. And her own DNA would be jumbled and reformed and she'd be a descendant of someone else in the family line...?

Her head was starting to ache from the effort of trying to work out the possibilities.

"Mrs. Collins," said Mr. Deeley, "I must here bid you a good night."

Charlie's mind abandoned the conundrum.

Mr. Deeley had taken her hand once again—and was kissing it.

A gentle kiss, Charlie mused, slightly taken aback. Very bold, all things considered. She nonetheless allowed her fingers to linger in his for something more than a moment. It was a tender gesture, a sweet gesture, a gesture most definitely lost in the straightforward courtships of the 21st century.

"Good night," she said, thoughtfully, "Mr. Deeley."

CHAPTER 8

Charlie was dreaming about the wagon in the shed at the back of the Old Vicarage. In her dream, the wagon was no longer broken and ramshackle and in fourteen assorted pieces scattered around the floor. It was whole and assembled and useful again.

And in this dream, the upper part of the wagon's box was painted a beautiful glossy black, and its wheels and underneath bits a brilliant scarlet, and the lower half of its box a delicious chocolate brown.

The wagon was being drawn through the cobbled streets of Stoneford by Jolly, one of Horace Inkersby's handsome Clydesdales. It went past the newsagent, the bakery, the hardware shop, the Indian takeaway, the grocery and the chemist. It passed the banner exhorting everyone to Save Stoneford Village Green and Poorhouse Lane from Unscrupulous Developers.

And seated at the front of the wagon, holding the reins that guided Jolly towards The Dog's Watch Inn, was…

Bother.

She hated waking up before dreams were finished. It was like getting dug into a really brilliant novel, reading almost to the end, and discovering the last five pages were missing—along with the answer to the mystery that the author had spent the previous 400 pages plotting.

She stared at the tiny window set deep into the thick wall of Mary's little bedroom, and, for a moment, was altogether confused about where—or, indeed, when—she was.

But then, she remembered. She was in 1825. It was all very odd, lying on a mattress stuffed with horsehair, on top of a wooden frame that had straw instead of a box spring. Tucked between linen sheets and a colorful quilt which appeared to have been stitched together from scraps of old frocks. On top of a bed that was situated exactly where her trendy lion-pawed cast-iron old-but-new-again bathtub was, two centuries into the future.

And it was morning. Charlie could hear noises downstairs, the sure signs of a household awake: children's voices, Sarah in the kitchen.

What time was it?

No such thing as a handy alarm clock beside Mary's bed, although there was, downstairs in the sitting room, a big ticking timepiece that you had to wind by hand.

Charlie reached for her phone, unsure whether or not the answer would be British Summer Time, or original 1825 time.

She switched it on and was amused to discover that it was half past seven. And even more amused to find that her phone's internal calendar had opened to 1825, and that today was Friday, July 1.

She was less than amused to discover that she was down to 82% on her battery.

Quickly, she disabled all her phone's apps, and switched it off again. She had no way to recharge it. Even though Michael Faraday had invented a primitive electrical motor four years earlier, mains electricity would not exist for another six decades.

At home her day would have begun with all of those things you took for granted. A toilet that flushed. A bath that had hot and cold running water. A good face scrub with lathering concoctions guaranteed to moisturize, cleanse and restore. Teeth cleaning. Anti-perspirant.

And a practical consideration. Something rarely, if ever, mentioned in the research. Her period was due at the end of next week. How was she going to manage that? Obviously, she'd have to ask Sarah. Delicately.

Assuming she was still going to be here.

Assuming she wasn't suddenly hurtled forward in time again, through whatever accidental means had brought her here in the first place.

Well. The toilet was easily accomplished. The chamber pot was tucked away under the bed. She supposed she could grow used to it, just as she could grow used to the absence of hot water on demand, unless it was from that large pot hanging permanently over the kitchen fire.

A bath.

Not likely.

There was a bath, a container kept outside in the garden, tipped against the back wall of the cottage. But it would require numerous trips to the community pump down the road, and a good deal of firewood to heat it all to a comfortable temperature. A bath in Sarah's cottage would be not so much a morning ritual as a major event.

If she was still here on Monday—and she rather hoped she would be—Charlie made up her mind to tackle it, when Sarah and the children were out for the day, and she had the kitchen to herself.

A good wash would have to suffice for now. She wondered whether it would be good manners to go downstairs, clad only in her nightgown, to inquire about the possibility.

There was a knock at the door. And then Sarah herself poked her head inside the room, with the offer of a bowl, a large jug of warm water, a little bit of hard, scented soap, linen for ablutions, and a toothbrush.

"Of best boar's bristle," she said, laying the items out on a small table under the window. "I had not thought to inquire whether you had brought your own. But here is Mary's. I have rinsed it well, and she has no objection to sharing. And some toothpowder. I make it myself, copied from a recipe that I understand is popular in London."

Sarah leaned toward Charlie, confidentially.

"It has a little gunpowder in it. But the effects are tolerably excellent, and the taste is disguised with the rind of oranges."

She smiled, revealing teeth which, Charlie had to admit, were very white, and without decay. Gunpowder obviously had many uses.

"Thank you," she said.

"I shall leave you to your toilet. The children come to the vicarage with me at nine, so there is still a little time for conversation over breakfast."

• • •

Breakfast was simple and surprisingly leisurely, compared to the haphazard things Charlie threw together in the microwave and ate while she pedalled to the museum. It was more like the breakfasts she used to have with Jeff, laughing over the toast, arguing over who'd used the last of the Marmite and then making up in the shower. And occasionally in bed, which caused hurried calls to their respective employers, apologizing for accidentally switching off the alarm clock, promising to be in before noon.

Breakfast in 1825 was thick slices of home-made bread, toasted over the fire by Jack, and pats of butter that had been heavily salted to keep it from spoiling, and dabbles from a large and seemingly permanent pot of honey.

"It comes from Mr. Ashe, our favourite beekeeper," Mary explained, spooning a generous dollop over her toast.

There was tea, and fresh cream, and boiled eggs from Mrs. Horton's chickens, who ran free in a yard ruled by a noisy cock. Charlie had heard him at dawn, crowing his dominionship over his hens, the village, half of Hampshire and all the ships at sea.

"This," she pronounced, cutting herself another thick slice of bread, "is lovely. Did you bake it yourself?"

"Of course!" Sarah replied, surprised. "Do you not bake your own breads?"

"I never seem to have the time. Usually I just pick something up..."

"What?" Jack said, cleverly, "Off the floor?"

He laughed outrageously at his joke, and Charlie was momentarily reminded, in both his innocent humour and his infectious laugh, of her father. Something passed down from Sarah, then. A fragment of DNA that had survived the generations. It was curiously fascinating. Her father—and therefore, she herself—were both descended from someone not yet born. But in this half-brother of the yet-to-be, there was a little genetic bookmark.

"I'm so busy picking things up off the floor, Jack, that I don't have any time left to bake bread. I'm an incredibly disorganized person, really. Often I don't even eat breakfast."

"That is very naughty of you," Mary replied. "Breakfast is the most important meal of the day."

And there—another bookmark—Charlie's Auntie Nora, her dad's sister. Maddeningly sensible. A teacher of six- and seven-year-olds, who yearly went on Agatha Christie-like train journeys, carrying all of her clothes in one canvas knapsack. Sending postcards home which read: *Eating bread and goat's cheese in Lugano. This afternoon: a bathing establishment on the lake.*

And Auntie Nora's favorite admonishment: *Breakfast is the most important meal of the day.*

Here it was, in the flesh. The theory she'd been talking about with Nick, the persistence of memory. That you carry, in your genes, the vestiges of things passed down from the DNA of your ancestors.

"Catherine," Sarah inquired. "Will you join us at the vicarage? We finish morning lessons at twelve. I can introduce you to the Reverend and Mrs. Hobson, and then, I thought, perhaps a picnic. In the garden."

Mary and Jack were beside themselves. "Yes please!" they shouted, almost in unison.

"That would be lovely," Charlie replied. "As I should very much like to see the room where you give your lessons."

She desperately wanted to visit the vicarage. She knew its windows and doors and nooks and crannies by heart. She'd explored them all in quiet moments when it was raining outside, and the buses filled with pensioners and schoolchildren had splashed off towards the motorway.

"What will you do to occupy yourself until then?" Sarah inquired. "I have some interesting books…"

She leaned her head towards Charlie, and whispered confidentially.

"I have two written by an Anonymous Lady which are exceedingly good. *Sense and Sensibility*, and *Pride and Prejudice*."

"But those are by Jane Austen!" Charlie said, surprised.

Sarah was also surprised. "Has she a name, then?"

"Yes, of course! But…" Charlie racked her brain to remember the details she had gleaned from the assorted Janeites that Sam knew. "Her true identity was made known only after she died."

Sarah looked truly horrified. Her face fell. "My lovely Anonymous Lady is dead?"

"Yes—some years ago." Charlie was struggling again. "I'm so sorry…"

"Never to be another *Mansfield Park* or *Persuasion*?"

"But she has such a following," Charlie said. "Everyone knows who she is. People dress up in her clothes and have elaborate teas and dances. Mr. Darcy's more popular than Jesus…"

"I daresay in London," Sarah replied, sadly. "But we are somewhat more removed here in the country. News is always reluctant to arrive in a timely fashion."

"Your lovely Anonymous Lady," Charlie assured her, "is destined never to be forgotten."

But Sarah was still unhappy, and would not be cheered as she cleared away the breakfast things.

Charlie poured herself another cup of tea. "This morning I thought I might explore the village," she said, carefully. "And that manor on the hill…"

"The manor that belongs to Monsieur Duran?" Jack inquired.

"Yes," said Charlie, with a glance at Sarah.

"Monsieur Louis Augustus Duran," Tom added, with an atrocious French accent. "Zee most important monsieur in all of Grande Bretagne. *Tout alors.*"

"Yes," Sarah replied. "And I wish he would go back from whence he came, *tout alors*. He is easily the most annoying gentleman I have ever had the misfortune to have discourse with."

Mary leaned across the table, balancing herself on her hands. "Mama is not fond of Monsieur Duran," she said, in a very loud whisper.

"So I gather," Charlie replied.

"He has proposed marriage," Sarah continued. "Five times. One might conclude, after a less than enthusiastic response to the first two attempts, that a willing wife might better be sought elsewhere. But no."

She collected the remaining breakfast plates, and carried them to the sideboard.

Charlie was going to say something further, a gentle attempt at persuasion, a hint that perhaps Monsieur Duran might not be as vile and contemptuous as he appeared. And that perhaps Sarah only needed to observe him to arrive at a more measured conclusion. But there was a perfunctory tap at the kitchen door that stopped her.

Jack was seated closest, and it was he who jumped up from his chair to answer the knock.

It was a young woman dressed in a maid's uniform, holding a large and loosely wrapped parcel.

"Begging your pardon, ma'am," she said, with a small curtsey. "I am Martha, from the manor. Monsieur Duran has bid me deliver this to you, along with his greetings, and his fond hope that you will agree to attend the ball on Saturday to welcome his father to England."

She offered the parcel to Sarah, but it was Jack who seized it, and laid it on the table in front of his mother.

"Is there any message you wish me to convey to Monsieur Duran?" Martha inquired.

"No message," Sarah replied. "But you may convey the gift back to him, as I am singularly opposed to its receipt."

"Oh no," Martha said. "I cannot. Monsieur Duran has forbidden me to accept a refusal. If you wish not to acknowledge this token of his absolute affection for you, then you may do as you wish with it. But he will not allow its return."

"This man is more hellishly annoying with each advancing day," Sarah said, to Charlie. She turned to Martha. "Very well. You may report to Monsieur Duran that the package has been delivered, with the understanding that I harbor no affection for him, absolute or otherwise. And that there exists no obligation for further discourse upon my part, nor upon his. I cannot state it more plainly. Your task is therefore complete. Good morning."

"Good morning, ma'am," Martha answered, with another small curtsey, and then, she was gone.

Jack closed the door.

"What is inside?" Mary inquired, excitedly. "May we see?"

"I am tempted to convey it straight into the fire," Sarah replied. "Unopened and unseen."

"Just a quick look," Charlie suggested, her own curiosity piqued.

"Three times he has sent me an invitation," Sarah said, undoing the string. "Three times I have refused."

She unfolded the paper. Inside was a gown, exquisitely stitched, of finest pale silk gauze, with a blue leafy pattern worked in flossed silk, and trimmed with silk netting and blue satin.

"You'll have to go to the ball now," Jack said.

"I shall not," Sarah replied, firmly. "I do not wish to be paraded before his friends like his most recently-acquired horse. Nor do I wish to share his matrimonial bed, which I am certain would be as repugnant as he is. He seeks only to possess me. I would be despised by the entire village if I agreed to become his wife. Or pitied. So there you have it."

She wrapped the gown up again, and placed it on the sideboard, beside the unwashed breakfast plates.

"Children—it is time for our lessons."

CHAPTER 9

Dr. Allen, the psychiatrist-on-call at the hospital, had completed her morning rounds, and her assessment of the patient.

"This character, Mrs. Collins, is intelligent and bright," she said, sitting with Nick and Sam in the private visitors' lounge at the sunny end of the ward. "If slightly agitated."

"Yes, but what about Charlie?" Sam asked.

"Well, for the time being, she isn't Charlie. She believes she's Mrs. Collins. So I think you should go along with her. It's temporary. She'll come round. But she shouldn't be left on her own. She'll have to stay with you, Sam."

"Can't you keep her in here?"

"I'd take her home with me," Nick said, "but I think there might be strenuous objections. Regency etiquette being what it is. Or was."

"She's entirely without the foundations of any sort of mental disturbance profound enough to necessitate a prolonged stay in hospital," Dr. Allen replied. "Rather like old Mr. Abbott who lives over the bakery and for the past two months has insisted he's King George the Third."

"Mr. Abbott should have been taken into care years ago," Sam said.

"But he's in no danger of self-harm, Sam. And he's not contemplating harming anyone else. It's the same with Charlie. She's quite all right, really...except for her belief that she's Catherine Collins. It'll right itself. Keep an eye on her. Are you going to the Quiz Night at The Dog's Watch next Tuesday?"

"No," Sam said.

"I might," Nick replied, good-naturedly. In her other life, Dr. Allen was Wendy, whose husband Bill was quite a good mate of his.

"We'll see you there, then." Dr. Allen stood up. "Perhaps if you show her all things that Charlie's familiar with, something will click."

"We could take her to the museum," Nick suggested. "She's due at work in an hour anyway. Though I suspect they'll probably give her the day off. Under the circumstances."

"She's all yours," Sam replied. "Bring her back in time for supper."

It was a ten minute drive along the coast road from the Royal Memorial Hospital to the centre of Stoneford. Nick parked his car in the little visitors' lot in front of the museum, then went around to the passenger side to unbuckle Mrs. Collins, and assist her out.

"Oh!" she exclaimed, catching sight of the historical sign identifying the building as the old St. Eligius Vicarage. "But this is where my cousin Mrs. Foster is employed! Have you brought me here to meet her?"

"If you see her, I'd be happy to be introduced," Nick replied, humorously. "Shall we go in?"

Just inside the museum, in what had once been the front hall of the vicarage, there was further sign, welcoming visitors, explaining that admission was free, and pointing the way to the exhibits and the toilets. Nick led Mrs. Collins through to the old kitchen, where Charlie's desk was, still strewn with papers from yesterday's projects.

"'Morning, Charlie!" Natalie King, the museum's office manager, waved from her desk beside the fireplace. "And Nick! What a nice surprise!"

"Good morning," Nick replied. "I'm afraid Charlie's a bit upset...she spent the night in the hospital."

Natalie's face fell. "Oh. Oh yes, of course. It's Jeff, isn't it. Five years, yesterday. I'm so sorry, Charlie. You mustn't come in to work today. I'll manage."

"Why does everyone insist that I am Charlie?" Mrs. Collins whispered, behind her hand, to Nick. "He must be very highly regarded in the village, for I have heard his name mentioned unfailingly since my arrival."

"She's got a touch of amnesia," Nick provided, to Natalie.

He turned to Mrs. Collins.

"Charlie's a 'she'…a sort of nickname. And you look remarkably like her. You must forgive peoples' confusion."

He paused.

"Does anything seem familiar…?"

"Nothing whatsoever," Mrs. Collins replied, "save for the fireplace, which is very similar in shape and size to the one in my cousin's cottage. But I find my appetite is getting the better of me, Mr. Weller. I was discharged from the hospital with no thought given to sustenance. Might there be something approximating breakfast nearby?"

There was indeed something approximating breakfast nearby.

Nick's house had originally been constructed as a small chapel on what had once been the edge of the village. Over the decades, the chapel had been transformed from a stone and brick ruin into a tidy living space. And as the village had been modernized, so had the former chapel's insides. It was now functional and bright, with two bedrooms and an open plan living room, and a loft upstairs, underneath the vaulted ceiling, held up with fine oak beams. It was the perfect sort of place to house Nick, his cat and his research, and his wife and children, on those occasions when they graced him with a visit from London.

Nick unlocked his front door, then stood aside, allowing Mrs. Collins to enter first.

"What an interesting design," she remarked. "I must admit, Mr. Weller, that from what I beheld on the outside, within I expected pews and a pulpit. I had half a mind to believe you were a pastor. Although given your choice of clothing, I should believe God to have quite a sartorial sense of humor."

Nick considered his shirt, which today was bright red, with yellow hibiscus flowers. He had an entire closet filled with God's sartorial sense of humor. His Hawaiian shirts kept him cheerful, even on those days when gloom threatened to descend with the rain, and his leg was aching beyond the reach of his prescription painkillers.

But Mrs. Collins' attention had turned to more pressing matters.

"Mr. Weller," she said, quietly. "I do not wish to be indelicate, and, indeed, I find myself blushing as I speak, but I am in need of your convenience. Might you direct me towards it…?"

"But of course," Nick replied. He led her to the bathroom, beside his bedroom. "There you are."

"Oh!" she exclaimed, observing the toilet, the sink, the bath and the shower. "You are most fortunate. There was a similar chamber at the hospital, very near to where I was confined! I was greatly amused by these clever waterworks."

She walked to the sink, and turned on the tap.

"There is nothing like this where I live. London would benefit greatly from such an invention."

She pushed down the flush handle on the toilet, laughing delightedly at the gurgling result.

"And as for this…I was so predisposed by its ingenuity that I undertook a study of it, over and over, last night—ceasing only when a bad tempered woman in a white costume arrived to make known her objections."

She beckoned to Nick, and then whispered:

"She advised me of its true purpose. And bade me make use."

Nick left her to it.

And in the meantime, to the accompaniment of numerous flushes and running tap water, he set the table for breakfast: cereal and orange juice, toast and butter, tea with milk.

Mrs. Collins still had not reappeared, so Nick went up to the loft. It was his workspace, an open gallery over the living room which was reached by a short, steep staircase. It was hell to climb, and even more hell to come down again, when he was jousting with sleep and wanting only to collapse into bed.

He'd spent a lot of last night up there with Charlie's laptop, running diagnostics and watching while rows of code tumbled down the screen in a furious waterfall of letters and numbers. He'd been determined to locate the malware he was certain had invaded it, jumbling its internal workings and scrambling its normally well-ordered bits into a fevered battle.

But his investigation had come up short, and he'd staggered down to bed with more questions than answers.

He switched it on again now, and double-checked the steps he'd initiated in order to try and identify whatever worm, trojan, malware, adware, spyware, polymorphic or metamorphic code had caused it to hiccup the day before.

Whatever it was…it appeared to now be gone.

"Damn," Nick said, to himself. He hadn't wanted the piece of coding to disappear. He'd only wanted to isolate it, so he could take it apart and study it.

There was one last place he hadn't looked: Charlie's family tree program. The initial pathway, he strongly suspected, of the first contagious infection.

Opening the program, he clicked on the series of names in the tree's top index, going back, back, back…right the way back to 1825, and Sarah Elizabeth Foster.

Nothing there. Nor there. And then…as the cursor landed on Sarah's square…the screen flickered uncertainly.

Sarah's square flashed a brilliant mauve.

And there was a very subtle ripple in the loft beyond his desk and the laptop…a lapping crease in time and space which Nick just managed to catch out of the corner of his eye.

Was that his imagination?

His pragmatic mind wanted him to believe it was.

His pragmatic mind suggested that a second visit to Sarah Elizabeth Foster's square would be the ideal scientific response.

And so, he clicked again.

Again…the flicker.

"You bugger," Nick said, under his breath.

This was clearly no ordinary virus.

And Mrs. Collins was, at last, emerging from the loo.

"Oh that I had the comfort of one of those in London!" she exclaimed. "I should not wish to leave my house ever again!"

She spied the table, set for breakfast. And the remote control for Nick's TV, which he'd inadvertently left beside the sugar bowl.

"What is this curious device?"

Nick hurried down the impossible stairs.

"It switches on the TV."

He demonstrated, to Mrs. Collins' astonishment.

"This button changes the channel, and this one adjusts the volume."

"Look!" she said, excitedly, as a program about antiques began showcasing collectors' chamber pots. "The very same as the one underneath my bed in London. But a hundred and forty pounds! Goodness. I paid nothing like that for mine. And it's from Wedgwood. These little people know nothing about your convenience, Mr. Weller. You must advise them immediately, before they squander a small fortune on outmoded pottery!"

CHAPTER 10

So, in spite of Monsieur Duran's very persuasive gift, there would still be no contemplation of marriage, no discussion of it whatsoever. Not even an opportunity to approach the subject delicately and from the standpoint of a perfectly convenient Grand Summer Ball.

As Sarah and the children departed for the vicarage, Charlie set out for the manor, deep in thought and in a very poor mood.

On television, in books, in films, whenever travel in time was embarked upon by fictitious adventurers, the prime directive was always clear: never interfere.

Because if one interfered, even to the smallest extent, one risked altering the future exponentially. Everything that happened, everything that was recorded as having happened, was set in stone. Otherwise, how else could she—Charlie—have existed in Stoneford two hundred years from now?

She knew what Nick would say. He'd argue quantum mechanics and throw chaos theories at her, and make her brain hurt with the possibility of parallel universes and paradoxes. And then, at the opposite end of the argument, there was Jeff's simple logic. We are who we are, and where we are, because something happened, or didn't happen, in the past. It doesn't matter *how* we got here, it matters *that* we got here.

And she knew what Sam would say, too. Hang the complexities. Do what needs to be done.

Sam had very little patience for Charlie's ancestral adventures. Whenever they had conversations about history, she'd made it very clear she would much rather have been talking about multi-bladed mechanical scarificators and bloodletting cups than birth, marriage and death records from 1851.

Only one question really needed answering. If you were to find yourself transported back in time…and if you were faced with resolving a dilemma…should you act, or not act?

And what if the answer was that you had to act, in order to cause the future to happen? What if you were the lynchpin upon which everything else hung? And if you didn't act, would you cause history to change, and not necessarily for the better?

Charlie was descended from Sarah Elizabeth Foster and Louis Augustus Duran—of that she had no doubt whatsoever. It was written in the parish books, and in the census results, the marriage and birth certificates, the school records, the lists went on and on.

And if she did not interfere, none of those ancestors would come to be—and neither would she.

It was simple. They had all existed. She existed. Therefore, her interference was not only expected—it was mandatory.

She stopped to think further.

Nick would argue she couldn't be in two places at the same time. There was only one of her, and if she was here, now, she couldn't also be in the future, where he was. Therefore, if she messed up, and made the wrong decision resulting in the wrong reaction…then she might never actually inhabit the future. Which wasn't an altogether displeasing solution, considering what she knew awaited her, two centuries on.

But there, again, was Jeff's straightforward logic creeping into her mind. If you are here now, then obviously you did make the right decision when you were called upon to act, or you wouldn't have existed at all in the future, in order to make this journey back.

Put that way, it made perfect sense.

Except, she was someone else in this version of history. She wasn't Charlie Duran Lowe at all. She was Catherine Collins.

And that was a complication she suspected not even Nick would have an answer for.

• • •

At the edge of the village, the cobbled road gave way to a cart track, which meandered up the side of the grassy hill, first this way and then that way, in a gentle ascent to the top. Two centuries on, this would be called Manor Lane, and it would be widened, and paved, and made accommodating to tourists in large cars laden with luggage.

Now, it was not much more than two ruts carved into the turf by the wheels of wagons, and flattened by decades of footfalls.

At the crest of the hill, she could see Mr. Deeley leading an energetic horse out of the stables. He paused as he spotted Charlie, trudging up the cart track, then waved, and waited for her to arrive.

"And so," he said, as she approached, slightly out of breath and convinced that climbing hills in long frocks and 19th century footwear was nothing short of madness, "it is my pleasure to discover our paths cross once more. The view of the sea from here is, as you will note—if you turn around—unparalleled."

Charlie did as she was told, and turned. She knew the view well, but it was different now, unencumbered by houses and shops, buses and cars. And the English Channel, normally chock-a-block with marine traffic, was decidedly absent of freighters and ferries, barges and tankers and cruise ships.

"Fabulous," she said, as a magnificent three-masted, square-rigged vessel sailed into view, its sheets gleaming white.

"I have often stood here, pausing in my work, to imagine far-off lands," Mr. Deeley said, his voice revealing something of the nature of a confession. "I have had some schooling, although I was often admonished for expending too much energy on dreaming, and not enough on practicalities such as the Rise and Progress of Geography and Astronomy, the Divisibility of Matter, and Perpetual Motion."

"We are all dreamers, Mr. Deeley," Charlie smiled, turning her attention away from the sea, and back to shore. "There would be no inventions and no explorers, and nothing new in the world at all, if someone didn't first dream about them happening."

"If only you had been in charge of my education, Mrs. Collins," Mr. Deeley mused, "and not the very aged and imaginatively diminished Reverend Hopwood Smailes."

Charlie laughed. Mr. Deeley was lovely. And quite unlike any gentleman she'd known before. If this was what early 19th century Stoneford had in store for her, she would have no objection at all to remaining here.

"The household is in a state of disarray this morning," Mr. Deeley added, "as the greater Monsieur Duran is expected to shortly arrive from Amiens."

"Why is he called the greater Monsieur Duran?"

"Because he is the father of the lesser Monsieur Duran," Mr. Deeley said, with an amused smile, as the crack of a gunshot blasted across the hilltop.

"What was that?" Charlie asked, alarmed.

"There, Marie-Claire," Mr. Deeley said, soothing the horse with a tender touch on her neck, and a carrot from his pocket. "That would be the lesser Monsieur Duran. Attempting to shoot hedgehogs."

"Oh no! How horrible! I must stop him at once!"

"Fortunately," Mr. Deeley added, as Charlie set off at double-speed towards the source of the gunshot, "his eyesight is even less effective than his aim."

The lesser Monsieur Duran was, at that precise moment, holding court in the kitchen garden, squinting down the length of his flintlock pistol. He was, Charlie judged, about five foot four. And therefore quite befitting his description.

Some ten feet away, his quarry, a young hedgehog, had curled into a defensive ball under a leafy lettuce.

Behind Monsieur Duran, a red-faced, white pinafored woman Charlie assumed was the manor's cook, and a gentleman she thought could be the manor's gardener—bespectacled and cloth-capped, with rolled-up shirtsleeves and suntanned arms—looked on with something akin to humorous apprehension.

Beside Monsieur Duran, a dour-faced butler dispensed the accoutrements of reloading and re-firing.

The hammer thus half-cocked, Monsieur Duran poured a measure of gunpowder into the flintlock's barrel, rammed in a lead ball wrapped in a tiny bit of rag, and finished with a further addition of gunpowder to the pan. He fully cocked the hammer—and fired again, missing the hedgehog by several feet. Before he could reload once more, Charlie was upon him.

"What are you doing?" she demanded. "Hedgehogs are endangered! And you are abominably cruel!"

Monsieur Duran lowered his pistol, and glared at the impertinent young woman who had dared to challenge his singular domain. The dour-faced butler followed suit.

"And who," Monsieur Duran inquired, "are you?"

"I am Mrs. Collins," Charlie replied, without hesitation, surprising herself.

"Mrs. Collins," Monsieur Duran said, mocking her. "I do not know the person, Mrs. Collins. In fact, I think I do not wish ever to know the person, Mrs. Collins." He waved her away with his gun, impatiently. "Be gone."

"Monsieur Duran—sir," Mr. Deeley interrupted. "I have made this lady's acquaintance upon a previous occasion. She is a cousin to Mrs. Foster."

Monsieur Duran raised an interested eyebrow. "Madame Foster? Indeed."

"I will be gone," Charlie decided. "It was interesting but not altogether pleasant meeting you."

But before she could turn away, Monsieur Duran had seized her hand, and had planted a disgustingly wet kiss upon it. "*Enchanté*, Madame."

Charlie removed her fingers from his before he could insult them further.

"*Enchanté* yourself," she replied, haughtily. "I am seriously not impressed."

She succeeded in turning her back on Monsieur Duran at last, but he called after her. "Please stop a moment, Madame! Will you do me the great honour of joining my father and myself for lunch tomorrow? We will dine at noon. It will be no imposition."

Charlie faced him. "I think not, Monsieur Duran. In fact, I can think of nothing I'd rather do less."

"But I do not accept *non* as a response," Monsieur Duran persisted. "And my mind is made up. I shall expect you at twelve o'clock tomorrow. I will not consume a morsel on my plate until you arrive."

"Then I fear you may expire from starvation," Charlie replied, pleasantly. "Good day, Monsieur Duran."

Mr. Deeley caught up to her outside the stable.

"Not the most auspicious of introductions," he ventured. "But you have, at least, now become acquainted with my employer."

"I hate him," Charlie said. "I cannot believe we are related."

Mr. Deeley paused. "You are a member of Monsieur Duran's family?"

"No," Charlie said, quickly. "Not yet."

Her mind was racing.

"I meant—if Sarah marries him. We will then be related."

"I see nothing to convince me that is likely to happen in my lifetime. Or yours. And you know, of course, that by inviting you to lunch, Monsieur Duran hopes to persuade you to convey his… advantages…to Mrs. Foster…?"

"Painfully obvious," Charlie replied. "And since I have no plans to attend, I have become, in fact, his disadvantage."

Mr. Deeley laughed.

"In that case," he said, "I am presumptuous and bold, but I am inspired by your courage and the impetuousness of your spirit. May I borrow a leaf from Monsieur Duran's book…and inquire if I may call upon you at Mrs. Foster's cottage? You will note that I merely inquire. I am not so reckless as to impose upon you without invitation."

Charlie looked at him. "Oh," she said.

"You are offended?"

"No—no—only surprised. This is…most unexpected."

"Might Mrs. Foster object because Monsieur Duran is my employer?"

"I cannot believe she would find you disagreeable," Charlie smiled.

"Might you inquire, then—if it is not too forward a suggestion—about the possibility of my being invited to tea?"

"I would be very pleased to inquire about the possibility of you being invited to tea," Charlie replied. "When?"

"This evening."

"This evening," Charlie laughed. "You are indeed impetuous, Mr. Deeley. But I do not consider it too forward a suggestion at all. I shall make the necessary inquiries, and you will have your answer this afternoon."

CHAPTER 11

Her mind dancing with thoughts of Mr. Deeley coming to tea, Charlie was about to trudge down the hill and back to the village, when she saw an open wagon drawn by two very fine horses, creaking its way up the rutted cart track to the top of the rise.

Seated behind the horses, coaxing them along with a gentle rein, was a gentleman of middling age, quite handsome and fair, though his hair seemed to be less in evidence than it might have been in his younger years, and the fairness was tempered in places with grey.

He wore a brightly coloured waistcoat that was decorated with clever embroidery and delicate hand-stitching. And his many bags and cases were jumbled behind him in the wagon, attesting to a carefree disposition, as well as what Charlie judged was likely a lengthy stay. Beside him, occupying pride of place on the seat, was a musical instrument. A 19th century guitar. Not entirely dissimilar, Charlie thought, to its 21st century six-stringed acoustic cousin.

"This," Mr. Deeley said to Charlie, "will be the greater Monsieur Duran."

The wagon, at last, reached the top of the hill.

"Good afternoon, sir," Mr. Deeley ventured, warmly. "I trust you have enjoyed a pleasant journey."

"The sea air was as bracing as it was beneficial to my constitution," the greater Monsieur Duran replied, climbing down from the wagon. "May I be introduced to this charming young woman?"

"Certainly. She is Mrs. Catherine Collins, from London, visiting a cousin who lives in the village. Mrs. Collins, Monsieur Duran. The greater."

"I am most delighted," Monsieur Duran replied, with a small bow.

"As am I," Charlie replied, amused. The man was considerably taller than his son. And altogether more agreeable.

Monsieur Duran turned to acknowledge the manor's gardener, who had arrived, slightly out of breath from running.

"And where is my repellent progeny?"

"He was earlier discharging his pistol at harmless wildlife," the gardener replied. "However I believe that he is now in the process of interviewing a new housemaid."

"My condolences to the poor girl. Take this, Mr. Rankin."

The greater Monsieur Duran passed the musical instrument to the gardener, who considered it with great interest.

"It is the latest from France," Monsieur Duran provided, removing the item from Mr. Rankin's hands, turning it around, and replacing it, right way up. "You must pluck the strings here, and press down with your fingers on the long bit there. The Gypsies are particularly good at it."

"I do not suppose it will ever supplant the pianoforte in the parlour, will it," Mr. Deeley mused.

He glanced over his shoulder.

"Ah—here comes your son."

A somewhat dishevelled Louis Augustus Duran approached the small gathering with a distinct absence of enthusiasm.

"Louis!" his father exclaimed. "My dear child!"

He planted a kiss on either side of his son's cheeks.

"Father," the lesser Monsieur Duran acknowledged, begrudgingly.

"What have you for lunch? My journey has been long, and I wish for something substantial and not detrimental to my waters."

Without waiting for a reply, he considered Mr. Rankin—and the guitar—with amusement.

"Have you any asparagus, sir?"

"There is some in the kitchen, fresh from the garden," Mr. Rankin replied, "I will ask Mrs. Dobbs if she will blanche it for you."

He departed, carrying the guitar a little awkwardly, and at arm's length.

"Let us not stand about," the elder Duran pronounced, handing the horse reins to Mr. Deeley, and beckoning his son follow him to the manor's front door. "Idleness leads to insufficiency, and I had quite enough of that when you were a child."

The walk down the hill was a lot easier for Charlie than the trudge up.

The morning had turned brilliantly sunny and the air was sweet and fresh. There was no industrial muck, no exhaust from cars and lorries on their way to Bournemouth and Southampton, no jet effluent from planes caught in circular holding patterns above Heathrow and Gatwick.

Charlie was still smiling, thinking about Mr. Deeley, as she approached the jumbly row of cottages and houses that together made up what was known as the Poorhouse.

As she walked past, she caught a glimpse of some of the paupers who lived there, supported by the parish.

A pale-faced young woman, barely more than a girl, was sitting in the sun, looking after an infant who was experimenting with the idea of walking.

And a very old man, grizzled and threadbare, was hunched on a stool beside her, diligently taking apart a length of worn rope and pasting the strands onto a flat scrap of wood to fashion a seascape.

"Hello," Charlie said, bending over to have a closer look. "That's quite good, that is."

The old man ignored her.

"It's very good!" Charlie tried, again.

"He cannot hear you," the young woman said. "He is as deaf as a post, poor Old John. But he is very good with his hands, as he was once upon a time a sailor, and he knows the ropes, inside and out."

She gently tapped Old John on the shoulder, and then, when she had his attention, pointed to Charlie, and smiled.

"Aye," Old John grinned, displaying an alarming absence of teeth. "Thank ye."

And he returned to his seascape, without further discourse.

"What is your child called?" Charlie inquired.

"His name is Daniel." The young woman paused. "I have not seen you here before."

"I am Mrs. Catherine Collins," Charlie said. "I am visiting from London."

"London," the young woman said, with a sigh. "I had thought I might see London one day. Before this." She nodded at her son.

"Are your circumstances so unfortunate?" Charlie asked, with care.

"Most unfortunate," the young woman replied, unhappily. "Two years ago, I was employed in the household of Monsieur Duran. But I was relieved of my position, through no fault of my own—other than a poor innocent's misguided trust in a rogue."

There. Again. Her forebear, the despicable Monsieur Duran. The young woman had been economical with the details, but Charlie could guess what she meant.

"Monsieur Duran is Daniel's father?"

"He will not admit to it. I was dismissed the moment I confided in him. My mother and father have disowned me. I have a sister who visits, upon occasion, to bring clothing for me and the little one... but she must do so in secret, or she would be disowned as well."

And here, the young woman began to weep, wiping her eyes with a thin shawl, and her nose with the back of her hand.

"What is your name?" Charlie asked, kindly.

"I am called Eliza Robinson."

"Perhaps fortunes will change," Charlie said, hopefully. "Perhaps, in the future, you may find Monsieur Duran a kinder soul...perhaps the addition of a Madame Duran will transform the household..."

"I do not think kindness is a word familiar to Monsieur Duran," Eliza replied. "And I cannot imagine any woman wishing to marry him, for he is a tyrant."

She leaned forward, as if to confide in Charlie.

"He possesses cruel and unnatural tendencies," she whispered.

"Unnatural...?" Charlie faltered.

"He derives pleasure," she whispered again, "from subjecting innocent maids to his horrific fantasies."

She swallowed.

"He prefers them to be tied up. Helpless. Subject to his every whim. And if you should weep and beg him to cease…"

She swallowed again, and Charlie was afraid she might burst into tears on the spot.

"…it only serves to inflame his ardour more."

"Oh," Charlie said. How could she possibly encourage Sarah to marry him now?

"Furthermore, he is possessed, and interrogates you, demanding that you answer questions about his invention. And if you should answer incorrectly…he punishes you. Severely."

"Monsieur Duran is an inventor…?" Charlie asked, not quite willing to allow her imagination to consider her ancestor's private inclinations.

"He wishes to be an inventor. I would not credit him with the title, as he has met with very little success, and it will never be accepted in polite society."

"What is his invention?"

"A contraption," Eliza replied, "like a chamber pot, but enclosed in a room of its own, and relying upon water brought in from the outside to empty its contents. It was my duty to attend to this ridiculous contrivance."

Charlie tried to recall something—anything—about the history of the flushing toilet. Somehow, she felt, she would have known if her great grandfather, six generations into the past, had lent his talents to this most important item of plumbing.

"My sympathies," she offered. "It cannot have been easy for you."

"Nothing in this life has been easy for me," Eliza replied. "Perhaps in the next, I shall find my redemption."

"Certainly a life free from the unceasing demands of Monsieur Duran," Charlie agreed, comfortingly. "I am very pleased to have made your acquaintance, Miss Robinson. I shall bid you a good morning, with the hope that we will talk again soon."

And she continued on her way, walking past several Gypsies who were knocking on doors with offers to mend pots and pans, and the dodgy-looking fellow with the eye patch, who she'd seen speaking with Lemuel Ferryman yesterday, going into the butcher's shop carrying a dead rabbit.

And it wasn't until she'd walked all the way to the top end of the Village Green, and was about to cross the road and take a shortcut to the vicarage through the St. Eligius churchyard, that she realized… if Daniel Robinson was the son of Louis Augustus Duran—acknowledged or not—then he was, in fact…one of her ancestors.

Charlie knocked upon the front door of the vicarage. It was answered by a stout woman carrying a bad-tempered infant.

"Hello," Charlie said. "I am Mrs. Collins—cousin to Mrs. Foster. Has she told you of my arrival from London?"

"Indeed she has," the woman replied. "I am Mrs. Hobson. Will you come inside?"

Charlie stepped into the front hall. It looked the same, except that two hundred years into the future, there would have been signs giving directions to the visitors. It was a little disorienting to see what appeared to be framed portraits of all of Reverend Hobson's clergy-minded forebears decorating the walls instead.

"I have heard so much about your vicarage, I feel as though I have been acquainted with it intimately," she said.

"Well, you have found us all at sixes and sevens today," Mrs. Hobson replied. "Mr. Hobson has received some rather unexpectedly good news. Mrs. Foster will be instructing the children in the lesson room, if you would care to join her."

Charlie dodged two of the smaller Hobson offspring, who, too young for schooling, raced in front of her waving a large white home-made flag, screaming with mischief, and causing two alarmed-looking cats to seek shelter beneath a table.

Mrs. Hobson disappeared with her infant, and so Charlie knocked on the nearest closed door. It was opened by Sarah.

"My dear cousin! Do join us!"

Two centuries in the future, this room would be made over into the Ladies, Gents and Disabled Toilets. Charlie entered.

Five Hobson children—three boys and two girls, ranging in age from six to fourteen—were seated around a crowded table with Tom, Jack and Mary Foster. All were preparing, with varying degrees of enthusiasm, to sew buttons onto squares of cotton.

Resuming her place at the head of the table, Sarah consulted a linen hussif that was embellished with intricate embroidery. Inside its pockets were needles and pins, and a thimble, a measuring tape and a wooden piece wound with a selection of threads. And there were buttons. All manner of buttons—wood, bone, mother-of-pearl and pewter and china. Buttons wrapped with thread, and buttons covered with fabric.

She tumbled the collection onto the tabletop, then held up a length of cotton thread, and a large needle.

"It is much easier if you make a little knot in the end of the thread before you pull it through the needle," she said. "That way it cannot slip out. Would you like to demonstrate, Mrs. Collins?"

Charlie had not threaded a needle since she was in school, and learning, with not much success, how to make an apron she knew she would never in a million years wear. She'd given the rather poor result to her mum, who had put it on and promptly spilled barbecue sauce down its front. It was never seen, or mentioned, again.

Charlie managed, however, to poke the thread into the eye of the needle, and after pulling it through to make a double strand, knotted the ends together.

"There you are," Sarah said. "Simple and straightforward. Would you like to sew a button for us, Mrs. Collins?"

"I would rather it were you," Charlie replied, handing her back the needle and thread. "I am somewhat out of practice."

Sarah laughed.

"What a pleasant humour you possess, my dearest cousin. Only last month you wrote to tell me of the success of your most recent delicate embroidery."

Sarah picked up a large brass button that looked as if it had come from a seaman in the Royal Navy, and one of the cotton patches.

"Watch, children, as I draw the needle and thread through the fabric. You can see that because of Mrs. Collins' knot, it is well anchored and will prevent the button from becoming loose later."

Jack nudged his older brother. "I am going to sew my button onto the bottom of Mary's pantaloons."

"Master Jack," Sarah said. "Kindly name the four great ancient monarchies."

"The Assyrian," Jack replied, readily, but then he paused. "The Persian?"

"The Grecian," Mary finished, "and the Roman."

"Very good," Sarah said, as there was a further knock upon the door, and a befuddled-looking gentleman in clerical clothing poked his head into the room.

"I am so terribly sorry to interrupt," he said, with some hesitancy. "But might I have a word with you and your cousin, Mrs. Foster?"

"Of course!"

Sarah left her needle and thread in Mary's custody.

"You may instruct Jack in the art of the button hole," she said, to Mary, and to the children in general: "Do try to behave while we are gone."

Reverend Hobson escorted Sarah and Charlie into the front room which, two centuries into the future, would house the museum's Travellers Display. It was very cluttered. Mrs. Hobson had taken up residence beside the fireplace and was nursing the bad-tempered infant. The two children who had earlier terrorized the cats were playing at her feet, building a fortress out of wooden blocks.

Charlie searched, unsuccessfully, for a chair that was not occupied by something damp that had been hung up to dry in front of the fire.

"Oh dear," Reverend Hobson said, mopping his forehead with a large white handkerchief.

"Do stop dithering, Mr. Hobson," Mrs. Hobson said, with a slightly perturbed look.

"Mrs. Foster," Reverend Hobson began. "I am afraid we have received some rather dreadful news."

"It is not so dreadful for ourselves, Mr. Hobson," Mrs. Hobson corrected. "In fact, it is a matter I consider long overdue in arriving."

"But I fear it will be terribly inconvenient for you, my dear Mrs. Foster. Fortunately, your cousin who is visiting from London is nearby to assist you, should you be overcome by our dispatch."

He glanced at Mrs. Hobson, who smiled back, benevolently.

"I—we—are being assigned to another parish. There. I have said it. Oh dear."

"Bournemouth," Mrs. Hobson provided, disconnecting the infant from her breast. "A significantly increased population. With a significantly increased congregation. We shall miss you, of course, Mrs. Foster."

"We are promised a very large house," the vicar added, hastily.

Speechless, Sarah looked first at Reverend Hobson, and then at his wife. And then at the infant, who, rather loudly, was objecting to the interruption of his lunch.

"Is there no possibility Mrs. Foster might continue her employment with you as governess in Bournemouth?" Charlie asked, as Mrs. Hobson rearranged herself, and connected her infant to the other breast.

"My dear, we would have it no other way," she provided. "But there is a governess who is already in place. She is the unmarried daughter of the vicar who has, with utmost misfortune, recently departed this life. She has known no other home. I am told she is very plain and most unlikely to find a husband, and so, of course, we must exercise our Christian generosity…"

"Of course," Sarah said, struggling to maintain her composure. "I understand. And the vicar who is coming here in your place? Have his children no need of instruction?"

Reverend Hobson looked as if he needed very badly to relieve himself. "The Very Reverend Hopkirk is advanced in years. As I understand it, Mrs. Hopkirk has produced eleven offspring, nine of them surviving infancy…but alas, dear Mrs. Foster, the youngest is herself now a woman close to your own age…"

"If there is anything we might do for you," Mrs. Hobson added, quickly. "We shall, of course, provide a reference…"

"Yes. Thank you." Sarah replied.

"When are you leaving?" Charlie asked, rather more to the point.

"Very quickly, I am afraid," said Reverend Hobson. "It is somewhat of an urgent nature, as the congregation has been left without spiritual guidance…"

"Within the month," said Mrs. Hobson. "If not sooner."

Sarah's hand was upon the door.

"I must return to the children," she said, quickly, before tears could betray her composure. "As I am more than certain the lesson room has by now descended into chaos."

CHAPTER 12

The lesson room had indeed descended into chaos, if not outright war. In one corner, two of the Hobson brothers had seated themselves on top of Jack, who was flat on his back on the floor, objecting loudly. Meanwhile, the third Hobson brother—not being terribly concerned about the inclusion of anatomy—was in the process of sewing a large wooden button onto the middle of Jack's shirt.

In another corner, one of the Hobson sisters had removed her petticoat, the other had cut it up into squares, and the two of them, plus Mary, were busily stitching the shapes together to make a flag.

Only Tom was uninvolved, lounging in the window seat, sketching a picture of a horse that was not unlike Mr. Deeley's favourite, Marie-Claire.

All eight children stopped cold as the door to the room was flung open, and Charlie entered with Sarah.

"What in heaven's name," Sarah demanded, "is going on in here?"

The garden behind Sarah's cottage was much the same as Charlie's. The exceptions were the apple trees, which were smaller. And the surrounding stone wall, which was newly built and lacked the moss and lichen that, in Charlie's future, would texture into fuzzy greens and slippery golds and delicate browns.

Charlie sat on a blanket with Sarah, underneath the largest of the apple trees, doing her best to enjoy the picnic that had been planned at breakfast, but which was now not a very happy occasion at all.

Spread across the blanket was a feast. A freshly baked veal

and ham pie, still warm from the fire. A salad, with tomatoes and cucumbers and lettuce, and a dressing made from oil and vinegar. And more of the delicious bread that they'd had for breakfast, with butter and cheese.

And there was a sponge cake, made into four squares, pink and white, each separated by layers of strawberry jam, with whipped cream on top. Very like a Battenberg, Charlie thought—though the cake itself would not appear for another sixty years, commemorating the 1884 marriage of Queen Victoria's granddaughter to Prince Louis of Battenberg.

"And how have you managed to make these squares such a lovely pink colour?" Charlie inquired.

"A little cochineal," Sarah confided. "A tiny touch here and there provides the cheeks—as well as the cake—with a healthful bloom."

Their quiet contemplation was interrupted by Mary, running into the garden from the house, crying loudly.

"Whatever's the matter?" Sarah asked, opening her arms to comfort her.

"I don't want to go and live in a hayloft like Great Uncle Hamish!" Mary sobbed.

"I am certain we will not have to live in a hayloft," Sarah reassured her. "And please tell Jack to stop saying such ridiculous things."

Mary ceased her tears, and turned her attention instead to a rabbit she had just seen hopping past the four lilac bushes at the bottom of the garden.

Sarah looked at Charlie. "You are miles away," she said.

"I am. I apologise."

Charlie pulled her thoughts back to the picnic. She'd been thinking about the lesser Monsieur Duran's invitation to lunch tomorrow. An hour or two earlier, she had dismissed it as a foolish request. But now…

Now, everything had changed.

"You are fortunate to be able to remain in this cottage," she said.

Sarah poured a glass of lemonade for herself, and another for Charlie.

"Indeed," she agreed. "Although it was owned, at first, by Mr. Foster's uncle, who built it with his own hands. When he died childless, it was passed down to Mr. Foster by way of an inheritance. We were living in Christchurch at the time, and came here to take possession."

So, Charlie thought. She'd been right all along. Stoneford had not been Sarah's home at all. If only she'd thought to look at the parish records in Christchurch.

"When Mr. Foster was swept to his death, as his widow, I assumed ownership of the cottage. If only I also had possession of the deed to the two plots of land that I was given as my birthright."

There, Charlie thought. The very question that had been perplexing her for two years.

"What has become of that deed?" she asked. "I know we exchanged letters in which it was spoken of, but my memory has failed me concerning the details."

"It was lost," Sarah replied, despondently, "by Mr. Foster. But surely you must recall this? I was inconsolable."

"I do remember," Charlie said, sensing it was better to tell an untruth than to risk upsetting Sarah further. "Please forgive me."

"The title was mine," Sarah said, as if repeating it again now might somehow result in a different outcome. "The land was owned by my father's ancestor, Mr. John Harding, who had a farm here. The land was passed down, father to son, until my own father departed this earth. As the first born, and as I had no brothers, the title reverted to me. But when I married, everything I owned became the property of Mr. Foster. Who lost it, Catherine. Lost it. Everything."

She looked at her cousin, hopelessly.

"I am so sorry," Charlie said, meaning it.

Sarah's expression became more stoic.

"I believe that cruel advantage was taken of Mr. Foster. I have never been privy to all of the details…but he had, just before he died, fallen under the influence of certain men. Who smuggled and gambled. And were liberal with their drink. And the deed was taken from him to account for a debt which was worth far less than the value of what the paper represented."

"Do you know who took it?" Charlie asked. "Was it Lemuel Ferryman?"

"Lemuel Ferryman?" Sarah laughed. "Alas, no. If he had, I would know where to go to demand its return. The gentleman—and I use the word with prejudice—remains unknown to me."

Charlie was confused. How had Lemuel Ferryman ended up with the land, then? Had history been changed?

"And now," Sarah continued, "although we have a roof over our heads, I am shortly to be without means to provide food and clothing for myself and my children. I must count my pennies. There will be nothing extra for cochineal...or sponge cake."

The universe might yet right itself, Charlie thought. Perhaps, in the end, the union of Sarah Foster and Louis Augustus Duran would be created, not out of love, but out of necessity.

"Perhaps," she ventured, "it would not be such a bad thing for you to attend Monsieur Duran's Grand Summer Ball."

Sarah looked at Charlie.

"It would be a very bad thing," she countered, "as it would do nothing but signal to Monsieur Duran that I am considering his proposal of marriage. No. I would rather spend my days washing other peoples' soiled linen than consider a union I do not want, to a man I cannot possibly love. So let that be an end to the speculation."

CHAPTER 13

Nick needed to walk.

He switched off Charlie's laptop, a precautionary move. There was no telling what it might get up to with Mrs. Collins sitting downstairs, acquainting herself with two months' worth of *Coronation Street* on his digital recorder.

Rather than resort to yet another concoction of pharmaceuticals for his aching leg, Nick's preferred remedy was a gentle stretch, followed by a slow and steady plod about the village.

"Breakfast was all right...?" he checked.

"Breakfast was delicious," Mrs. Collins replied, without removing her gaze from the large TV screen. "I have not previously had occasion to eat Superfruity Shredded Wheat. It is yet another invention that London would surely benefit from."

She made a face at the television.

"This creature, Tracy Barlow, is easily the most annoying individual I have ever had occasion to meet. She needs to be married off to a gentleman who might instill in his bride some common manners. And very soon."

"You could get a job scriptwriting," Nick laughed. "I'm going for a walk. Would you care to join me?"

"I would rather not," Mrs. Collins decided, after a moment. "I would rather stay behind to see what becomes of Tracy Barlow. And her interfering mother. Goodness, if I were to live in their street I believe I should be quite apoplectic by now."

"Promise me you won't touch anything, or go anywhere, while I'm out," Nick said.

"I shall remain steadfastly seated in this chair, Mr. Weller."

And so, Nick set out, deep in thought, taking his familiar route, down the grassy drive to the road. His journey took him past a row of post-war red brick houses, and then an older group of whitewashed dwellings, their front gardens splashed with antique roses, their tall Victorian chimneys reaching into the blue morning sky.

A theory was beginning to take shape in his mind. Until now, he'd believed that the woman who now sat in his front room, caught up in the drama at The Rovers Return, was his cousin Charlie. And Charlie had simply undergone some sort of brain blip the night before which had convinced her she was someone else. That much had made sense. Charlie often lost herself in time, immersed in her family tree research, or some new historical project for the museum.

Last night, she'd simply gone one step too far. Perhaps it had something to do with the damage she'd allegedly done to Ron Ferryman's property. Possibly the shock of it had been too much for her, and, coupled with the anniversary of Jeff's death, it had caused her to retreat, temporarily, into the *persona* of Mrs. Collins.

Nick went around two corners, which took him to the High Street running along the west side of the Village Green. He popped into the Village News for a paper, and then decided to buy some boiled barley sugar sweets as well. He lingered over a copy of *All About Space* until Gavin, the proprietor, cleared his throat and he was forced to buy a copy if he wanted to finish reading about pulsars and antimatter.

Nick carried his purchases outside, and crossed the road.

That was what he had believed had happened to Charlie. A temporary brain blip.

Until now. And nothing in his experience, or in his research, could adequately explain it.

The makings were there, like all of the ingredients for soup, waiting to be stirred and cooked. Sprites were real. And tachyons, in theory, did exist. And there had been that one bold lightning strike, cracking into the Village Oak and across the roofs of nearby cottages.

Was Mrs. Collins, in fact, not Charlie at all, but someone from another time?

And if that was the case…where was Charlie?

It was too early for Emmy Cooper to be feeding the pigeons on the green, and far too early for the village children to be kicking a football around. The grassy triangle was deserted.

Nick wandered over to the old oak, still deep in thought. He barely noticed the heavy machinery that Ron Ferryman had parked nearby, an ever-present reminder of what he had planned as soon as he was granted permission by the council. The tree was looking very sad, he thought, treading through an overnight dropping of dead leaves.

Nick's phone buzzed and he reached into his pocket. His eldest daughter was learning to drive and had been hinting about a car for her birthday, in a month's time.

He unlocked the screen.

A text message.

But it was not from Naomi.

It was from Charlie.

Nick read it over, quickly, and then went back and read it once more, this time very slowly.

His first thought was that she was playing an amazing practical joke on him.

And then, his first thought was replaced very quickly by a sobering second thought. It was not a practical joke at all. It was real. And it was the answer to his theory. If Mrs. Collins had appeared from somewhere in the past…then Charlie must obviously have gone where Mrs. Collins had been.

Nick read his cousin's message a third time, and made note of the date at the top of the screen. Sent on Thursday, June 30, 1825.

1825.

Completely impossible.

Yet there it was, in black and white, on his mobile.

I seem to be back in 1825, Nick.

The Village Oak's got some kind of Wi-Fi thing going!

And then:

Do you or Sam know anything about a cousin, Catherine Collins? Married to someone who died before 1825. Need to find out more.

Nick did the logical thing.

Greetings from now to 1825, he wrote. *Message safely received. We know about Catherine Collins. Will try to find out more.*

He read over what he'd written. Too brief. He added a post-script.

Will try to work out how to bring you back. Don't panic.

He touched Send, and watched as his message hung for a moment in cyberspace, as if trying to decide for itself whether this was a genuine request, or a joke. And then...it was gone.

Sent.

And now his phone was ringing properly. A caller.

Edwin Watts. Antiques Olde and New, a shop at the bottom end of the green, where the tour buses stopped.

"Edwin," Nick said. "Sold that Commodore 64 yet?"

"Oi," Edwin said back. "Less of your humor, mate, and a bit more attention to your nearest and dearest. I've got your cousin here and if she don't stop stabbing at me with her sword I'm ringing the coppers."

"I thought," Nick said, "that you promised me you'd stay put."

"The window box ceased to function," Mrs. Collins replied. "And, as I was unable to summon its tiny inhabitants for further amusement, I became weary of my surroundings, and thought I might acquaint myself further with the environs of your village."

"You on drugs?" Edwin Watts said, narrowing his eyes at her.

Mrs. Collins lowered the antique sword so that it was pointing at Edwin Watts' heart, and not his neck.

"Do not vex me, sir. I am skilled in the use of this weapon. My lately departed husband fought under the Duke of Wellington."

Edwin Watts raised his hands a little higher in the air.

"I think you ought to put that down," Nick suggested. "Really."

"I shall," Mrs. Collins replied, "when Mr. Watts agrees that the sword rightfully belongs to me."

"You're bonkers," said Edwin Watts.

"You are my witness," Mrs. Collins replied, lowering the weapon at last, and placing it on a display table next to a collection of runny glass bottles and a selection of vintage Victorian hand bells. "This is the undress sword of a British Cavalry officer. It was fashioned in 1796, and it was in use at the Battle of Waterloo. As you can see here, and here, and here."

She indicated a series of nicks and deformations in the long, heavy blade.

"It's yours," Edwin Watts said. "For nine hundred and fifty quid."

"And I shall have it, sir," Mrs. Collins replied, "though I intend to pay nothing for its retrieval. For I know it to be the very same sword that my late husband brought back from the battle. It is a sword given to him by Lieutenant-Colonel Sharpe, a reward for his bravery in attempting to save the life of a fallen Cavalry officer. It is that fallen man's sword. See—here—it has his initials carved into the back of the guard. An F and an H. It disappeared from my residence some months ago, under mysterious circumstances. And you, sir, appear to have been responsible—and if not you, then some wicked accomplice. And, for that, I intend to remove it from your possession now."

"I'm calling the coppers," said Edwin Watts.

"She's not herself," Nick answered, hastily. "She's under a lot of stress."

"Nine hundred and fifty quid," Edwin Watts replied, picking up the phone. "Or it's the Old Bill."

CHAPTER 14

With much energetic advice from Tom and Jack, and a great deal of giggling from Mary, the large table from the kitchen had been moved into the sitting room.

A white linen cloth had been placed over its top, and spread across the cloth was a light supper that had been hurriedly put together by Sarah using leftovers from their picnic lunch. As well, there would a very fine soup, with turnips and carrots and onions, and mushrooms and parsley, and salt and pepper and stock, which was still simmering over the fire in the kitchen.

This was, all agreed, a Very Special Occasion.

"You have gained an admirer," Sarah remarked, to Charlie.

"I must confess," Charlie replied, "I have discovered Mr. Deeley to be an unexpectedly pleasant surprise."

"If only the same could be said of his employer," Sarah said, dipping the ladle into the soup to sip, and taste.

There was a jaunty knock at the door, which Charlie went to answer.

"An even more unexpected surprise," she laughed.

It was Mr. Deeley, and he had picked a cheerful bouquet of wildflowers on his way down the hill from the manor.

He presented them to Charlie with a bow.

"Thank you, Mr. Deeley. Please do come in."

"A pleasing combination," Sarah remarked, to herself, as she put away the soup ladle and stepped forward to welcome Mr. Deeley. "And it certainly does not lack for want of simmering."

• • •

The veal and ham pie was just as delicious cold as it had been warmed for lunch. And there was another salad, there being no shortage of little farms surrounding Stoneford, and therefore, an almost endless supply of greens and other offerings from their fields.

There was fresh bread and butter, and there was a feast of cheese: two kinds of Cheddar, a generous helping of Cheshire, and a fine wedge of Wensleydale.

And afterwards, there was a trifle. Charlie had managed to concoct it, recalling a recipe she'd read in a six-months-old women's magazine in her dentist's waiting room. She'd incorporated biscuits, custard, cream, and rather a lot of wine, which she'd discovered lurking in a corked bottle in the cupboard next door to where the candles were kept.

Seated at the head of the table, Sarah poured tea for their guest.

"I apologise, Mr. Deeley, for the meagreness of our fare. No doubt you are accustomed to more lavish meals in Monsieur Duran's household."

Mr. Deeley laughed. "There is no meagreness in the fare here, Mrs. Foster."

He glanced impishly at Charlie.

"And I expect that my appetite, having been tantalized this once, will in future be well rewarded."

"I do not think you will be disappointed, Mr. Deeley," Charlie replied. She looked at Sarah.

"This morning I had the pleasure of meeting Monsieur Duran's father. He has come to visit from France."

"Has he?" Sarah said, plunging into the trifle with a very large spoon. "And does Monsieur Duran's father share his son's infelicitous distemper?"

"Fortunately, he does not," Mr. Deeley replied.

"He's a count, you know," Tom offered, as Charlie passed his bowl up to the top of the table.

"Yes," Jack added. "And he lives in a very draughty chateau near Amiens that he hates."

"And," Mary said, "he has six dogs, three cats, and four pet geese, who are all named after French kings: Charles the Wise, Charles the Bald, Charles the Simple and Charles the Fat."

Sarah spooned a small helping of trifle into Tom's bowl.

"Goodness, children," she said. "How on earth have you managed to acquire this knowledge?"

"Because Mr. Deeley acquainted us with Monsieur Duran's father when he came to visit from France the last time," Tom answered. "And I should like a slightly larger portion of trifle than that, Mother, thank you."

"Last summer," Jack added, "Monsieur Duran's father showed me how to cut silhouettes from coloured paper."

"Last summer, Monsieur Duran's father showed *me* how to stand on my head," Mary countered, not to be outdone.

"Perhaps you might consider going to Monsieur Duran's ball tomorrow night," Charlie said, "in order to acquaint yourself with the person who is held in such high esteem by your children."

"Certainly not," Sarah replied, perfunctorily.

"I should like a much larger portion of trifle than Tom, please," Mary said. "And I do think you should go to the ball, Mama."

"If only to give the greater Monsieur Duran the opportunity to teach you to stand on your head as well," Mr. Deeley suggested, cheekily. "And I should like a much larger portion of trifle than Mary, please."

An hour or so later, the plates and bowls, glasses and cups and saucers, knives and forks and spoons had all been carried to the sideboard in the kitchen for washing up. Headstands and silhouettes had been discussed and dissected, as well as the greater Monsieur Duran's eclectic and peculiar menagerie, and all of the French kings from Charlemagne onward. And there had been delicate confirmation by Mr. Deeley of the lesser Monsieur Duran's apparent obsession with the invention of a sanitary water closet.

Mary, Jack and Tom, Mr. Deeley and Charlie were all now gathered around a small pianoforte in the sitting room. Addressing the keyboard, Sarah played a pretty melody she had learned from her mother, but had found no occasion to perform in recent years.

She was a competent musician, Charlie thought. Not overly musical, but educated ladies in Sarah's time were expected only to master those skills which were consequential to domesticity. Cookery and sewing. Embroidery. How to draw and how to dance. How to speak passable French, how to recognize countries on a globe. And how to play the pianoforte, whether they had a talent for it, or not.

Sarah finished, competently, to polite applause.

Charlie stood up.

"May I?"

"Of course!" Sarah exclaimed. "I expect you have had much more opportunity than I to entertain, living in London. The lower keys are fond of sticking a little—it is the sea air. But otherwise, the tuning is tolerable."

Charlie took Sarah's seat at the keyboard. It had been a very long time since she'd done that.

Five years.

She used to rock out the tunes. Jeff had a day job, in Southampton, in an office. But every weekend, she used to join him and his musician friends, playing at a club, or sometimes just practising in an upstairs room over a pub.

Charlie had a portable electric keyboard she used to carry around to all their gigs. The drummer, the bass player and the fellow on rhythm guitar were old enough to be their parents. And Jeff was their lead guitarist, twanging away on his old Fender Strat, channeling Hank Marvin when they invariably reverted to *Apache* or *Wonderful Land* at the end of an evening.

She'd given away the electric keyboard. And the Strat had been tucked into its hard travelling case. Charlie had not opened it since Jeff had died.

Here and now, she had suddenly felt a long-buried leap of anticipation. There was someone in attendance that made her want to play.

She sat at the pianoforte, and picked out the first tune that came into her mind. Used to be her favourite, that one. One of Jeff's favourites, too. The one that made him joke that he was channeling Hank Marvin. *F.B.I.*

But the pianoforte keys didn't bend the way guitar strings did. And without that accompanying guitar, it all sounded a bit…eerie.

"Will you permit me to join you?"

Charlie glanced up, surprised, to find Mr. Deeley dragging his chair over to hers.

"The senior Monsieur Duran may have excelled at silhouettes and headstands," he said, making himself comfortable beside her, "but his lasting contribution to my proficiency in social intercourse has been a passable intimacy with these keys. Show me the notes. We can play a duet."

F.B.I. as a piano duet. The idea made Charlie smile. A song never intended for the piano at all, now arranged for four hands. She played the simple introduction on the lower keys for Mr. Deeley.

"Just do that, over and over again."

Mr. Deeley obliged, with a far more competent ear than Sarah possessed. In fact, Charlie thought, he was quite brilliantly, and improvisionally, good!

She joined in with the melody line, filling the sitting room with the joyous harmony she and Jeff had shared two centuries later, in the future—but now, through the oddity of a timeslip, a tune transposed back into 1825.

The duet finished with a grand flourish, and to much delighted laughter.

Mr. Deeley stood up to bow, and Charlie performed a slightly unsteady curtsey.

"Later on I'll teach you the special Shadows' Walk that goes with that song," she promised, whimsically.

"I believe there might be opportunity for an excellent dance to accompany this piece," Mr. Deeley remarked. "If circumstances were favourable, I would introduce a version of it at tomorrow night's ball to amuse and entertain Monsieur Duran's guests."

"Oh!" Charlie exclaimed. "Will you be there?"

"I shall be," Mr. Deeley confirmed.

"How so?" Sarah inquired. "Surely Monsieur Duran would never allow his groom to attend such a grand function…"

"He would not at all," Mr. Deeley agreed. "However, at the annual celebration three years ago, a trio of musicians had been hired, and the pianist was discovered, too late, to be entirely too fond of imbibing. He was found beneath his instrument midway through the evening, having lost control of most of his faculties, and, indeed, an embarrassment of his bodily functions. The Grand Summer Ball teetered on the verge of disaster, until it was suggested to the lesser Monsieur Duran by the greater Monsieur Duran that I might be an excellent replacement. And so I was summoned—and I performed exceedingly well. Thus saving the evening, as well as the reputation of the gentleman of the manor."

"How fortuitous for the lesser Monsieur Duran," Sarah remarked. "I hope you received compensation for your contribution."

"A half day away from the stables," Mr. Deeley said, "which I spent at the seaside, with a picnic lunch, the sun, and an enjoyable book. And an invitation, assured each year by the greater Monsieur Duran, to the Grand Summer Ball. Although I am certain he only does it to annoy his son."

Sarah smiled, and Charlie laughed.

"Would you do me the honor of allowing me to escort you to the aforementioned ball tomorrow night?" Mr. Deeley asked, turning to Charlie very formally, and looking rather serious.

"But I haven't been invited," Charlie said. Impulsively, Mr. Deeley took her hand, and got down on one knee.

"Mrs. Collins, would you therefore do me the very great honor of accepting my invitation?"

"I would be greatly honored, Mr. Deeley," Charlie said, pulling him to his feet.

Mr. Deeley, looking very relieved, turned to Sarah.

"Your presence at the ball would also honor me greatly, Mrs. Foster."

"No," Sarah replied, with finality. "I thank you for your kind invitation. But no."

Their conversation was interrupted by a knock upon the kitchen door.

Charlie went to see who it was.

"Mr. Rankin," she said, recognizing him from their brief meeting at the manor. And there was Marie-Claire, saddled and waiting patiently in the road beyond, her reins looped through the garden gate.

"Good evening, Mrs. Collins," Mr. Rankin said. "I must speak with some urgency to Mr. Deeley."

"Of course. I'll fetch him for you."

Charlie returned to the sitting room.

"Mr. Deeley," she said. "It is your gardener. Mr. Rankin."

She paused.

Rankin. No. Couldn't be. And yet…

"He requires your attention."

Mr. Deeley obliged, excusing himself, and with a bemused look, followed Charlie back to the open kitchen door. Mr. Rankin was bent over in the garden, examining the tall foxgloves growing up on either side of the path.

"Ned," said Mr. Deeley. "Do Mrs. Foster's flowers meet with your approval?"

Mr. Rankin stood up.

"The flowers are handsome and well-tended," he said. "And I am sorry to interrupt your evening, Shaun, but the lesser Monsieur Duran appears to be in urgent need of our assistance."

His first name was Shaun. Charlie had wondered what it was, but hadn't been certain of the etiquette involved in finding out.

Mr. Deeley was Shaun, and Mr. Rankin was Ned.

She smiled as she followed Shaun Deeley and Ned Rankin down the road. Tom and Jack had decided to trail along as well, although Mary had been forbidden by Sarah, and had therefore been left behind, in a very poor mood indeed.

They walked in a small group towards The Dog's Watch Inn,

with Mr. Deeley leading Marie-Claire.

"I heard a very pleasant melody as I walked up the road to the cottage," Mr. Rankin commented. "Was that you, Shaun?"

"It was," Mr. Deeley confirmed. "Ably assisted by the talented Mrs. Collins. Did you like it?"

"The music was unfamiliar to me," Mr. Rankin replied, with a great deal of thought. "Yet it was not displeasing. I found it…" He paused, to think of the word. "Indelible."

"I shall play it again for you at the manor," Mr. Deeley promised. "You will be able to learn it on Monsieur Duran's guitar."

Lemuel Ferryman, Charlie knew from her research, was an enterprising individual whose father had been a butcher, and whose father before him, an undertaker. In fact, the entire Ferryman family seemed to have prided itself on their canny ability to detect what would always be in demand.

Fanny Ferryman, Lemuel's older sister, was the madam of a highly-sought after house of ill repute in a notorious neighborhood in Portsmouth.

And Edgar Ferryman, their younger brother, was a tax collector.

"Mr. Deeley," Lemuel Ferryman said, greeting him at the door to the inn. "And Mr. Rankin. And half of the Foster family. I appear to have no shortage of diversions this evening. If you would be so kind."

He nodded at a group of locals who had gathered in a circle in the centre of the floor, creating a kind of improvised boxing ring.

Charlie, Tom and Jack stayed where they were, in the safety of the doorway, while Mr. Deeley and Mr. Rankin waded into the crowd.

Occupying the centre of the boxing ring were the lesser Monsieur Duran—looking rather the worse for wear, Charlie thought, his shirt-tails askew, his buttons torn open, his face bloodied—and a gentleman Tom recognized as George King, from the village.

"He is the older brother of Rose," Tom provided, "who was employed as a housemaid at the manor. But she was dismissed last week."

"For the honour of my sister," Mr. King said, landing his fist squarely on the lesser Monsieur Duran's nose, "I swear, sir—you shall die!"

Another villager, identified by Tom as John Wallis, who had been given temporary custody of George King's tankard, cheered him on. "You tell him, sir! Remind the *croque-monsieur* just who it was won the Battle of Waterloo!"

Mr. Wallis's friend, a soldier called Henry Cole, who, according to Jack, was missing most of his left arm as the result of an altercation with one of Napoleon's best swordsmen, drained his own mug of ale. "Send the damnable frog back to his stinking swamp!" he said, wiping his mouth on his sleeve.

"You are all beneath my consideration," the lesser Monsieur Duran scowled, drunkenly. "You are all the commonest of scum!"

"A fine way to speak to the citizens of the country that offered you sanctuary," George King countered. "It is a great pity Madame la Guillotine was not able to entertain you in her parlour following your peasants' popular revolt!"

The lesser Monsieur Duran responded to this with a wild swing at Mr. King's nose, missing it completely.

Clearly unused to hand-to-hand combat, and even more clearly, somewhat of a coward when it came to actual physical pain, the lesser Monsieur Duran then immediately lost his footing. The momentum propelled him backwards and directly into Mr. Wallis' awaiting arms.

Mr. Wallis immediately propped the lesser Monsieur Duran upright, which allowed Mr. King to respond with a neat upper cut to his chin, sending him to the floor, where he lay for a moment, stunned.

The assembled villagers cheered, toasting George King's victory with their ale.

"A swift kick in the canards would suit him well now!" Mr. Cole suggested, encouragingly.

"Come on!" Mr. King shouted, at the crumpled heap that was the lesser Monsieur Duran, cowering on the floor. "Up! I will not strike a man when he is down!"

The lesser Monsieur Duran, ever mindful of his own sense of

self-preservation, wisely remained where he was.

"*Vous êtes un cochon dégoûtant,*" he replied, sourly, spitting out some blood, and most of a tooth.

George King removed his tankard from Mr. Wallis's hand and hurled the dregs of its contents at the lesser Monsieur Duran's face. "Get up! And speak the King's English while you call England your home, you snail sucking swine!"

"Good evening, gentlemen," Mr. Deeley said, good-naturedly, at last deciding the time had come to take action. "Monsieur Duran, sir, you seem to be in need of some assistance. Come—we will ensure your safe journey back to the manor."

Mr. Deeley bent down, firmly grasping a left arm, while Mr. Rankin took hold of the right. To a chorus of boos, the lesser Monsieur Duran was hauled to his feet.

"You leave him to us, Shaun," Mr. Wallis advised.

"We shall see him home safely," Mr. Cole added, in a voice that was less a reassurance than a promise of certain malice.

"We never learn, do we, sir," Mr. Rankin added, in the lesser Monsieur Duran's ear, as he and Mr. Deeley assisted him past Charlie, Jack and Tom, and deposited him, head first, face down and mostly sideways, over Marie-Claire's accommodating saddle.

CHAPTER 15

Do you or Sam know anything about a cousin, Catherine Collins? Married to someone who died before 1825. Need to find out more.

"Mrs. Collins," Nick began, his notepad at the ready, and his excellent note-taking pen—which he'd been given the Christmas before by Naomi—poised above it. "Please tell me..."

What? He had no idea where to start. Please tell me everything about your life, from the very beginning until now? Whenever now might happen to be?

Mrs. Collins wasn't even listening to him. She'd found Nick's iPod, hidden under some papers on his desk. And she would not now relinquish it, having discovered three Shadows tunes that Charlie had transferred over from Jeff's collection years earlier: *Apache, Wonderful Land* and *Atlantis*. As well as a number of songs by Cliff Richard, and the full soundtracks for both *Summer Holiday* and *The Young Ones*.

"But this is wondrous," she marvelled, holding her hands over the ear buds, to the exclusion of all other sounds, including Nick's voice. "If only these musicians were to inhabit the sitting rooms of London, we should witness an expeditious end to the torment of ponderous women who cannot sing, inflicting songs on a pianoforte they cannot play!"

"Might we get on with my questions?" Nick said, very loudly.

She'd agreed to be interviewed in exchange for Nick paying for her sword. It was an expensive trade-off. But Charlie was worth it.

With great reluctance, Mrs. Collins removed the ear buds, and switched off the iPod.

"Can you tell me your full name?"

"Certainly. I was born Catherine Mary Harding, in Christchurch, in the county of Hampshire. Although, as you know, my married name is Collins."

"And how are you related to Sarah Foster?" Nick asked.

"I am the eldest daughter of Mrs. Foster's father's youngest brother," Mrs. Collins replied, patiently.

Nick took a moment to think this through. Family relationships had always confounded him, in spite of his having a meticulous brain when it came to fundamental science.

Seeing his confusion, Mrs. Collins continued: "My cousin's name before her marriage to Mr. Foster was also Harding. Her father was Mr. Ebenezer Harding, the eldest of five siblings, who were, in order of birth following him, Mr. Bernard Harding, Mr. Darwin Harding, Mr. Lyndon Harding and Mr. Osbert Harding. The last, Mr. Osbert Harding, is my father."

Mrs. Collins paused, to give Nick a chance to write it all down in his notebook.

"Ah," he said, as it all began, slowly, to make sense. "First cousins, then."

"I have five sisters, all younger, all happily married, all happily contributing to my father and mother's occupation as doting grandparents. I myself am childless, for I am widowed, as my dearest Mr. Collins was sadly taken from me five years ago, a victim of pneumonia."

Mrs. Collins stopped again, and waited for Nick to catch up.

"And your husband's name was…?"

"Mr. Joseph Collins, of London. We were married on Sunday, the 27th of August, 1815 at St. Mary's, Lambeth, following his return from Belgium, where he fought as a Private with his regiment at Waterloo. You have already heard about the sword, which was given to my husband to reward him for his bravery."

Nick acknowledged the weapon—which was resting upright against his desk—with a renewed appreciation.

"And your birthday?" he inquired.

"The second of September, 1796," Mrs. Collins replied. "I am very close in years to Mrs. Foster, who was born on the 16th of August, 1793."

"And Mrs. Foster was married…when?"

"She and Mr. Aiden Foster were wed on Saturday, the 28th of May, 1814, in Christchurch. They relocated to Stoneford when Mr. Foster's uncle died without issue, and his home was bequeathed to the newly wedded couple."

Mrs. Collins was showing signs of impatience.

"This device has enticed my imagination," she decided, putting the ear buds back in, and switching the iPod on again. "And this gentleman who is singing about going to where the sun is shining brightly and the sea is blue—a most appealing voice."

Nick abandoned the interview. But he'd gathered enough information to convince him that Mrs. Catherine Mary Harding Collins was exactly who she claimed to be. And the answers she'd provided had done more to shake his faith in pragmatic science than anything—anything—ever before encountered in his long and, until now, completely unremarkable career in Physics.

Charlie knew how to research her ancestors, and had come up with blanks when Sarah Foster was concerned. But Mrs. Collins had provided all of the answers.

Still sitting at his desk, with Mrs. Collins happily singing along to Cliff Richard, Nick composed a new message to Charlie that contained all of the information she'd asked for. He re-read it several times before making the final decision to launch it into whatever ripple in space and time was going to allow it to reach its destination, two hundred years in the past.

Stay calm, he finished. *Hope this helps.*

He touched Send, and watched the little screen.

Nothing.

For a moment, Nick had a horrible thought. Charlie's partially disinfected laptop was sitting nearby. What if he'd wiped out the only connection there was to his cousin in 1825?

And then, he remembered. Charlie had mentioned it in her message. The Village Oak.

• • •

111

The growl of heavy machinery coming from the direction of the Village Green was as alarming to Nick as it was surprising. He quickened his pace, as much as his damaged leg would allow.

Ron Ferryman did not have the Village of Stoneford's permission to proceed with any kind of work on the green, regardless of his highly touted claim to the property. The bulldozers were there purely for show, meant to intimidate—in much the same way that Reg and Ron had generated fear, followed by compliance, in the schoolyard they'd tyrannically ruled as children.

As he crossed the road, Nick saw, to his horror, that a crew of tree cutters, armed with chainsaws, had assembled a few yards away from the Village Oak. They were prevented from actually approaching the tree by a group of angry-looking villagers who'd arranged themselves in a defiant circle around its trunk, their arms linked in solidarity.

"And what the hell do you think you're doing?" Nick demanded, confronting Ron Ferryman, who was trying his best to look important in a blue hardhat and a bright yellow high-visibility vest.

"What the hell do you think I'm doing?" Ron Ferryman countered.

The Brothers (as they'd been referred to in the schoolyard) had never been able to bully Nick, in spite of escalating threats and several intimidating confrontations in the lane behind the church.

"Whatever it is, it's illegal," Nick replied, standing his ground.

"And inevitable, Weller. I've brought in my own experts, and they've advised me that tree's not likely to survive. It's coming down. I don't see why there should be any further delays."

"And what have your experts concluded is the cause of the tree's declining health?"

"Failure to thrive?" Ron Ferryman guessed.

"Failure to survive having poison poured into its roots," Nick corrected.

Nick realized, as he said it, that Mike Tidman had only theorized that was what was killing the oak. He hadn't officially said anything, publicly. It was Charlie who'd confided to him what Mike had said about the poison. And tests were still being done.

"Watch yourself, Weller. I'd say that kind of statement constitutes slander."

In the schoolyard, Ron was the boy who could be counted on to provide names and details to the headmaster whenever there had been mischief afoot. Unless, of course, the mischief had involved himself, or his brother.

"No slander," Nick said. "I've merely stated a fact. Poison has been identified as the probable cause of the tree's failure to thrive. Did my statement include any names?"

"Names were inferred."

Ron Ferryman turned to the circle of villagers surrounding the oak. "You heard him."

"I heard nothing of the sort," replied one of the tree-protectors, a retired bus driver named Morris Adams who had once saved a little boy from drowning by jumping into a river.

Another of the protectors, Peter King, who was behind the campaign to save the hedgehogs, tapped his hearing aid. "What did you say, Ferryman? Your digger's making a terrible racket!"

"I'd advise you to step out of the way," Ron Ferryman said, sourly, to Morris Adams. "Before I set the police on you."

"Go on then," Morris Adams replied. "Fetch the Stoneford Constabulary."

"One of 'em's down the pub," Peter King added, "and the other's in Southampton on a course."

"Typical," Ron Ferryman said. "Never about when they're needed most."

"Haven't caught your vandal yet, then?" Peter King taunted. "Too quick on his feet?"

"It was a 'she'," Ron Ferryman replied. "And 'she' will be arrested on Monday, once her 'medical complications' are proven to be nothing more than amateur stalling tactics."

"Your family wouldn't have a claim to this property," Nick said, "if it wasn't for our family letting it go two hundred years ago."

"Then I shall be forever indebted to Mrs. Lowe for her ancestors' lack of foresight and utter stupidity," Ron Ferryman answered.

"Can you produce the papers?"

"You know as well as I do they no longer exist. They were destroyed by fire."

"Then I challenge you," Nick said, boldly, "to prove your official ownership."

The assembled protectors—most of them in their senior years and all of them with ancestors who had grown up alongside Ferryman's forebears—muttered their collective agreement.

"Another stalling tactic," Ron Ferryman replied. "Very well. I'll bring in the solicitors."

He retreated—but only as far as the safety of one of his hired bulldozers, in the lower corner of the green. He was followed, in short order, by the workmen with their chainsaws.

Taking out his mobile, Nick placed himself in close proximity to the ancient tree. Then, standing just outside its circle of protectors, and glancing up into the spreading branches and wilting leaves, he touched Send.

It had to work this time. If not…

He watched the little screen as the message he had prepared for Charlie hovered uncertainly in the space between Here and There.

And then…it was gone, replaced by two simple words:

Message Sent.

CHAPTER 16

In the cottage kitchen, a bucket of water was simmering over the fire. There had been an excited recounting of events at The Dog's Watch by Tom, with actions handily provided by Jack. And Charlie was now helping Sarah wash and dry and put away the plates and knives and forks from their tea.

For Charlie, who, two centuries into the future, tended to rely solely on her dishwasher, it was a sobering experience. There were no powders or tidy pouches containing pre-treat, food-dissolver, rinse and shine.

There was a bowl with hot water for washing, and a second bowl for rinsing. And there was a soft brown soap supplied by Mr. Rigby, the same man who provided the tallow candles. He was distantly related to Lemuel Ferryman, and he rendered animal fat at his premises on the other side of the village.

"Thankfully downwind," Sarah said, as she washed, and Charlie rinsed, and at the end of the line, Mary dried, employing an old piece of linen that had been cut from a worn out bed sheet.

The dried and polished plates were stacked on the sideboard with the hope that Jack or Tom would eventually put them away.

It was, Charlie thought, a profoundly optimistic wish. Clearly, Jack and Tom considered the kitchen the domain of females, and had made themselves conveniently scarce.

"I do believe," Sarah remarked, casually, to Charlie, "that you have managed to capture the affections of Mr. Deeley."

Charlie glanced at Sarah. "And what would you think about that?" she inquired, with care.

"It is his employer I dislike. Mr. Deeley is…" Sarah searched for the words, then smiled. "…very good with his hands."

Charlie laughed. Then caught herself. For a moment, she had almost considered it a possibility. But she was not of this time. And her mind had been so overwhelmed with the events of the past two days, she had not allowed herself to contemplate what might come next.

But now she was contemplating it. Quite seriously. What would happen if she didn't go back?

It was not unpleasant here. Dreadfully inconvenient, yes. And she couldn't begin to imagine how she was going to manage when her period was due…or if she was suddenly in need of a tooth to be filled…

But…there was Mr. Deeley. As she had been sitting with him, her hands beside his on the piano keys, her heart had been filled with such a soaring joy. Something she'd forgotten. Something she now realized she had missed, in all the years since Jeff had died, and now yearned to have back. Something she'd lost…and had now rediscovered.

And the thought of it suddenly—and unaccountably—caused tears to well up in her eyes.

"My dear!" Sarah exclaimed. "It has been five years! Your time of mourning is long over. There is a season for everything…and our time on this earth is so fleeting. You have allowed yourself to grieve…but now, I am certain—I am more than certain—you must allow yourself some happiness."

Charlie looked at the spot on the kitchen wall where, two centuries on, a five-year-old calendar hung, permanently reminding her of the month and day that Jeff had ceased to be.

"Think of it!" Sarah continued, "You and Mr. Collins had so longed for children…"

"It isn't that, Sarah. It's…" How could she possibly explain?

"And you could not ask for a better prospect than Mr. Deeley. He earns a good wage. And his future employment is secured."

"You will marry again, Sarah," Charlie said, trying desperately to change the subject. "And you will have two more children. A boy and a girl. Augustus and Emily."

Sarah opened the kitchen door, and tipped the soapy water out into the bare patch of earth behind the foxgloves.

Mary followed, with the rinsing bowl. "Augustus," she said, with great thought. "I believe I should quite like to have a brother called Augustus."

Sarah laughed. "Augustus indeed. I think not."

She took the two bowls back inside, as Mary, acquitted from dish rinsing, seized the opportunity to disappear into the sitting room.

"But it is true," Charlie protested. "I have a way of...seeing things. A way of knowing what is in your future..."

Sarah's smile faded, and was replaced by a worried frown. "Do you read the cards? And see patterns in tea leaves and upon the palm of the hand? The Gypsies who live in the New Forest practice these dark arts..."

"No—nothing like that!" Charlie assured her. "It's like a...a sort of understanding. And the understanding is that you will marry again."

Sarah was looking increasingly uncomfortable.

"And you will live a good long life, Sarah, with grandchildren, and great-grandchildren. You must believe me when I tell you this."

"And what does your special understanding tell you about your own future?" Sarah countered. "Will you marry again? Will you have children and grandchildren?"

"I wish I knew," Charlie answered, unhappily.

"It does seem a great shame," Sarah said, "that you cannot foresee what is next for yourself...yet you are uncommonly certain about what is in store for me. A Gypsy woman named Esmerelda read my tea leaves at the Village Fair last year. And she was of much the same opinion as you. Another marriage. And other children. But I cannot see the logic of such things, Catherine. It is the stuff of fancy and conjecture."

"There may be an opportunity to fulfill Esmerelda's prediction at tomorrow night's ball," Charlie said. "There are sure to be guests, a complement of unattached gentlemen of means, who Mr. Deeley would happily contrive to make your acquaintance."

The idea had only just come to her. Convincing Sarah to attend the Grand Summer Ball would be half the battle won. A partial result was better than no result at all.

"Oh, indeed," Sarah laughed. "And having successfully

dispensed with the lesser Monsieur Duran, I shall then marry one of his contemporaries. And give birth to a son I shall name Augustus, so that each time Monsieur Duran passes him in the village, he will be reminded of his unfortunate decision to send me a gown."

She paused to dry her hands on the old piece of linen Mary had left hanging by the fire.

"A not altogether displeasing scheme," she admitted.

"And so you *would* consider taking another husband?" Charlie asked.

"Of course I would," Sarah replied. "But the more pressing question might be, would a gentleman of means, who has either managed to avoid marriage into middle age, or who has suffered a tragic loss and has now ended his grieving and is of a mind to remarry, be willing to consider me? With three children of my own, and nothing to bring to the union but a cottage and an independent mind."

She paused again.

"No," she decided. "No. I will not risk it. Mr. Deeley may accompany you to the ball, but I shall stay behind."

"And Monsieur Duran...?"

"Monsieur Duran," Sarah said, hanging up the tattered piece of linen, "is welcome to amuse himself. As I'm quite certain he does. Unceasingly."

She would not interfere. She would not. She had done her best, and still could not convince Sarah to change her mind.

Charlie excused herself, and went outside to think.

There was still the lunch tomorrow, with Monsieur Duran and his father.

There was still time for the lesser Monsieur Duran to say something—anything—that she could take back to Sarah as an offering.

Even if it was to be a loveless marriage, she would have security and comfort. She would be looked after, as would her children...and her two future children, thus guaranteeing the orderly progression of descendancy.

And perhaps, she thought, hopefully, Monsieur Duran might confine his…unnatural habits…to clandestine affairs with his maids, and reserve the marital bed for more traditional practices.

Charlie shook her head. What was she thinking? This was madness. She needed to walk. By herself. She needed to clear her mind.

It was a lovely summer's evening, and without the ever-present reminders of life in the 21st century that Charlie was used to. There were no jet trails criss-crossing the sky and no aircraft glinting their way to and from Gatwick and Heathrow. There were no whining car engines, no diesel lorries taking an illegal shortcut past the Village Green. And there was nothing of the foul exhaust that they left in their wake.

It was, in fact, very, very quiet. And the twilight was scented with woodsmoke and garden flowers and something that she could only describe, in her imagination, as *green*. Shrubs and trees and grass: a wilderness kind of smell that had been lost when paved roads and frantic commerce had inflicted their brand of civilization on the countryside.

She walked along the cart track that was Cliff Road. There were no lights. There was barely habitation at this end of the village, though in the future it was destined to be populated by expensive houses with even more expensive views, sun decks and swimming pools. This was where Sam would live with Roger, in a house they could barely afford, but one which allowed Sam a cachet of wealth and privilege.

A little further along, the track sloped down to the familiar shingle beach. The moon was rising, shining like a brilliant silver lantern in the indigo sky. It illuminated the sea and the pebbles and the strip of sand dunes where, centuries later, a long row of brightly painted little beach huts would stand, status symbols for holiday weekenders.

Charlie stood in the twilight and listened to the soft *whish* and *shirr* of the tide lapping in and out.

She looked out over the dark deserted stretch of water between the beach and the Isle of Wight, two miles in the distance.

Not quite deserted.

There was a boat. Charlie could see it by the little light that was still lingering on the horizon. There were two men aboard, rowing, and there was cargo.

Smugglers?

She stepped back and crouched down behind some tall tufts of beach grass, so that she was not so visible. She watched as the men landed on the rocky part of the shore, about a quarter of a mile to the west. There was a small ravine, there—Stoneford Bunny—which was heavily wooded and, in the future, would be protected as a nature conservancy. Now it was just an overgrown and uninhabited little valley running back from the gravel and clay cliffs, with a surprise patch of quicksand at its foot. Perfect for smuggling contraband, as only the Stoneford locals would have the knowledge to enable them to navigate past the dodgy bits.

Near the ravine, at the top of the cliff, was a farm. Charlie could see a lantern, shining from one of its windows.

Two hundred years later, that farmhouse would be long gone, and the land it once sat upon would be in danger of falling into the sea, as the edges of the cliff-tops were unstable and eroding. A tunnel was rumored to have once run from Stoneford Bunny to Beckford Farm, but nobody had ever been able to locate it.

Watching silently from her hiding place in the tall grasses, Charlie had absolutely no doubt that the tunnel existed, and would shortly be employed by the three gentlemen—all wearing dark clothing—who had appeared from nowhere with a hand-drawn cart to greet the two individuals from the boat.

Said boat was divested, quickly, of its cargo of casks and containers, with few words spoken. And then, as Charlie watched, an argument erupted. She couldn't hear exactly what was being said, but there were raised voices. And one of the gentlemen who had appeared from the gulley seemed to be disputing something the other four fellows had no quarrel with.

The argument escalated. There were threats. And gesticulations. And then—a decisive act. The disputing gentleman was suddenly attacked by one of the others. Struck from behind with an oar, he collapsed onto the shingle beach where his throat was cut with the single decisive slash of a flashing blade.

"Bollocks!" the murderer swore, and Charlie saw that, in his haste, he'd also managed to cut himself.

Frozen with fear, she watched as the murderer rifled through the clothing of his victim until he found what he wanted—a folded piece of white paper. The victim's body was then bundled into the boat.

The two men climbed back aboard and rowed out into the deep, dark water.

The two smugglers left behind on the beach scurried and scuttled and hoisted the casks from the sand onto their cart. Then, as silently as they had arrived, they departed, disappearing into the ravine.

Far away on the water, in the moonlight, the body of their companion was tipped over the side of the rowboat, and the vessel continued on its way, back to the Isle of Wight.

The beach was once again deserted.

Charlie stayed where she was, concealed in the marram grass, until she was certain the two gentlemen with the cart would not be returning—and that the two men in the boat would not be changing their minds about which shore they preferred.

Then, taking off her shoes—they were full of fine sand—she crept back towards the Cliff Road, reflecting on the sobering fact that the argumentative gentleman who'd had his throat slashed was the same dodgy fellow with the eye-patch she'd seen earlier, outside The Dog's Watch, talking to Lemuel Ferryman.

And, that the smuggler who'd done the coshing and the slashing and who'd removed the piece of paper from the dead man's clothing bore a not uncanny resemblance to Lemuel Ferryman himself.

CHAPTER 17

Twilight had progressed to night by the time Charlie had negotiated her way back along the gentle climb of the Cliff Road to the village. It was dark, but the moon was full, and the road was familiar. It had been a very long time since she had actually attempted the ascent, her preferred mode of transport consisting of two wheels, not two very tired legs. And her shoes, which were meant to be worn in the museum as part of her costume, and which were off her feet as often as they were on, were beginning to rub in all the wrong places.

Still shaken by what she had witnessed, and wondering whose husband or brother or son would be missed by dawn, she walked up the hill as quickly as she was able. She missed her vintage Elswick Ladies Town Bike, with its wicker basket and bright blue paint. Jeff had found it abandoned by the side of the road one day, a rusted relic from the 1960s. He'd lovingly restored it for her.

At last, she reached the spot where the Cliff Road abruptly changed its name to the High Street, where the village properly began. There was a little more light here, as some of the inhabitants were still burning late-night candles and rushes. Charlie could see their flickering glow through the windows of little cottages.

As she walked past the collection of dwellings that made up the Poorhouse, Charlie noticed, standing in the dark little lane, a shadowy figure which, upon closer inspection, she determined to be Eliza Robinson.

And Eliza was not alone. Her back was pressed to the brick wall of the house, her full attention focussed upon a young man of a similar age to herself, who was similarly engaged in what Charlie observed was a fairly passionate kiss.

What caught Charlie's attention more than the kiss, however, was the sudden appearance of young Daniel Robinson, Eliza's son, from the open doorway beside her.

He ought not to have been awake at that hour. He ought to have been fast asleep in his cot. But there he was, and while his mother was otherwise preoccupied, he'd obviously made up his mind to explore as much territory as his little legs—and their newly acquired walking skills—would allow.

In fact, he was not so much walking as running. And, with his face wreathed in joy and a delighted laugh, he was off to explore his world. He shot straight out from the doorway and into the lane, his itinerary taking him directly out to the High Street.

Charlie's first instinct was to run after him. And, from habit, to check right and left before darting into traffic.

Not that she should realistically have expected anything other than an occasional horse.

As it happened, there were two horses. Galloping. And behind them was a coach—which was travelling at breakneck speed towards The Dog's Watch Inn.

With an alarmed shriek, Charlie rushed into the road, scooping Daniel up and hurling both herself and the infant onto the grassy verge that belonged to the western edge of the Village Green. The two horses—and the Royal Mail coach from London to which they were attached—clattered over the spot where they had been a moment earlier without slowing.

For his part, Daniel remained momentarily composed. And then nonplussed. And then, he began to scream. Not because Charlie was squashing him into the dewy grass—she'd remedied that almost immediately. But because his glorious adventure had been thwarted and, to make matters worse, the thwarting seemed to be related to the Royal Mail coach, which he was used to seeing arrive in the afternoon, and certainly not in the middle of the night.

Young Daniel's wails had one predictable effect: the immediate appearance of his mother, Eliza, running, horrified, from the darkened passageway, followed closely by her amorous young man.

"Here you are," Charlie said, graciously, delivering Daniel into Eliza's custody. Several hundred yards in the distance, the Royal Mail coach disembarked its payload and its passengers, its driver apparently unperturbed—or unaware—of the deadly accident that had very nearly taken place.

"Thank you! Oh, thank you!" Eliza gasped, erupting into sobs herself as she hugged Daniel close. "Oh! I should never have brought him downstairs with me! But he would not settle! And to leave him alone would have been worse! Oh Jobey, whatever would we have done?"

Jobey, the young man whose interests had been wholly focused on Eliza in the cobblestoned lane, stepped forward.

"We are grateful to you," he said, to Charlie. "I am called Jobey Cooper…"

And here, he paused, as if Charlie ought to have known who he was.

She did not…and yet—she did. Cooper.

An ancestor of old Emmy Cooper…?

"Jobey lives in a Gypsy camp in the New Forest," Eliza said. "And it would not do for it to be known that he is keeping my company. He would be thrown out by his family."

"So that is why you must meet in secret…?" Charlie asked.

"We are man and wife in the eyes of God," Jobey replied.

"And we will be married by the Vicar soon enough," Eliza added. "But until then…you will not breathe a word to anyone of what you have seen this evening, will you, Mrs. Collins?"

"You may consider me a trusted confidante," Charlie replied. "I shall say nothing."

"Thank you," Eliza said. "And thank you, too, for your fortunate timing…for if you had not happened along when you did…I cannot bear to think what would have become of Daniel."

"You have our gratitude for your assistance," Jobey added. "For I love Daniel as if he were my own, and when we are married, I intend to give him my name."

"And when he is old enough to understand," Eliza said, "I shall ensure he remembers always the visitor from London who saved his life."

"Thank you," Charlie replied. "It was a pleasure to meet you, Mr. Cooper, although I wish it had been under more auspicious circumstances."

She took her leave, and walked on to the Village Green.

What had nearly happened there?

What had nearly happened was that Daniel Robinson was very nearly Not. And if he had been knocked down and killed…everything that had come afterwards would have been irrevocably altered.

What would come afterwards?

She paused to think.

Emmy had shared a little knowledge about her forebears with Charlie. Her ancestors had been saddlers, generation upon generation of them, until the advent of motor cars and buses had put them out of business. Saddlers going all the way back to the early 19th century, and Daniel Cooper, his very fine leather work reputed to be the best, the sturdiest, and the most well-crafted in all of Hampshire.

Jobey Cooper intended to give Daniel Robinson his name.

So if the life of Daniel Robinson Cooper had been extinguished on this night, Emmy Cooper would never have been born.

And there was something else. For if Daniel Robinson was indeed the son of Louis Augustus Duran, and if Jobey Cooper did indeed marry Eliza Robinson and adopt Daniel as his own…then she and Emmy Cooper were, in fact, also related. Distantly and rather untidily. But related, nonetheless.

It was a very odd feeling. If she had not acted, history would have been undone.

Her interference had ensured that what was to be—what she knew to be—would actually be.

And it wasn't until she was halfway to the Village Oak that she remembered something else old Emmy Cooper had once told her, one day when they were sitting together on the bench, tossing stale bits of bread crust to the pigeons.

Emmy had told her that her middle name was Catherine. And

that it was a name which had been passed down to all of the females in her family, beginning with Daniel, who had given it to his firstborn, a daughter. The reason for choosing that name had been lost in time.

Charlie now knew the answer.

And the newfound knowledge made her smile.

She *had* done the right thing.

At the top end of the green, Charlie could see the Royal Mail coach, getting ready to depart after its brief stop at the inn. And she realized that the colours she had dreamed about the night before—the ramshackle wagon that had been put back together—the beautiful glossy black box, the wheels and the underneath bit a brilliant scarlet, the lower half of the box a chocolate brown—were exactly the colors that the Royal Mail coach was painted.

As Charlie continued her walk past the Village Green, with the large old oak at its heart, she had a thought. She would make a note about Eliza and Jobey and the stagecoach on her phone's To Do list. She would also make note of the murder she had witnessed on the beach.

She retrieved her mobile from the bosom of her frock, where it had been comfortably sitting for most of the day and half of the night.

She switched it on.

77% battery.

Not good. She'd have to borrow Sarah's pencil and paper to transcribe this later.

But something else she saw on her mobile's screen made her heart leap. Two messages had arrived. Quickly, she retrieved and read them.

They were both from Nick.

One acknowledged receipt of her message.

And the other, somewhat longer, was packed with information about her distant cousin, Catherine Collins. The woman whose identity she'd borrowed, the woman who had now given her name to all of Daniel Robinson Cooper's future descendants.

"Catherine Collins, born in Christchurch."

Charlie read the words aloud, making them real.

"Husband named Joseph—yes, he's come up in conversation. Former soldier. Died in 1820 of pneumonia."

She shook her head, sadly.

"Would have lived if they'd had antibiotics."

She paused.

It wasn't as if she was Catherine Collins. But the oddest thing was…she felt like Catherine Collins.

Will try to work out how to bring you back, Nick had written. *Don't panic.*

Charlie switched off her phone.

Nick had mentioned nothing about Sarah and Louis Augustus Duran. Perhaps other things in the future had already been changed as a result of the circumstances whirling around her now.

But she had to know.

Composing the words quickly, she keyed her message back to Nick.

Please reconfirm Sarah Foster and Louis Augustus Duran marry 30 July 1825. Look it up. St. Eligius parish records.

Charlie paused, thinking about what she wanted to say next.

Not sure I want to come back, Nick. Convince me.

No. That would worry him.

Instead, she decided to ask another favour.

Please find out everything about Shaun Deeley. Born about 1790. Groom at the manor. Urgent. PS. Louis Augustus Duran is a complete wanker.

Smiling, she clicked Send, and watched while her phone paused—and continued to pause—for so long that Charlie began to be almost convinced that she'd imagined it all.

And then the little symbols appeared, and the signal strength grew strong, and she knew she had not imagined it. Her message was not going to disappear by some cruel whim of the universe— whichever universe it was that she happened to be occupying.

Message Sent.

CHAPTER 18

There was a text from Sam.

Come and see, she'd urged, and so, after finishing his supper and rinsing his dishes in the sink, Nick wandered back to the Village Green.

He discovered it had undergone something of a transformation.

News of his earlier face-to-face altercation with Ron Ferryman had obviously spread, fuelled in large part by his assertion that poison had been administered to the tree's roots.

And Ron's defensive rebuttal to Nick's inferred guilt had only served to fan the flames.

In the space of a few short hours, the vigil had become an Event. There were spotlights and floodlights. And all manner of tents had been spontaneously erected.

A striped one offering kebabs and coffee, tea and cakes, baguettes and mineral water. A purple one displaying hand-made wall-hangings, silkscreened t-shirts and knitted caps (all profits donated to The Committee to Save the Village Green and Poorhouse Lane). A plain one put up by the vicar of St. Eligius, in case anybody's soul required uplifting, saving, or simple ongoing sustenance. And a small army surplus tent in the far corner, emanating mysterious scents and peaceful philosophies, along with photocopied leaflets on passive civil disobedience.

Nick had no idea where they'd all come from. Other villages and towns, obviously. Stoneford wasn't big enough to have created this, in such a short period of time.

Someone had lit a bonfire in a large steel barrel, and an impromptu concert had sprung up around it. Nick recognized three of the members of Jeff Lowe's weekend tribute band, with their six and twelve-string acoustic guitars. They were joined by two sopranos and a tenor from the St. Eligius Choir, and the entire McDonald family from the grocery next door to the Indian takeaway (eight children, Paddy and his wife Moira, Nana and a Jack Russell terrier named Lola). And a man in a hat, with a tambourine in one hand and a cabasa in the other, who Nick couldn't recall seeing before, but he seemed like a nice fellow and he knew the words to all of the songs.

At the base of the Village Oak, a group of new age hippies were offering incantations intended to infuse healing from root to leaf tip.

And next to them were a group of travellers Nick remembered had been camping on the site of the old Beckford Farm near Stoneford Bunny. They were facing a court-ordered eviction next week as the land they were occupying was on dodgy footing, its eroded overhangs deemed likely to tumble into the sea at no moment's notice. Their presence was obviously welcomed by the new age hippies, and the two gatherings were sharing their food, drink and philosophies—as well as good vibrations for the tree.

Nick watched, fascinated, as a TV news crew set up a base with a good view of the oak, and their female reporter checked her hair and makeup in a mirror in advance of a live hit for their nightly broadcast.

"Nick!"

It was Sam, in jeans and a silkscreened Village Green t-shirt from the purple tent. And Mrs. Collins, who seemed at last to have been persuaded to change out of her Regency frock into something similar.

"Come and have some tea!"

Nick joined his cousins, who were sitting on the grass with their backs to the low stone wall, Mrs. Collins' dangerous-looking sword resting upright between them.

"I see you've come ready for combat," he remarked, humorously, perching on top of the wall.

"She won't let that bloody thing out of her sight," Sam said. "You've started something, you know, Nick. People have been Twittering. Googling. Liking it on Facebook. The Stoneford Village Oak is trending."

"This is a brilliant device," Mrs. Collins added, seizing Sam's mobile. "And I have very much enjoyed the Twitter. I have nearly one hundred followers. Is this not an excellent achievement?"

"Exceedingly excellent," Nick replied, amused. "And you don't mind being disguised as a boy now?"

Mrs. Collins considered what she was wearing.

"I find your clothing tolerably comfortable," she judged. "Although what is worn beneath is rather more confining than what I am used to."

Nick found a more comfortable position on top of the wall. The evening was cool and dewy, and it was going to play nasty havoc with his leg.

"I'll just see if I've got any messages," he said, taking out his own mobile, while Sam poured him a cup of tea from her thermos, and Mrs. Collins sent a tweet to her followers, telling them about the weather and the spag bol Sam had made for dinner.

Nothing.

Perhaps, Nick thought, it really had all been a fluke of astronomy and physics. And there would be no more messages to and from the past.

But it had worked, before. Once coming his way, and twice going back.

Perhaps there was too much interference from the TV vans, with their antennas on top of tall poles. Perhaps it was all the reporters, with their wireless mics. A group of them had just chased Ron Ferryman into The Dog's Watch Inn, shouting questions about the disputed ownership of the two properties and the ludicrousness of sending earth-filled trucks down a cobbled lane with only inches of clearance on either side.

The idea of Charlie lost forever in time and space sent a shiver of dread through Nick. It did not bear thinking about.

He watched with amusement as Reverend Wolsley, detecting a lull in the need for immediate spiritual guidance, slipped out of his tent and walked furtively to one of the idle bulldozers behind the oak. There, with a pious acknowledgement skyward, he made a quick sign of the cross, then set about letting the air out of all four of the vehicle's tires.

How did the oak transmit its signals, Nick wondered. Had it been charged with some kind of trans-chronometrical Wi-Fi?

Wi-Fi.

Of course.

He'd switched it off.

Nick flipped the wireless signal on again.

There was a bleep.

His heart leaped.

A message.

And it was from Charlie.

Relieved, he began to read.

And then he burst into laughter.

"What?" Sam said.

"Oh, do you tweet also?" Mrs. Collins inquired, craning her neck to try and read Nick's screen. "Do let me see. What is your twittername? Mine is Troublemaker. A suggestion from Mrs. Palmer. Is it not both humorous and apt?"

Nick pulled his mobile away, hiding it from Mrs. Collins' view, as he read Charlie's message.

"Mrs. Collins," he said, thinking he might save himself a trip to the crypt at St. Eligius, "Do you recall your cousin Mrs. Foster marrying a fellow named Louis Augustus Duran?"

"Indeed I do not," Mrs. Collins replied. "But I have certainly heard about the gentleman, as my cousin has written to me often of his unceasing proposals of marriage."

"Oh," Sam said. "I can help you there. There's a painting. A portrait. I was going to tell Charlie about it next time we met up. It's in our attic in an old trunk that has all sorts of ancient family things in it. I was up there the other day looking for Great Uncle Percy's collapsing telescope. I saw the portrait and thought, Charlie'll be interested in that. It's Sarah Foster and Louis Augustus Duran. Dated 1827. Man and wife."

Mrs. Collins looked confused. "This news plays havoc with my sensibilities, for how can a painting possibly be dated two years hence, and yet be currently located in an attic? And worse, portray a union which I am certain has never taken place? And shall never, if my cousin has any say in the matter?"

"Can I see the painting?" Nick inquired.

"What...now?"

"Yes, please. Now. Very much now."

"If you must." Sam got to her feet, and helped Mrs. Collins up. "I don't understand the sudden urgency. But anything to oblige."

Nick quickly finished the message he was composing to Charlie, then added a little something extra, and clicked Send.

And then he slid off the top of the wall, and followed Mrs. Collins and Sam back to Sam's car.

CHAPTER 19

"I'll fetch it," Sam said, parking her Civic in the driveway of her house overlooking the sea. "There's only space for one person in the attic. You two can wait in the front room with Roger. He's getting ready for a re-enactor event that's been scheduled for next month, and he's trying to summon up the courage to tell me about it. Since that weekend does, unfortunately, happen to coincide with our ninth wedding anniversary."

Roger Palmer was polishing his replica Brown Bess musket, and looked up, startled, as Sam opened the door to the front room.

"Evening, Rog," Nick said, with a wave. "Still got Napoleon on the run?"

"Evening, Nick." Roger looked uncomfortable. "Char—Mrs. Collins. Sam."

Nick noted that Roger had brought his entire 33rd Regiment of Foot re-enactor kit in from the garage, and had unpacked it, and spread it out over the sofa, the armchair, and most of the floor.

"I didn't think you'd be back so soon," Roger said, to Sam. "Dear."

"Nick wants to see that painting."

"Which painting would that be?"

Sam was already halfway up the stairs. "The one in the attic!" she shouted, over her shoulder. "The one I told you about!"

"Mr. and Mrs. Louis Augustus Duran," Nick provided, looking for somewhere to sit. Most of the places he would normally have chosen had been appropriated by the accoutrements of a 19th century soldier: red wool regimental coat, cartridge pouch, belts, scabbard, haversack, water bottle, knapsack, and assorted other necessaries including brushes, buffing sticks, mess tins, mugs and pewter spoons.

Mrs. Collins removed a dangerous-looking bayonet from one

end of the sofa, and sat down with her sword.

"I think I should quite like to join you as you stage The Battle of Waterloo," she decided. "My late husband shared many a tale with me of his skirmishes in Belgium."

"Well," Roger said. "I did enjoy our excellent dinner conversation this evening, Mrs. Collins. You are, surprisingly, quite an expert on the Cavalry. And its weapons."

"And the First Duke of Wellington," Mrs. Collins supplied. "Also known as Field Marshal Arthur Wellesley, whom I had the great honour of meeting some years ago. I do believe he will one day become Prime Minister of this country."

Roger gave Nick another very uncomfortable look.

"I understand your Napoleonic weekend's going to clash with your wedding anniversary," Nick said, humorously, changing the subject.

"Sam tell you that? Bloody hell. I'll be hoovering all of downstairs for the next two months to make up for that."

"The family name was Wesley," Mrs. Collins continued. "Irish. It was changed to Wellesley in 1798. I may also reveal that, based upon personal observation, he possesses an uncommonly large nose."

"Found it!" Sam shouted, clattering down the stairs, rushing into the front room.

She propped the painting up on the sofa, and stood back.

"There. Happy now?"

The portrait, inside an ornate gold frame, was of middling size, about two feet long and one foot wide. It had been painted in oil, and had not been particularly well cared for, which was a shame, Nick thought, as the result was a webwork of tiny cracks that crinkled over its entire surface.

He studied the painting at length, and the note affixed to its back. *Monsieur and Madame Louis Augustus Duran, 30 July 1827, on the Occasion of the Second Anniversary of their Wedding.*

"Handsome couple," he remarked. "Even if he is a complete wanker."

"Wanker?" Mrs. Collins inquired. "An entirely new word which I confess provokes my curiosity. Is it some form of local commerce?

Does wankering involve the extrication of juices and animal matter?"

"Something like that," Nick replied, trying very hard not to laugh.

He snapped a photo of the portrait with his phone, and then another for good measure.

"Now, would either of you mind giving me a lift back to Stoneford...?"

At the Village Green, the hippies were debating whether or not to chain themselves to the oak. And one of the TV crews, alerted by their rather impassioned discussions, were in the process of setting up an interview with their leader, a dreadlocked 52-year-old who was performing a shaman-like incantation which had, apparently, the week before, successfully brought round his youngest daughter's very ill pet rabbit.

Nick found a quiet spot beside Ron Ferryman's deflated bulldozer. Keying a message into his phone for his cousin, he attached one of the portrait photos, and touched Send.

"There you go, Charlie," he said. "Proof of nuptials."

Returning to his house, and addressing his computer, Nick got back to his theory. What he needed was a concise history of Stoneford, the Village Green, and the tree at the centre of it. And he knew exactly where to look.

During quiet moments at the museum, Charlie had compiled a website. She'd mined newspaper clippings and old brochures, printouts from historical archives and minutes from meetings. Photographs she'd discovered in squeaky wooden office drawers and falling-apart boxes in forgotten-about cupboards.

And Charlie was a stickler for detail. She knew her stuff. If anyone wanted obscure details about the village, they fired off messages to her. She always replied. Quickly if she had the answer at the top of her head. Always thoroughly. And taking somewhat more time if she needed to go digging to locate the facts.

Really, Nick mused—as he looked for one page in particular that he knew was there, because he'd been responsible for putting the entire website online—Charlie was far more comfortable in the past than she was in the present.

The thought struck him as strangely appropriate.

And at the same time, it triggered that nagging worry. What if he couldn't bring her back?

What if Charlie was destined to remain in 1825…communicating with him with 21st century technology…until…

It didn't bear thinking about.

Until her battery ran down and her mobile stopped working.

Charlie would be lost, forever, in time.

Nick pushed the thought from his mind. He wouldn't, couldn't, allow it to happen. And he'd found the page he wanted.

During the summer of 1825, a massive bolt of lightning had struck the upper branches of the Village Oak, causing a small fire which was immediately doused by the rain.

The ancient tree did not suffer any lasting damage. However, several large branches could be found on the green the next morning. The entire population of the village had turned out to watch as the windfall was taken to a local carpenter, one Mr. Haddock, who was able to fashion a commemorative bench from the rescued pieces of wood.

A bench which could, to this day, be found at the northern end of the green, next to the birdbath commemorating Mrs. Tamworth's early contributions to women's suffrage.

Nick checked the date of the lightning strike.

"Damn."

He'd been hoping to harness the electricity to try and bring Charlie back. But this one was a month too early: June 1. And there were no further records of anything similar.

He wondered whether it would be feasible to search the Met Office website for a record of all thunderstorms along the south coast that same year.

No. Not feasible at all. Their statistics didn't go back that far.

He supposed he could try contacting someone at the weather office. Or do a Google search…

Here was something, on a meteorological blog site: *1825 proved to be a very dry summer, although we experienced a notable hot spell in July.*

Nick shook his head. This was the kind of meticulous research that could take months, if not years.

And he didn't have months.

He wasn't even sure he had days, given the rate at which Charlie's phone battery was going to be used up.

There had to be another way.

He re-set his mind, forcing it to go right back to the beginning, and start over.

Perhaps all of his research into sprites and tachyons and the energy generated by lightning strikes was a discovery of distraction, rather than a discovery of cause.

What if the lightning strike had been merely coincidental?

And what if Charlie's journey backwards in time had more to do with the rogue virus that had invaded her computer, than with the electrical surge that had been produced by the storm?

Perhaps the virus itself had contained both the mechanism and the jolting surge of power to trigger time travel. Something like a binary tachyon particle?

And that was what needed to be harnessed?

Nick opened Charlie's laptop, and switched it on.

If he could dissect the coding in the malware and find out what made it tick…and if he was able to isolate that theoretical particle, and train it to obey his commands rather than the commands of its original author…and if he could then bottle it and send it back to Charlie in 1825 with instructions for use…problem solved.

Nick let his breath out.

This was going to require another cup of coffee.

CHAPTER 20

It was, Charlie thought, completely un-Jane-like. And had she been anyone but herself, transplanted from the future with all of the attitudes and independence that the 21st century had equipped her for, she almost certainly would never have done it.

But she had made up her mind that she would, after all, accept the lesser Monsieur Duran's invitation to lunch at the manor. Because she quite liked his father. And she felt she would not be so much at the lesser Monsieur Duran's mercy, as long as the greater Monsieur Duran remained in the room.

And she had a second motive. A few extra private moments with Mr. Deeley.

Dressed in one of Catherine Collins' fashionable London frocks, with a straw bonnet and a shawl, she made her way up the hill from the village. Mr. Deeley, however, was not to be found with his horses.

"He is with Mr. Rankin," Albert, the young boy who worked in the stables, advised.

"And where might I find Mr. Rankin?"

"Across from the scullery," Albert replied, without providing any further details.

Charlie set out in search of the scullery. She had visited the Manor Bed and Breakfast on many occasions, and knew the approximate historical layout of its rooms, even though there had been a good deal of refurbishment over the years. The scullery had been on the bottom floor, next to the kitchen. Some of the servants' quarters were down there too, in modern times their adjoining walls knocked down to create a reasonably spacious place for the guests to eat breakfast.

Charlie found her way back to the vegetable garden, and from there, located the door that led to the passage where the kitchen was. And the scullery. And Mr. Rankin's room, from which were emanating the unmistakable sounds of a guitar being played. Or attempting to be played. Gathering her courage, she knocked on the plain wooden door.

"That's done it, Ned," Mr. Deeley said, laughing. "Cease and desist orders from above." He opened the door, and was surprised— and then very pleased—to see Charlie.

"Are you lost, Mrs. Collins?" he inquired, cheekily. "Luncheon is being served upstairs."

"I am not lost, Mr. Deeley," she assured him. "I have arrived a little early. To visit Marie-Claire. I've brought her a treat." She produced a lump of sugar, which, just as cheekily, she offered to Mr. Deeley.

He accepted. "I shall deliver this to her," he promised, "with your fondest wishes."

"You are very welcome to keep it for yourself," Charlie teased, "with my fondest wishes. Might I come in...?"

Mr. Deeley looked doubtful. "I do not think that wise, Mrs. Collins."

"Leave the door open, then. I assure you my intentions are completely honorable."

Mr. Deeley looked to Mr. Rankin for guidance. None appeared to be forthcoming, however, and so Mr. Deeley made up his own mind, and stepped aside to admit her.

It was a tiny room, furnished with a wooden wardrobe, a narrow bed, a small table and a chair. There was a window, high up on the wall.

"Hello, Mr. Rankin."

Mr. Rankin, who'd been sitting on the bed with his guitar, was quickly on his feet.

"Good morning, Mrs. Collins."

"I know a little about that instrument, Mr. Rankin."

"I have encountered several of these in recent years," Mr. Rankin supplied. "I have seen them being played by the Gypsies. But I must admit, I am confounded by the complexity of its construction."

He demonstrated.

"It is a trifle awkward to hold. And if one strums the strings thus..."

139

He drew a tentative finger down all six strings at once.

"…one is not presented with an overly pleasing result."

"In fact," Mr. Deeley added, "it is an altogether horrible result."

"May I?" Charlie asked.

Mr. Rankin gave her the guitar, and she sat down in the chair.

"If you follow the greater Monsieur Duran's somewhat vague instructions…and place your fingers here, on the long part…"

She pressed down three of the strings on the upper neck, to create a G major chord.

"You are then able to influence the creation of quite a nice sound. And it is not, in fact…"

She drew the fingers of her right hand down all six strings.

"…half bad."

"Excellent," said Mr. Deeley, impressed.

"And furthermore, if you were to pick out the melody that you overheard coming from Mrs. Foster's cottage the other night…"

From memory, Charlie recreated the lead guitar line from *F.B.I.* She'd watched Jeff play it so many times.

"…you might find yourself very pleased indeed."

She returned the guitar to Mr. Rankin.

"You try."

Stoneford Manor's gardener attempted to copy what Charlie had just shown him, with middling results. He tried a second time, haltingly. And on the third try, managed to reproduce it almost perfectly.

"You have a good ear," Charlie judged. "Well done!"

"I am intrigued by the thought of genteel young ladies eschewing the parlour pianoforte for this much more portable instrument," Mr. Deeley remarked.

"I am amused even more," said Mr. Rankin, "by the idea of genteel young ladies being attracted to young marriageable gentlemen who are proficient at playing this much more portable instrument."

He placed the guitar in Mr. Deeley's hands.

"You must ask Mrs. Collins to instruct you, too."

• • •

Upstairs, in the Great Dining Hall, luncheon had been delayed by fifteen minutes, half an hour, nearly an hour.

Charlie entered the room to find the lesser Monsieur Duran pacing the floor, pressing a muslin bag filled with ice against his face, which bore cuts and bruises from the altercation at the inn the night before.

Not far away, his father was seated at a long, polished table, reading a book with quizzical amusement.

"Madame Collins!" the lesser Monsieur Duran exclaimed. "I am pleased you have undergone a change of your mind. Be seated. You know, of course, my father."

"I do indeed," Charlie replied. "Good afternoon, sir."

"Good afternoon, Mrs. Collins," the greater Monsieur Duran replied, standing, "will you take the chair beside mine?"

"I would be honoured," Charlie said.

The lesser Monsieur Duran was anxious to impress.

"This table," he provided, "was imported by me, at great expense and effort, from our *chateau* in Amiens. Around this table we have entertained innumerable members of *la noblesse*, before, during and after *la Révolution française*. You sit, Madame Collins, in the *fonds de chaise* of my country's history."

"I am certain," the greater Monsieur Duran added, humorously, "that the bottom of Mrs. Collins' chair is most appreciative of this exclusive opportunity."

His son ignored him.

"I have instructed the cook to follow a prescription for lunch which has been laid down by your famous John Simpson. I hope you will convey to Madame Foster the eating pleasantries to be found in *A Complete System of Cookery, on a Plan Entirely New, Consisting of Every Thing that is Requisite for Cooks to Know in the Kitchen Business*. It is a considerable cooking book. It affords a completely different feast for every day of the year. And it has been published by a gentleman who has been employed at the home of the Marquis of Buckingham. I hold this book in exceedingly high estimage."

"I shall inform Mrs. Foster of your epicurean triumph," Charlie promised.

There followed two complete courses of food, which in themselves would have been enough to have filled the insides of both Monsieur Durans several times over, as well as half a dozen visitors, and all of the household staff.

The gastronomical parade began with a *soup santé*, then progressed to a haunch of lamb, served with chervil sauce. A beef steak pie. *Risoles*, peas and asparagus (much to the delight of the greater Monsieur Duran). A *souties* of rabbit and mushroom. And finishing up, Rhenish cream and an apricot tart.

"I have it in my mind," the greater Monsieur Duran said, as Alfred, the butler, removed the last of the rabbit and mushroom, and Martha, who had apparently replaced a recently sacked Rose King, arrived with the sweets, "to abandon the *chateau* in France."

"I beg your pardon?" his son inquired. "Did you not enjoy the rabbit, Madame Collins?"

"I am certain it was delicious," Charlie lied. "But I found myself quite full after the beef steak pie. Truly."

"It is far too large," the greater Monsieur Duran supplied. "And it gives me indigestion."

"The rabbit?" his son inquired, confused.

"The *chateau*. The rabbit was *soutied* to perfection."

"Sir, you surely cannot consider divesting yourself of my birthright!"

The greater Monsieur Duran waved away his son's panicked concerns.

"I shall leave it in the care of your brother."

"Gaston!" The lesser Monsieur Duran was barely able to contain his contempt. "Your rooms will be overrun with stray cats and consumptive orphans!"

"Far more preferable," his father replied, "than the atrocious poets and half-dressed courtesans which you would install as permanent house guests."

"A foible of my youth," the lesser Monsieur Duran explained, nervously, to Charlie. "Which he has never let me forget. It is not the case now, I assure you."

"We all have youthful foibles," Charlie assured him, humorously.

"Foibles which gave your mother the vapours, might I remind you. From which she did not recover."

The greater Monsieur Duran accepted a generous slice of apricot tart from the silver platter proffered by Alfred, while the lesser Monsieur Duran added the last three drops of red liquid from a small stoppered bottle to his wine, downing it with one swallow.

"The blanched asparagus was delicious," the greater Monsieur Duran remarked. "Please give my compliments to Mrs. Dobbs. And also to Mr. Rankin."

"Thank you, sir," Alfred replied. "I shall."

"Do you require more laudanum?" the greater Monsieur Duran inquired, of his son. "We cannot have you languishing in pain."

"It is nothing," his son assured him. "I am in otherwise excellent health."

"I am pleased for you. As is, I am certain, Mrs. Collins, who will happily convey the state of your physical wellbeing to Mrs. Foster."

"Happily," Charlie confirmed.

"In any case, Gaston is not likely to sell the property. You may sort out the question of ownership between yourselves, after I am gone."

The lesser Monsieur Duran eyed his father with suspicion.

"Where is it you are you going?"

"I was speaking…" The greater Monsieur Duran gestured in the general direction of an upper corner of the room. "…metaphysically."

"And where will you live if it is not in the *chateau*?" the lesser Monsieur Duran demanded.

"Well," said his father. "I have had this thought. That possibly, I might come to live here. With you."

The lesser Monsieur Duran, now thoroughly alarmed, attacked his apricot tart with a vicious stab of his fork.

"I will not have it!" he fumed, hurling the unfortunate implement against the wall.

Just as quickly, he acknowledged Charlie's look of alarm.

"*Excusez-moi.* I am not myself. A temporary affliction. It occurs rarely."

Dutifully, Alfred retrieved the fork from the floor, and replaced it, silently, with another from the sideboard.

"I can think of nothing more challenging to my sensibilities than bracing walks in the damp English countryside," the greater Monsieur Duran continued. "And I shall stock the pond with ducks. Whose purpose will be ornamental rather than gastronomic."

"You shall not!" the lesser Monsieur Duran shouted, with very bad grace. "*Pardon*, Madame Collins. Your indulgence, *s'il vous plaît*."

"My dear son. You have no say in the matter. Since the manor is, in fact, owned by myself. And not by you."

"But you gave it to me," the lesser Monsieur Duran replied, with a pout.

"I did not. I loaned it to you, so that you might have somewhere tolerable to live while domiciled in England. You are very welcome to join your brother in Amiens if you find the arrangements displeasing."

Here, the greater Monsieur Duran paused, and tasted his apricot tart.

"Delicious," he judged, with a nod towards Alfred. "Again, my compliments to Mrs. Dobbs."

"I shall convey them, sir," Alfred replied.

"Now then," the greater Monsieur Duran continued. "What is this I hear about your latest all-consuming interest, Louis? A sanitary water closet which is able to wash away effluent with the mere flick of a wrist? You must show Mrs. Collins your efforts as soon as we have finished our meal, and you have recovered sufficiently from your wounds to afford us a tour."

"I do, in fact, know how to create Rhenish cream," the greater Monsieur Duran was saying, to Charlie, as they walked down the grand staircase from the dining room. "It is not the fashion for a man to be a master of cookery, but I consider all subjects worth pursuing, and I am not averse to learning them all. It is a delightful concoction consisting of the finely beaten yolks of eight eggs added to one quart of jelly, which is then strained and moulded and garnished with oranges."

"It's delicious," Charlie remarked. She made a mental note to try her hand at it later.

The lesser Monsieur Duran's sanitary water closet was contained in a small construction at the back of the manor, within shouting distance of the scullery.

The building was of brick, with a solid roof and a window for ventilation, and a good wooden door that provided privacy but which would render the interior, Charlie thought, somewhat dark and very foreboding when shut.

"And so," the lesser Monsieur Duran announced, "here it is. My invention."

"And how does this invention function?" the greater Monsieur Duran inquired, amused.

"If you would care to sit," his son replied.

Obligingly, the greater Monsieur Duran seated himself upon a wooden shelf within, which contained a suitably placed opening.

"You do not find this too assaulting to your delicate constitution?" the lesser Monsieur Duran checked, turning to Charlie.

"Not in the least," she assured him.

"Very good."

The lesser Monsieur Duran's eyes grew bright, his own constitution aided considerably by the laudanum he had ingested with his wine.

"Imagine you have deposited your contribution. It will be there."

The lesser Monsieur Duran here directed Jane, another housemaid, who had been summoned from her own lunch, to open a hinged door beneath the shelf. Obligingly, his father parted his legs, to reveal a receptacle made of glazed and fired clay. Not unlike, Charlie thought, the chamber pot under the bed in Mary's room at the cottage.

"In there?" the greater Monsieur Duran inquired, peering down between his legs.

"It is in there, yes," his son replied.

"And...?"

"And here, we have the water."

The lesser Monsieur Duran turned a small spigot which was

affixed to the brick wall behind the wooden bench, and a trickle of water could be heard travelling along a pipe.

"And where is it this water comes from?" the greater Monsieur Duran inquired.

"It is stored in a cistern outside the rear wall."

"And it finishes its journey there?" the greater Monsieur Duran asked, indicating the glazed clay bowl.

"Indeed it does," his son replied, with a good deal of pride.

"And so my contribution is contained in a bowl with the addition of water. And then…?"

"And then," the lesser Monsieur Duran replied, "at the end of the day, the maid removes the bowl and discards its contents into a pit some yards hence."

He turned to Charlie.

"It is very clever, is it not? Madame Foster will consider herself fortunate, should she choose to alter her name to the Countess Duran."

"I cannot help but think," the greater Monsieur Duran mused, "that there may be an additional step to this. Which you have not yet invented. Or considered."

"I cannot imagine what that might be," his son replied, a touch indignantly. "Come, let us return to the house. I have drawings of the cistern which may impress you more."

CHAPTER 21

It was Saturday afternoon, and at the Village Green, the new age hippies and the travellers had been joined by a troop of South American musicians who were touring England with their charangos and pan pipes.

As well, Nick observed that three politicians who had travelled down from London were now holding an important meeting with the Parish Council in the St. Eligius tent, temporarily vacated while Reverend Wolsley conducted an afternoon wedding in the nearby church.

There were reporters from several regional newspapers, and two tabloids, and three more television crews had arrived with their satellite vans, cameras, lights and microphones.

Nick negotiated a path through the villagers, the hippies, the travellers, the musicians, reporters and TV crews, to the tree. There, he found Mike Tidman, on his knees on the ground, delicately coaxing tiny spadefuls of contaminated earth out from around the oak's damaged roots.

"Anything new?" Nick asked.

"Well," Mike replied, "we've identified the poison. Hexazinone. Not even approved for use in this country. Kills the leaves repeatedly until the tree's strength is sapped and it dies. Whoever saturated this old girl's roots knew exactly what they were doing."

"The Ferrymans always know exactly what they were doing," Nick said, glaring at Ron and Reg, who had granted an interview to a sympathetic business reporter from one of the London papers. "Can you save her?"

"I'll certainly give it my best shot," Mike promised. "It'll involve digging down at least three feet to excavate all of that contaminated soil. Then we'll surround the roots with charcoal and microbes to help break down the herbicide. And then we'll have to replace what we've removed with clean topsoil. And there's no guarantee it'll work. But it'll put a stop to any more damage. After that, it's up to this old girl."

Mike gave the tree's massive trunk a reassuring pat, then stopped. Something was poking out from between two of the oak's gnarled and ancient roots.

Gently, he coaxed the object free.

It was a stoppered glass bottle, old, its glass runny, attesting to its handmade origins. Nick could see that inside there was a folded piece of paper, brown around the edges and most certainly fragile from having been buried in the earth for a good many years.

"Is there a historian in the house?" Mike mused.

"There is," Nick replied. "But she's not here. Charlie Lowe. You spoke to her the other day."

"Ah yes," Mike said. "Perhaps she should have the honours, then. Something for the museum."

He gave Nick the bottle.

"She'll like that," Nick said.

But as he was considering whether or not to open the bottle to see what had been stuffed inside, he was accosted by Ron Ferryman, fresh from his interview with the business reporter.

"I believe we own the rights to whatever is found here," Ron said.

He removed the bottle from Nick's hand.

"Could auction this off for a tidy sum at Reg's pub," he mused. "Unopened, intact. Good publicity for The Poorhouse Lane Development. Exploiting Stoneford's sense of history and all that."

And he walked away, whistling, dropping the little glass bottle into the jacket pocket of his Savile Row suit.

As the carnival atmosphere on the green continued, Nick took up his accustomed place beside the stone wall, and constructed another message to Charlie.

I know you know, he wrote, thoughtfully, *but just in case. I have to caution you about interfering. Remember the Butterfly Effect. Would hate to think flapping your wings Over There would cause a hurricane Over Here. And wipe out the entire population of Stoneford.*

He paused, and smiled.

To more serious matters.

Still working on a way to bring you back, he wrote. *Looking into that virus on your laptop. Hopefully have answer in the next day or so.*

Nick paused again.

Try and save your battery, he added, and then: *Might not be too many more opportunities to chat.*

He clicked Send.

CHAPTER 22

Charlie had taken her leave.

And had altogether dismissed an offer from the lesser Monsieur Duran that he should accompany her down the hill and to the front door of Sarah's cottage.

"It's a pleasant day," she said. "I shall come to no harm walking by myself."

"But you will convey to Madame Foster my fondest wish that she herself should accept an invitation to lunch? You cannot fail to have been impressed by the fare. I am very wealthy. There will never be a famishment at my table."

"I will convey what I have observed to Mrs. Foster," Charlie promised. "Good afternoon, Monsieur Duran."

But as she made her way down the cart track, she was distracted, momentarily, by a sharp twinge of pain in her right side.

"Ow!" she exclaimed, surprised, pressing her hand to the spot.

Was it a cramp?

No. It was in the wrong place entirely.

A twisted muscle?

Indigestion? Too many raw egg yolks?

Her hand remained where it was.

The twinge was going now.

There.

Better.

She made her way back down to the village, and the Village Green, to see if there were any more messages from Nick.

Her phone was down to 68%. How could that happen? She hadn't used it for anything. Annoyingly, it was using up battery power by virtue of its mere existence.

But there were two replies from Nick. And the attachment he had promised, the portrait of Sarah and Louis Augustus Duran.

"Mrs. Collins!"

She glanced up, and saw Mr. Deeley, walking across the green towards her, from the direction of The Dog's Watch. Quickly, she switched off her phone and hid it.

"Mr. Deeley," she said, standing up.

"I am delighted to discover you here, Mrs. Collins. And happy to report that Mr. Rankin has mastered your song. He looks forward to playing it for you at the earliest opportunity. I trust lunch was not too disagreeable?"

"I am now well-acquainted," Charlie said, "with the lesser Monsieur Duran's abiding passion."

"As are all of us who are employed at the manor," Mr. Deeley replied, humorously. "Do you suppose there is any future to it?"

"I suppose there is," Charlie said. "Though not, perhaps, the exact design which Monsieur Duran has come up with."

"And what brings you to the green?" Mr. Deeley inquired. "Have you been bothering the hedgehogs again?"

Charlie smiled. "No. I have been having a conversation with the Village Oak."

"Ah," said Mr. Deeley. "I confess, I often hold similar consultations. And at night, discussions with the moon and the stars. Has the Village Oak imparted anything useful by way of advice?"

"Nothing yet," Charlie replied. "Although I am upset by my cousin's sudden misfortune and loss of income. If only she still had possession of the deed to the land she inherited. Do you happen to know anything about how Mr. Foster came to be parted from that? This village is small enough that, surely, there must be someone who knows the name of the person he owed the debt to."

Mr. Deeley was deep in thought, his brow furrowed.

"It is curious that you raise the subject," he said, "as this very afternoon Mr. Ferryman attached that same deed to the wall of the inn, so that it now occupies pride of place behind the bar."

"And what is Mr. Ferryman's explanation of how he comes to possess this most important piece of paper?" Charlie asked.

"He related a tale to those gathered at the bar," Mr. Deeley replied, "which involved a game of cards, a wager, and the result of the wager being the forfeiture of the document by its original owner."

So. That was what she had seen Lemuel Ferryman removing from the body of the smuggler on the beach. And that was how it had come to be in the Ferryman family's possession. One illegitimate transaction, followed by an even more illegitimate transaction.

"This mysterious 'original owner' was not the original owner at all," Charlie said, "but a rogue who stole it under very similar circumstances from Mr. Foster."

She stopped. It was best not to say anything more. It was best to keep quiet about what she had seen last night, lest she run the risk of becoming the next victim to disappear by the hand of Lemuel Ferryman.

She had another thought. "Do you think it possible, Mr. Deeley, that Mr. Foster did not accidentally fall into the sea...?"

"I would not like to say," Mr. Deeley replied, carefully. "There was a gale which resulted in very high waves. And there were many questions left unanswered about Mr. Foster's intent when he went walking upon the rocks that night. Some say he had arranged a meeting. Yet it seemed to others an inhospitable and unlikely location for a conference."

Charlie pressed her hand to her side and winced, as another twinge shot through her middle.

"Are you unwell?" Mr. Deeley asked, his face showing sudden concern.

"I have a pain," Charlie said. "Here."

She showed him, with her hand.

"I know of a surgeon in the village. The lesser Monsieur Duran consults him often, as he suffers greatly from bad blood, and requires a vein to be opened at regular intervals in order to release the malaise."

"I believe I am feeling less unwell now," Charlie answered, hastily.

And then, in the brilliant sunshine, and quite unexpectedly, Mr. Deeley kissed her. On the cheek. With impetuousness. Causing her to catch her breath in a way that she had not since the beginning of her relationship with Jeff, when their love was impulsive and dangerous and unlike anything she'd ever felt about another person.

"Until this evening, Mrs. Collins," Mr. Deeley said, with a highly satisfied smile. "I shall call for you at seven."

"Until this evening, then, Mr. Deeley," Charlie agreed.

She watched as he walked away, jauntily, his hands in his pockets.

And then she took out her phone again, and at last clicked on the photo that Nick had sent.

Sarah Elizabeth and Louis Augustus Duran. On the occasion of their second wedding anniversary, the 30th of July, 1827.

The tiny portrait was formal, what one would expect from its time. She was sitting uncomfortably and stiffly on a chair in her best frock. And he was standing by her side, his hand resting lightly on the back of the chair, near her shoulder.

Charlie made the picture bigger, zooming in.

It was Sarah. Her likeness was impossible to dispute.

But the "he" of the couple…the "he" was most definitely not Louis Augustus Wanker Duran.

"Mr. Deeley!" Charlie shouted.

Mr. Deeley, who had nearly reached the road that ran along the west side of the Village Green, turned around, his face a question mark.

"Does Monsieur Duran—the greater—share exactly the same names as his son?"

Charlie held her breath for the answer.

"They are both known as Louis Augustus Duran, yes," Mr. Deeley replied, with absolutely no inkling of the importance of his answer. "But the greater Monsieur Duran prefers to be known informally as Augustus. Why?"

Charlie's heart was in her mouth.

"And is there a Madame Duran?"

"There was a Madame Duran," Mr. Deeley supplied, "but ten years ago she became an invalid, and took to her bed, never to recover. Some say her untimely passing is the reason why the lesser Monsieur Duran carries such bitterness within himself. They were, by all accounts, very close."

So. There it was.

The answer. *The* answer.

History didn't need to be changed at all…

Only nudged.

"Mr. Deeley," Charlie said, excitedly. "Tonight we must absolutely ensure that my cousin is introduced to the greater Monsieur Duran!"

CHAPTER 23

The gown Monsieur Duran had sent Sarah was nearly a perfect fit.

"This does not surprise me in the least," Sarah remarked. "I am certain he watches me when I am in the village. I would not put it past him to have an eyepiece of some sort, mounted in a convenient upstairs window, so that he may spy upon my every going and coming."

"Never mind about him," Charlie said. "It is his father you must seek to impress."

She admired her own reflection in Sarah's dressing table mirror.

The bags that had come with Catherine, from London, had contained a frock which would not have been out of place at a society tea, or, indeed, a grand country dance. It was a deep indigo blue, and made of heavy silk, with red and gold embroidery and beads around the hem that reminded her of something Oriental, or Indian. The gown was finished with a simple satin ribbon, also deep blue, which was meant to be tied in a bow at the back of its high waist.

"It is very elegant," Sarah judged.

Charlie turned around.

"Will you tie the ribbon for me?"

Sarah obliged, and then looked in the mirror herself.

"It has been an age since I have had need to attend to my hair," she said, "or to contemplate a little extra colour for my face. I think a touch of cochineal and a fine dusting of talcum powder should suffice the cheeks. And another touch of red upon the lips. I have never been one to make a fuss over artifice."

"Nor me," Charlie assured her. "Although I have always been at a loss where my hair is concerned."

It was true. At home, in the 21st century, she washed her hair and ruffled it with a towel, and that was the extent of her attention. It wasn't laziness. Just a distinct lack of caring enough to bother.

"Then you must let me pin it up for you," Sarah decided.

She stood, and gestured to Charlie to take her seat in front of the mirror.

"When my husband was alive, he was very much taken with my skills at hair dressing. And I think a little posy of fresh flowers would not be amiss here, behind your ear…and some curls, I think, to show off your pretty face to Mr. Deeley."

It was as much a surprise to see Mr. Deeley in his formal attire, as it was for Mr. Deeley to behold the two ladies he was escorting to the Grand Summer Ball.

He cut, Charlie had to admit, a rather dashing figure, in white breeches and a white waistcoat, a white linen shirt and a dark coat, a neckpiece tied jauntily under turned-up collars, and fawn kid gloves.

"My compliments to the ladies," he said, as Charlie and Sarah departed the cottage, amid much waving and cheerful encouragement from Tom, Mary and Jack.

"Thank you, Mr. Deeley," Charlie replied. "Our compliments to the gentleman."

Mr. Deeley laughed. "Your presence will be brilliant lights during what might otherwise have been a very dull evening for me."

The Great Reception Hall had been decorated with fresh flowers and cuttings of English ivy from the manor's gardens. And there were hundreds of lit beeswax candles, in several large chandeliers, along the walls, and in silver candlesticks placed on tables in strategic locations. The entire room was bathed in a warm yellow light.

"Monsieur Duran hired an artist from Southampton to chalk the floor," Mr. Deeley revealed, as they joined the ladies and gentlemen who had already assembled inside.

"What for?" Charlie asked.

"Is it not the fashion in London?" Sarah replied. "The wood is chalked with elaborate and pleasing designs, so that the soles of our shoes will not slip as we dance."

"Of course," Charlie said. "Yes. I had forgotten. It has been too many years."

"Then let this occasion mark the official end to your mourning, my dear. I am certain your memory will recover once you have danced a set or two with our Mr. Deeley."

Three musicians were seated at one end of the great hall, a violinist, another who played the flute, and a third the pianoforte.

"Is that the one who three years ago lost control of an embarrassment of his bodily functions?" Charlie inquired, impishly.

"Happily not. Although we may yet discover him underneath a table at midnight, sampling the claret. He is known for his fondness of drink. But as his family is well-acquainted with Monsieur Duran, he must continue to invite him, or risk being ignored at similar social occasions himself."

The activity on the chalked wooden floor reminded Charlie of a long country linedance. It began with the ladies and gentlemen all facing one another. And then one couple met up at the top end of the two lines, and danced down to the bottom end. The entire process was then repeated, in turn, for the next gentleman and lady, and so on.

"It seems a very merry exercise," Charlie remarked. "Although one does need some semblance of coordination in order to carry it off well. I'm not sure I'm able to manage this without falling over."

"Watch what I do," Mr. Deeley suggested, "and you will not put a foot wrong."

"And make certain that you write Mr. Deeley into your card for the final dance," Sarah advised, "as I understand there is to be a grand supper at midnight, and the ladies are always escorted in by their partners."

This, Charlie did, with the pencil and card she had been given as they'd entered. It was slightly tricky as she wasn't used to the long white gloves that were apparently mandatory to prevent contact from sweaty hands.

A portly gentleman whose breeches were a trifle too tight in all the wrong places approached Charlie, Mr. Deeley, and Sarah.

"Mr. Deeley, would you do me the great honour of an introduction to the ladies?"

"Certainly," Mr. Deeley replied, turning to Sarah and Charlie. "Mr. Montagu desires to be presented to Mrs. Foster and Mrs. Collins. Mrs. Foster and Mrs. Collins, allow me to introduce Mr. Montagu."

"Of the Bournemouth Montagus," the portly gentleman added, with a slight bow. "Delighted. Would you honor me with the next dance, Mrs. Foster?"

Sarah's face briefly showed a hint of doubt, but since Regency manners forbade her to refuse unless she was tired or otherwise spoken for, she was obliged to accept Mr. Montagu's invitation.

Not to be outdone, and perhaps fearing that his opportunity might be delayed by another interested gentleman, Mr. Deeley addressed Charlie.

"And would you do me the great honor…?" he began, very formally.

"Of joining you for the next dance?" Charlie finished. "Yes, of course."

The exercise involved a good deal of clapping and skipping, and turning and hopping. And then another good deal of clapping and turning and skipping and hopping, all accompanied by a great amount of laughter. It ended up taking at least half an hour to complete, and finished with all of the ladies and all of the gentlemen returning to their straight rows, bowing deeply to one another, and then applauding their approval.

Charlie had to admit that she was, in fact, enjoying herself, as was Mr. Deeley, who was quite an excellent dancer.

Disengaging herself from Mr. Montagu, Sarah returned to Mr. Deeley and Charlie.

"Who is the fair-haired gentleman that I see in the corner," she asked, curiously, "engaged in conversation with the lady with the impossibly large feathers?"

"That," Mr. Deeley replied, "is the greater Monsieur Louis Augustus Duran. Will you allow me an introduction?"

"I would be very pleased if you would, Mr. Deeley."

Charlie and Sarah followed Mr. Deeley to the far side of the Great Reception Hall, where Augustus Duran was listening to an intensely dull discourse, delivered by Mrs. Montagu (of the Bournemouth Montagus), on the state of the country's cotton mills.

"Do excuse me," he interrupted, as Mrs. Montagu asserted, for the third time, that 13-year-olds were much more easily trained for mill-work than 16-year-olds. "Monsieur Duran, may I present Mrs. Foster. I believe you have already been acquainted with Mrs. Collins."

"Hello," Charlie said, with one of her small waves.

"Mrs. Foster, Monsieur Duran. The elder."

"I am not quite so ancient, Mr. Deeley," Augustus replied.

"Indeed," Sarah agreed. "You are not."

"I am delighted to make your acquaintance, Mrs. Foster. Mr. Deeley has spoken very highly of you."

Sarah smiled. "And I am pleased to make your acquaintance also, Monsieur Duran. Though I suspect by now your son has mentioned me in rather less glowing terms than Mr. Deeley."

Augustus laughed.

"My son has mentioned you, yes, a number of times. However I have not heard anything which could be construed as negative. Indeed, Louis' praises have consistently approached the superlative. But I now believe his words have failed to do you justice, Mrs. Foster."

"This gentleman is as charming as his son is revolting," Sarah whispered, behind her hand and not unkindly, to Charlie, who was quite unable to remove her eyes from the man who was destined to become her ancestor. He looked exactly like the individual in the painting Nick had sent her.

"Shall we join the next dance?" Augustus inquired. "I have not undertaken my constitutional today, and my spleen is looking forward to an energetic diversion."

"I would be happy to join you," Sarah replied.

"You must instruct your cousin to ensure the greater Monsieur Duran is pencilled into her card for the end of the evening, and supper," Mr. Deeley said, to Charlie, amused.

"I must do more than that," Charlie replied. "What would you say to a picnic, Mr. Deeley, tomorrow, after church? During which my cousin and your employer's father might further the friendship begun here tonight?"

"Mrs. Collins, I do believe you are dabbling in the fine art of matchmaking," Mr. Deeley teased. "Have you also a friendship in mind for me?"

"I do indeed, Mr. Deeley," Charlie replied. "Shall we dance?"

The next half hour was happily passed in the Great Reception Hall, during which Sarah, Mr. Deeley, Augustus and Charlie danced several reels, though not necessarily with one another, as etiquette dictated a frequent changing of partners.

During the last of these dances (a Quadrille in Reel time which involved a good deal of crossing and meeting and turning together) Charlie observed rather alarmingly that the lesser Monsieur Duran had contrived to position himself as close as possible to Sarah.

"We must watch over Mrs. Foster with care," she said, to Mr. Deeley, at their next opportunity of meeting up.

Mr. Deeley had noticed the same thing. "He changed places at the last moment with a gentleman who owns a nearby estate and is secretly enamored with Mrs. Montagu."

"You keep an eye on your employer," Charlie said, "and I'll look after Mrs. Foster."

"Agreed," said Mr. Deeley, as he turned, and continued the steps with a well-endowed young woman who had turned out to be Mrs. Montagu's unmarried eldest daughter.

The dance ended, and Charlie retired to a chair against the wall to catch her breath.

Sarah, however, had decided to continue, and was, Charlie noted, again happily partnered with Augustus for the set.

Charlie leaned her head back against the wall and shut her eyes. She was altogether exhausted. It might not have been Regency etiquette, but then most ladies from Jane Austen's time hadn't just travelled two hundred years from the future.

She let her mind drift as she listened to snippets of conversation from Mr. Deeley, who was standing nearby, discussing the best oil for leather saddles with Mr. Montagu.

And then, she was being coaxed awake.

"Mrs. Collins." It was Mr. Deeley. "Mrs. Collins, forgive me. I seem to have misplaced my employer. And, more inopportunely, Mrs. Foster seems also to have vanished."

She opened her eyes. Some time seemed to have passed. Had she been dozing?

"How have you misplaced him, Mr. Deeley?" she asked, trying to clear the haze from her mind.

"He was occupied by Miss Montagu during the dance. And Mrs. Foster was in the company of the greater Monsieur Duran. And then, when I looked again, the dance had ended, and my employer had abandoned Miss Montagu, and Mrs. Foster was nowhere in sight."

Mr. Deeley was joined by Augustus.

"My son insinuated himself into our conversation, and then they both withdrew. I considered it very bad manners on Louis' part; however he has always been one to flout polite convention."

"Did you see where they went?" Charlie asked, now wide awake and trying not to be alarmed.

"Alas," Augustus replied, "I did not."

Charlie was on her feet. "Then we must find her. Quickly."

The search was led by Augustus, who was far better acquainted with the upstairs floors of the manor than Mr. Deeley.

Discreetly, and with a better understanding than Charlie had previously credited him with, Augustus began with his son's bedroom. It was, to their very great relief, unoccupied.

Several other bedrooms were investigated, again to no avail.

"There is a small library," Mr. Deeley said, thinking. "It is situated in the west wing of the manor, next to the dining room. I was taken there once, when the lesser Monsieur Duran wished me to see a sketch of a horse in one of the books."

The Great Reception Hall occupied the center of the second

floor of the manor, and it was necessary for Charlie, Mr. Deeley and Augustus to negotiate their way back through its foyer in order to access the lavishly decorated west wing.

The door to the library was shut, but from within, very distinct voices could be heard.

"I do not consider this an appropriate conversation at all, Monsieur Duran."

It was Sarah.

"Nonsense."

Unmistakably the lesser Monsieur Duran.

"We are not the innocent and foolish young, requiring the chaperone. I wish to engage you in conversation, not in marriage. Though it is my hope the former will lead in brief time to the latter. Please, do sit."

"The intimacy of this room does not appeal to me, sir. I shall remain standing."

"If I may make a proposal…"

"I wish you would not, Monsieur Duran," Sarah interrupted. "I have not agreed to anything, although your imagination may have convinced you otherwise."

"You are wearing the gown. Which was presented by me."

"A presentation that was not anticipated, and which I accepted with the understanding that there would be no understandings," Sarah countered. "Did your maid not return my message to you? No future obligation upon my part, nor upon yours."

The lesser Monsieur Duran was clearly annoyed.

"Then what is the purpose of you attending here?" he countered, with impatience.

"I was invited," Sarah replied, "by Mr. Deeley. And encouraged by Mrs. Collins, who was anxious that I make the acquaintance of your father."

"Mr. Deeley," the lesser Monsieur Duran said, the irritation apparent in his voice. "And my father. These two persons persistently cause me undue vexation."

Mr. Deeley and Augustus exchanged a look.

On the other side of the closed door, there was an ominous silence.

And then: "Madame Foster, you have kept me in suspense for far too long. I am pleased that you have agreed to attend the ball. But I am displeased by the delays caused by your refusal of me. The gown suits you well. It would suit me much better to see it removed."

It was at that point that Sarah screamed, rather loudly. And there was a very loud thud.

In quick order, Augustus attempted to fling open the library door, only to discover it locked.

And then, employing a well-placed and solid kick, Mr. Deeley rendered the door both unlocked and open.

Augustus, Mr. Deeley and Charlie rushed into the room to discover the lesser Monsieur Duran crumpled on the floor beneath a small table, groaning and holding his head.

Sarah stood over him, a large leather-bound World Atlas at the ready, in the event he should recover his senses sufficiently to approach her again.

"Are you in need of assistance, Mrs. Foster?" Augustus inquired.

"No assistance is required," Sarah replied, "although, Monsieur Duran, I would be happy for you to escort me back to the dance."

She considered his son, underneath the table.

"I take my leave of you, sir. The conversation was not altogether engaging, and any agreements you may have anticipated as a result are not, I think, likely."

CHAPTER 24

It was Sunday, and nearly noon.

A late morning mist was lingering in the nearby trees as Sarah made her way up Manor Rise, followed, in order, by Tom, and then Jack, and lastly, Charlie, holding Mary's hand. The children were also in possession of three home-made kites, gleefully retrieved following that morning's sermon by Reverend Hobson, and promising a far more interesting occupation.

They negotiated the tricky bit in the curving cart track which always seemed to be muddy, in spite of there not having been any rain for nearly two weeks.

As the cart track meandered around the face of the hill for a second time, all of Stoneford became visible below, as well as the sea in the distance, and the manor above. And, under the shade of a spreading beech just ahead, two gentlemen appeared, both on their feet, both greatly anticipating the arrival of the small procession.

"Good afternoon, Mr. Deeley," Charlie said. "And Monsieur Duran."

"Good afternoon, Mrs. Collins," Mr. Deeley replied, with a welcoming smile.

"It is a lovely day, Mrs. Collins," Augustus acknowledged, "and what a pleasure it is to make your acquaintance again, Mrs. Foster."

"It is Monsieur Duran's father!" Mary shouted, rushing forward to demonstrate a perfect headstand, which, in turn, revealed a pair of handsome white pantaloons.

"Mary!" Sarah exclaimed. "Goodness! Manners!"

"There is no impropriety," Augustus assured her. "Only the exuberance of adventurous childhood. I have two sons and neither could ever be convinced to stand on his head. Your children, Mrs. Foster, are enchanting."

"Thank you, Monsieur Duran."

The two gentlemen had obviously been busy, as a grand luncheon had been laid out on a large white linen cloth. There were slices of ham and chicken, and asparagus with butter, and glazed carrots. There was a green salad and a fruit salad. And there were breads and cheeses, and lemonade and cake, all of it left over from the midnight supper.

"And do you judge the Grand Summer Ball to be a success?" Sarah inquired, sitting beside Augustus on a second linen cloth.

"A glorious success," Augustus replied, "in spite of the notable disappearance of my progeny, partway through the evening."

"It was whispered among the servants," Mr. Deeley supplied, "that he was put to bed by the butler, after suffering the ill effects of one too many bottles of fine French wine."

"If that is what Mr. Arrowsmith's very weighty *Outlines of the World* has come to be known as below the stairs," Sarah laughed.

She glanced at the book which Augustus had been reading just prior to her arrival, and which he had placed, face-down, on the cloth beside the chicken.

"Oh!" she exclaimed. "It is *Pride and Prejudice*. One of my favourites. But surely, Monsieur Duran—not one of yours!"

Augustus smiled. "I admire the individual and passionate nature of The Anonymous Lady's heroines. As I admire the realism, social commentary and individual character of the author herself. It is a shame she left us at such a middling age."

Sarah's eyes lit up. "What unusual qualities you possess, Monsieur Duran. A true appreciation for women of independence. And the wit of a philosopher! I was devastated to learn that she is with us no longer, for I had not been party to this knowledge. Yet you come equipped with the most recent information, all the way from France!"

Charlie joined Mr. Deeley, who was lounging on his back on the grass, his hands tucked behind his head as he studied the high, wisping clouds.

"What an amazing coincidence," she said, quietly, and not

without humour, "that the greater Monsieur Duran is such an ardent follower of Jane Austen and her work."

"It is unaccountably fortunate," Mr. Deeley agreed, also with humour.

"Have you read the novel?"

"I have not," Mr. Deeley admitted, "although I am at liberty to tell you that the greater Monsieur Duran was awake very early this morning, and was, according to Martha, very much taken with The Anonymous Lady at breakfast."

"How fortunate that your employer's library is so well-stocked."

"Indeed," said Mr. Deeley. "Although I suspect a large part of the collection remains unread. The lesser Monsieur Duran not being known for his proficiency with the written word."

There followed a sojourn of some forty-five minutes, during which the cold ham and chicken, the asparagus with butter, the glazed carrots, the salads and breads and a great deal of cheese were consumed, along with the lemonade.

Sipping from her glass, Sarah tilted her head towards the greater Monsieur Duran.

"I am most impressed with your mastery of English, Monsieur Duran. Unlike your son, who manages to insult the language at every opportunity."

Augustus took Sarah's hand, and held it with delicacy.

"I speak many languages," he assured her. "Fluently."

Sarah contemplated her three children, who had run into the meadow to fly their kites, while nearby, a consortium of sheep nibbled grass alongside mauve cranesbills and brilliant white yarrow.

"May I say, Monsieur Duran, that I am very pleased to discover you do not remotely resemble your despicable son in any way, shape or form?"

"You may say, Mrs. Foster," Augustus replied, graciously. "And I am, in turn, very pleased that you have made this fortunate discovery. I have myself known about it for some years. Although, I confess, I have not, to this point, been able to use it to any great advantage."

"Then it is my pleasure," said Sarah, "to inform you that I

perceive a very clear advantage making itself known today."

On the other side of the great cloth, where the butterflies and honeybees danced among the nodding yellow cowslips and buttercups, Charlie offered Mr. Deeley a morsel of cake.

"I do not believe," he said, "a more enchanting confection than this could possibly exist."

"Oh, Mr. Deeley," Charlie teased. "You trifle with me."

"There is trifle too…?" Mr. Deeley answered, hopefully.

Charlie laughed. "I do love you, Mr. Deeley," she said, impetuously, entirely ignoring the code of etiquette she was certain forbade such outrageous declarations.

"As I do you," Mr. Deeley replied, with sudden seriousness.

Charlie paused. He had surprised her.

And it was not an unpleasant discovery.

But it was completely unexpected.

She had not anticipated this at all.

"Head over heels," she said, slowly, as a small cloud drifted across the flawless blue sky, momentarily shadowing the sun.

Mr. Deeley looked up towards the manor, and frowned.

"Here comes a complication," he said, unhappily, getting to his feet.

Charlie stood also, and saw what Mr. Deeley had observed: the lesser Monsieur Duran, marching furiously down the hill, towards their meadow.

"Good day, sir," said Mr. Deeley.

But his greeting was not returned. Indeed, the lesser Monsieur Duran brusquely pushed his groom aside, and instead addressed Augustus, who had remained seated beside Sarah.

"You, sir, are required in France," he said, removing an important-looking piece of paper from a pocket, and waving it in his father's face. "My brother has dispatched this by messenger."

"I observed no messenger's arrival," Augustus replied, fixing his son with a steady gaze.

"Then you must have been otherwise distracted," the lesser Monsieur Duran answered, impatiently. "You must go."

Augustus took the piece of paper from his son's hand, and

studied the almost illegible scrawl that covered it.

"As you can see," the lesser Monsieur Duran said, "the matter is urgent."

"It may be urgent," his father replied, "however it is also impossible to decipher. What is the nature of Gaston's dilemma, that he so desperately requires my return to Amiens?"

Charlie could see that the lesser Monsieur Duran's temper was beginning to fray.

"It is the chateau," he said. "He believes it is under siege."

"Under siege?" his father inquired. "By whom?"

"By orphans. Cats. Dogs. Villagers intent on revolution. You know how he suffers from *l'hystérie*. He is in fear for his life."

Augustus considered his son with a less than charitable look.

"Your brother is to be congratulated on his ingenuity at managing to dispatch this letter without hindrance. I wonder why he didn't simply come along with it. Or seek assistance from one of his consumptive orphans."

"Unlike you, sir, he would never abandon the chateau."

The lesser Monsieur Duran looked at Mr. Deeley.

"And as for you," he said. "This picnic was your devising?"

"No," Charlie said, stepped boldly between them, "this picnic was my devising."

She faced Sarah squarely.

"I know who you are destined to marry, Sarah—and it certainly isn't this...wanker."

The lesser Monsieur Duran furrowed his eyebrows. "*Wang-coeur?*" he said. "What is this, *wang-coeur?*"

"Perhaps," Sarah ventured, quickly, smoothing her gown, "it is an expression of curiosity—from London."

"No, it is not an expression of curiosity," Charlie said. "From London or anywhere else."

"This picnic," the lesser Monsieur Duran continued, fixing his cold eyes on Mr. Deeley, "could not have occurred without the conspiracy of you."

He glared at his father.

"And you. And after last night, it is clear that you are both against me. So."

He again addressed Mr. Deeley.

"You are no longer in my employ. You may depart at your earliest convenience."

"No!" Charlie shouted—but Mr. Deeley touched her arm, silencing her.

"Sir," he said, evenly. "If I have offended you—"

"Enough!"

The lesser Louis Augustus Duran raised his hand to silence his groom.

"I have heard that Madame Foster has ceased to be employed with the vicar of the church in the village. This is true?"

"It is true," Sarah said.

"And you therefore have no means by which to support yourself?"

"That is none of your business," Charlie said.

"It will be my business, *madame*," the lesser Monsieur Duran replied, "in a month or two, when your cousin tires of scrubbing the soiled underthings of other people in order to have the meat and bread put on her table."

"I would rather scrub the filthy linen of strangers than any belonging to you," Sarah replied, boldly.

A thin smile appeared upon the lesser Monsieur Duran's face.

"I employ the servants for these tasks," he said. "You would have no need. But I believe you have been confused, Madame Foster. I believe that my father's attentions may have caused you to not know your own mind. No matter."

He looked at his father.

"Why do you still occupy here? You are henceforth banished. We shall see no more of you."

"I shall go," Augustus replied. "However I suspect your brother's delirium may well have been cured by the time I arrive. Or he will have been murdered."

"I sincerely hope," his son replied, impatiently and disingenuously, "that it is the former."

Augustus took Sarah's hand, and held it with great tenderness.

"I must take my leave, Mrs. Foster. I suggest we address this postponement at a more opportune time…"

Augustus here fixed his son with another penetrating glare.

"…before I succumb to an impulse thoroughly unbecoming my paternal affiliation."

He then turned to Charlie.

"It has been my very great pleasure to also make your acquaintance, Mrs. Collins. I look forward to our future friendship, as I intend to return to this village sooner, rather than later."

And with that, he departed, trudging up the hill by way of the winding cart track, and without looking back.

Charlie's spirit deflated as she watched him make his way back to the manor. She pressed her hand to her side. That pain. Again. And it was not getting better. In fact…it was becoming considerably worse. Last night's dancing had not done it any favours.

"With any luck," the lesser Monsieur Duran said, sourly, "my father's little boat will capsize in a gale as he crosses the channel."

"You," Charlie said, "are an exceedingly unpleasant individual, Monsieur Duran."

The lesser Monsieur Duran ignored her.

Emboldened, Mr. Deeley stepped forward. "Is this the same sort of banishment you arranged for Mrs. Foster's late husband?"

Monsieur Duran glowered at him. "You, sir, should also be gone."

"I will be gone, sir," Mr. Deeley answered, defiantly.

"Children!" Sarah called. "The picnic is finished! We are leaving!"

Playing in the long grass beside the meadow, where she had created a make-believe den for a flock of French fairies with gossamer wings and an English princess who was about to be crowned queen— and who also knew how to stand on her head—Mary was crestfallen. "But Monsieur Duran promised to teach me how to juggle!" she cried.

"Monsieur Duran has departed," his son replied, curtly. "And so should you, if you do not wish to incur my wrath further. Now—go."

CHAPTER 25

And so, they went, quickly and without further discourse, gathering up the remains of the picnic and carrying it, in three baskets, back to the tree-shaded garden behind Sarah's cottage.

At the bottom of the garden Mary was perfecting a cartwheel. Before the interruption of their picnic, the greater Monsieur Duran had imparted this new skill to her. He had observed her technique and judged her an expert, far advanced for her years. And certainly much better at it than Gaston, who had no sense whatsoever of up and down, and was far more likely to end up flat on his back on the ground and complaining about the ankle he had sprained falling off a wall when he was six.

"Perhaps," Sarah ventured, "we might send Tom and Jack back to the manor, to seek permission to collect your possessions, Mr. Deeley. Perhaps Mr. Rankin might be persuaded to assist in this endeavour."

Sitting beside Charlie on the grass, Mr. Deeley finished the last of the lemonade that they'd rescued from the picnic.

"I am certain Mr. Rankin would gladly oblige, though he would do so with a heavy heart, for he is my friend, and he will not be pleased to learn of the circumstances of my dismissal."

"Where will you stay?" Sarah asked. "Mary—do stop showing us your pantaloons. I am certain Mr. Deeley would much rather have another cup of tea."

"My friend Mr. Wallis will provide me with a bed until I am able to locate other lodgings," Mr. Deeley replied, as Mary, reluctantly, abandoned her cartwheels. "Tea would be most appreciated. And for you, Mrs. Collins?"

"Yes, thank you—" Charlie replied, but she caught her breath before she could finish her sentence, and bent over in pain.

"My dear," Sarah exclaimed. "You are unwell!"

"It is nothing," Charlie gasped.

"It is not nothing!" Sarah insisted. "You must come inside immediately and lie down. And I shall fetch the surgeon!"

"No," Charlie said, as the pain subsided a little, and she regained her composure. "No…please. I would rather you did not. I will go to the manor and request Mr. Rankin's assistance. I know where to find him, and I can slip inside without attracting undue attention from the lesser Monsieur Duran."

"If you are certain," Sarah answered, doubtfully.

"I am certain," Charlie assured her.

She was less certain about the pain than she had admitted to Sarah. Indeed, it was not nothing. And it was growing more persistent, like a nagging reminder that, inside, there was something going on that was not right at all.

Really, she thought, as she trudged up the rise for the second time that day, she could have done with some kind of diagnostic app on her phone. Something where she could key in her symptoms, and it would reply with a clever selection of suitable ailments and cures. Or a link to a website that would accomplish the same thing.

But her phone would not connect to the world wide web. She'd already tried. The best the old oak tree could manage was short messages and the odd attachment.

Which was, she thought, as she reached the top of the hill, in itself, something of a marvel. Considering what year it was. Considering what century.

Charlie decided she would ask Nick to ask Sam. The next best thing to the Mayo Clinic, having your own district nurse on call.

As she approached the kitchen garden, thinking she would slip inside the manor the same way she had before, she heard a familiar-sounding voice.

It was the lesser Monsieur Duran, pacing up and down between the rows of vegetables.

Charlie concealed herself just outside the gate in the brick wall, where she had an unobstructed view of the garden. The lesser Monsieur Duran was deep in conversation with someone she couldn't see.

Upon closer scrutiny, however, she realized he was alone.

"There is the risk, indeed," he reasoned, aloud. "There is the inheritance."

He reached the end of the lettuces, and turned.

"If my father decides now to remove me from the will, and everything is left to my brother…"

He paused.

"Gaston has not ever refused when I have demanded. On pain of intolerable suffering and miserableness. So. The will is easily resolved."

He continued pacing, until he had reached the cabbages.

"And now. Madame Foster. She will discover soon the marriage with me is preferable to poverty. I will husband her. Because once I make up my mind, I do not ever change it again."

Not, Charlie thought, her anger rising, if I have anything to do with it.

But she was very quickly brought back to reality. Her nudge hadn't worked. In fact, it had backfired. Badly.

She had no idea how Sarah and Augustus would manage to marry now.

"There remains," Monsieur Duran's son continued, from the carrots, "the complication of *les enfants*."

He bent down, and pulled up one of the plants.

"*Les enfants* are of course necessary to produce *les héritiers*. However they are mostly a nuisance and even more so usually in the way."

He tossed the uprooted carrot into a corner of the garden, and continued walking.

"I will send *les garçons* to a school. In Scotland. But *la fille*…"

He paused again, and contemplated a stand of rhubarb.

"*La fille* will not be of the marriageable age until ten years after now."

He broke off one of the leafy red rhubarb stems, and used it as a thinking stick.

"She might however live in France until the suitable husband is located."

He bit off the end of the stalk, and chewed it, thoughtfully.

"She might however cohabit with *cousine* Cosette. Her hearing is gone. And she is blind in one eye and confined to the bed. But Cosette has not ever been married and now requires a companion."

He took another bite of the rhubarb.

"The child will quickly learn the care of the elderly *invalide*. So. I will send a *lettre* to Cosette tomorrow." He threw the stalk of rhubarb after the discarded carrot. "And as for the interfering cousin from *Londres*...she is too much the unconstrained. This is not ever a good thing in *la femme*. I shall arrange her to go." The lesser Monsieur Duran turned again, and walked purposefully back to the scullery door, then went inside the manor.

Infuriated, Charlie followed him, ducking into the scullery so that she remained out of sight. She watched as the lesser Monsieur Duran walked quickly past Mr. Rankin's room and the kitchen, all the way to the other end of the hallway. The door at the end of the hallway was not locked. As Charlie continued to watch, the lesser Monsieur Duran entered quickly and quietly, closing the door behind him.

He was inside the room, Charlie judged, for no more than a minute. He reappeared quickly, shutting the door again, and beating a quick retreat upstairs by way of the servants' staircase.

Charlie waited a few moments more, then slipped out of the scullery and ran to the door at the end of the hallway. Opening it, she peeked inside.

It was Mr. Deeley's room. It could belong to no one else. There were many books, and framed paintings of horses, and several brass harness decorations being used as paperweights on a small side table.

Charlie peeked at what was written on the papers underneath the brasses.

Poetry!

Mr. Deeley was a secret poet, musing upon the sun, the moon and the stars.

For this, she loved him all the more.

The remaining furniture in Mr. Deeley's bedroom consisted of a narrow but neatly made bed, a chair, and an upright wooden wardrobe, varnished and very plain, and similar to the one in Mr. Rankin's quarters.

Curiously, Charlie opened the wardrobe door. Inside were drawers and shelves and hooks and hangers. And all of Mr. Deeley's clothes, smelling faintly of straw and stables and horses.

Charlie wasn't certain what the lesser Monsieur Duran had been doing in Mr. Deeley's room. Everything seemed neat and tidy. There were no signs of vandalism. Nothing looked out of place.

Confounded, she closed the wardrobe door again, and then slipped out into the hallway, to look for Mr. Rankin.

CHAPTER 26

"The lesser Monsieur Duran has always disliked me," Mr. Deeley said. "My services were inherited with the manor. My father was the head groomsman, and I naturally filled the position following his death. The lesser Monsieur Duran has never been an easy man to work for."

"He had no right to go into your room," Charlie maintained.

Mr. Deeley was more philosophical. "He is not one to respect the privacy of his household staff. But because of this, I made it a habit to exercise caution, and would never incriminate myself with a careless note left lying about, nor any other article which might be construed as less than respectful."

"You are very wise," Charlie said.

She had returned to the cottage with news of Mr. Rankin's agreement to facilitate the removal of Mr. Deeley's belongings the following day, Monday. She had also imparted to Sarah and Mr. Deeley the one-sided conversation she had overheard in the kitchen garden, followed by the lesser Monsieur Duran's subsequent and decidedly odd visit to Mr. Deeley's bedroom.

"Indeed," Mr. Deeley replied. "But in the end, it seems my wisdom did not serve me well at all. No matter. I will request a reference from the greater Monsieur Duran, and I will find employment in another country house, or at a stable. Perhaps Mr. Ferryman has need of an extra person at the inn, to help care for the overnighting of his guests' horses."

Charlie could think of other establishments which would make better use of Mr. Deeley's talents and skills as a horseman and groom, but she kept silent.

However Mr. Deeley's mention of Mr. Ferryman reminded her

of the conversation she'd had with him the day before, after her lunch at the manor and as he was returning from his visit to the inn.

"Mr. Deeley," she said. "Do you recall what you told me yesterday, about Mr. Ferryman's most recent acquisition?"

"I do," Mr. Deeley replied.

"It is the deed to your inherited land," Charlie said, to Sarah.

"*The* deed?" Sarah said, surprised.

The same," Mr. Deeley supplied. "He claims it as his own, won fairly and squarely after a game of cards."

"Then it has recently changed hands," Sarah lamented. "Again."

"I should like to see it," Charlie said, to Mr. Deeley. "Will you take me there?"

Mr. Deeley looked doubtful, but Charlie was adamant.

"It will not be the first time I have mixed with the inn's unruly customers," she reminded him. "And I will have you with me to keep my honor safe. I will not stop for a drink. I am interested only in viewing the deed, and bringing back my report to Mrs. Foster."

If, in the 21st century, there had been a selection of drinking establishments in Stoneford, Charlie—and indeed, most of the village's inhabitants—would have preferred to have taken their custom there. But there was no choice at all, and the nearest pub after The Dog's Watch was several miles away, in a village whose entire population seemed to embrace loud and completely incomprehensible rap music while downing their pints.

Here, in the 19th century, there were two taverns, but The Dog's Watch seemed to be the most popular. Constructed of brick that had been stuccoed and painted white, it was a single story high, and was attached to a two-storied establishment next door that formed the coaching inn. There were square sashed windows with working shutters. There was a sloping roof. And there was a six foot chimney that Charlie remembered in the 21st century had been struck by lightning three times in four years, much to the consternation of the customers within.

Here and now, in 1825, she could see the new red brick stable that Mr. Deeley had referred to, where horses could be put up for the night. Two centuries into the future, it would still be standing, its hayloft and wide wooden doors intact, though it would remain empty, its usefulness as a barn long since abandoned.

Charlie entered the public house with Mr. Deeley by way of the same doorway she'd always used on those days when she'd met Sam for post-work drinks. It was, in fact, the very same door. Although here and now, its hinges were not inclined to squeak or catch, and there were no splintered bits caused by someone's angry boots.

There were fewer people inside than there had been during the lesser Monsieur Duran's extraction two nights earlier. And so Charlie could see more of the room. She was astounded at how similar it was to Reg Ferryman's 21st century domain.

It had the same low, timbered ceiling. And the same massive dark brown beams extending down into the walls, which had been filled and plastered and painted white.

The same huge stone fireplace stood in the corner, complementing the same planked wooden floors and leaded windows.

The bar was far smaller than Reg Ferryman's, however, and certainly less decorative. It was merely the place where ale could be poured by Lemuel and carried away by his two assistants. One was a sallow-looking man with stringy hair and a look that suggested to Charlie he would be dead of consumption within the year. The other was a buxom wench who appeared to be on overly familiar terms with most of the male customers.

"Clara!" Lemuel Ferryman called. "This table wants serving!"

Clara.

Soon to become the second Mrs. Lemuel Ferryman, Charlie thought, remembering her research. In common law, anyway, the first and legal Mrs. Ferryman having departed in 1823, taking her two sons with her.

Clara.

Soon to become pregnant with Marcus Ferryman, if she wasn't already. And when Marcus was grown, he would marry; have sons and daughters, grandsons and granddaughters. Down through the centuries, the lineage would end, at last, with Ron and Reg, neither of whom had ever married nor, as far as anyone knew, been responsible for any offspring.

Clara removed herself from three particularly appreciative gentlemen, one of whom was very pleased with the fact that he'd been able to pinch her bottom without having his face smacked. Meanwhile, Mr. Deeley had spotted his two friends, Mr. Cole and Mr. Wallis, at a table close by the plastered wall where the bar was.

"Gentlemen," Mr. Deeley said, as they rose hastily to their feet. "I have the honour of introducing Mrs. Collins, who is visiting from London and is the cousin of Mrs. Foster."

Both Mr. Wallis and Mr. Cole bowed their appreciation.

"Mr. Wallis," Mr. Deeley said, to Charlie, "and Mr. Cole."

"Good afternoon, gentlemen," Charlie said, but her attention was diverted almost immediately by the piece of paper affixed to the wall beside the bar. She turned to Mr. Deeley. "Is that it?"

"It is," Mr. Deeley replied.

And before he could do anything to stop her, Charlie had dragged a chair across to the wall, and climbed up on it, the better to scrutinize the document.

It was the deed to two holdings, the first identified as "the land in the middle of Stoneford" and the second, "a piece of land in Stoneford, at Poorhouse ende".

The paper was made out in the name of John Harding, and dated 22 July 1729.

"John Harding," Charlie affirmed, aloud. Sarah's great ancestor, who had once worked the land around and in the village.

"A farmer," Lemuel Ferryman said, joining Charlie at the wall, "and a gentleman."

"Indeed," Charlie replied, turning to face him squarely—and making note of the grubby white piece of linen he had wrapped around his hand as a makeshift bandage. "As I understand it, this deed was taken from its legal owner in exchange for an unpaid debt. And as the debt was minor, compared to the actual value of the property, it was something close to highway robbery."

Lemuel Ferryman grinned, revealing an alarming absence of important teeth.

"In actual fact, madam, the exchange was made at a card game attended by myself, a local smuggler whose name escapes me, and my great friend Monsieur Louis Duran. It was the smuggler who won the game and was therefore owed the debt, and it was Monsieur Duran who suggested the deed by way of payment, as the gentleman in question was without other monetary worth. I had no say whatsoever in the matter."

"Is that blood?" Charlie inquired, pointing to a small blot of dull brown near the edge of the paper.

"I have no idea, madam," Lemuel Ferryman replied. "The stain was there when I took possession of the document."

"And how did you come to take possession of it?" Charlie asked.

"My friend Monsieur Duran won it back from the smuggler during a more recent game of cards. And made a gift of it, to me."

Charlie resisted the impulse to laugh. She had seen what had happened with her own eyes. And there were other witnesses, too. But they were also accessories to the murder, and if she dared to accuse him, what would happen to her? It didn't bear thinking about, even if she could prove it by drawing attention to his wounded hand. He would only make up some story about a temperamental pig or a recalcitrant chicken, resisting their fate as they were destined for the soup pot.

"A gift in exchange for a bottomless mug of ale, I have no doubt," Mr. Deeley remarked, from the table.

Lemuel Ferryman manoeuvred his large and greasy girth around Charlie, so that he was directly in Mr. Deeley's line of sight.

"Hastily spoken, sir, by someone who, it seems, is no longer in the employ of the aforementioned patron."

Mr. Deeley met Mr. Ferryman's hard stare with one of his own.

"An aforementioned patron who appears to be overly fond of dispensing with those who become a vexation to him," he said, evenly. "Aiden Foster, for one."

The level of noise in the room dropped suddenly and appreciably as the attention of the inn's drinkers was drawn to the conversation beside the bar.

"You have no proof of that, sir, and it would be unwise of you to pursue those thoughts further."

"Perhaps you know more about Mr. Foster's disappearance than you are willing to say," Charlie suggested.

A large vein in Lemuel Ferryman's right temple was beginning to throb with vexation. "It would be wise for you to reign in these accusatory statements," he replied.

Mr. Wallis raised his tankard to salute Mr. Deeley and Charlie. "I have heard similar," he said, taking a long drink, then returning his cup to the table.

"And I," added Mr. Cole, also drinking. "And upon more than one occasion."

"And since I am no longer in Monsieur Duran's employ," Mr. Deeley continued, "it appears I have little to lose by speaking my mind."

Lemuel Ferryman collected Mr. Wallis's empty tankard with his unbandaged hand.

"You are correct, sir," he replied. "In my establishment you may speak your mind. Or, you may stay and drink. You may in fact do either—but not both."

Mr. Deeley thought for a moment before responding.

"The proprietor of the Rose and Crown has no such conditions," he said, at last.

"The proprietor of the Rose and Crown is welcome to your custom, sir." Lemuel Ferryman turned to Charlie. "And yours."

"The proprietor of the Rose and Crown will welcome four new patrons this very afternoon," Mr. Wallis decided, as Mr. Cole finished his ale and wiped his mouth with the back of his hand.

The two gentlemen stood, and Mr. Deeley helped Charlie down from the chair.

"Good day to you, sir," he said, cordially, to Lemuel Ferryman, as all four left the inn.

• • •

"It is the genuine deed," Charlie judged, conveying what she had seen to Sarah. "Made out in John Harding's name, and dated 1729."

She had been safely accompanied back to the cottage by Mr. Deeley, Mr. Wallis and Mr. Cole, who had continued on to The Rose and Crown, on the western edge of the village.

Sarah stirred the supper she had made from the remains of the picnic, thickened into a stew over the kitchen fire.

"Such a valuable slip of paper," she said, sadly. "I wonder at Mr. Ferryman's folly, posting it on the wall of his inn. Anyone could remove it, following a convenient diversion of his attention."

"They could," Charlie supposed, "but what would be the point? Mr. Ferryman is not stupid. If anyone took it, they would never be able to show it anywhere, or use it to claim ownership. Mr. Ferryman has made witnesses out of everyone who drinks at The Dog's Watch. The deed is his."

Supper was brief, and conducted without much conversation. Afterwards, Sarah attended to some mending in the sitting room, and Mary and Jack read books by the window, and Tom sketched a likeness of a horse he had seen in the village.

Charlie excused herself, and made her way back to the old oak in the middle of the Village Green. There, in the early twilight, the annoying pain in her middle making itself known yet again, she eased herself down into a sitting position, her back against the tree's sturdy trunk.

She switched on her phone.

The battery indicator glimmered at her. 63% charge. 62%.

The sight of it made Charlie's heart sink.

At home, in the future, she never went anywhere without her recharger, which she kept in her bag.

But even if she'd had it with her now, there was nothing to plug it into.

A new message had arrived from Nick. This improved her mood a little.

I know you know, but just in case. I have to caution you about interfering. Remember the Butterfly Effect. Would hate to think flapping your wings Over There would cause a hurricane Over Here. And wipe out the entire population of Stoneford.

Well. She had interfered. Her intention had been only to nudge. But she had flapped her wings, and the bitter wind that was Monsieur Duran's vile son had roared down the hillside from the manor to destroy everything.

And there was nothing she could do about it now.

She shut her eyes and held her side as the terrible shooting pain began again.

If this was something very serious…and it certainly felt serious…then no amount of bloodletting and plasters and herbal tinctures and whatever else was in the medicine chests of 19th century Stoneford was going to make her better.

Charlie read the second part of Nick's message.

Still working on a way to bring you back. Looking into that virus on your laptop. Hopefully have answer in the next day or so. Try and save your battery. Might not be too many more opportunities to chat.

Easier said than done, Charlie thought.

She composed a reply, keying in her symptoms, describing them as accurately as she was able. *Please ask Sam what's wrong with me.*

If Sam could at least come up with a diagnosis, it would help her make a decision. The decision.

Began yesterday, she added. *Getting worse.*

She touched Send, and then switched off her mobile, and closed her eyes as the pain made her double over and gasp.

CHAPTER 27

It was amazing to Nick, but not in the least surprising, how the Village Green had become, in the space of something slightly more than forty-eight hours, the talk of Southern England and Wales, as well as a good part of the Midlands, and a small coastal village in Scotland which also had a green with an oak that was ailing, and therefore was supporting Stoneford in local solidarity, as well as online.

As for the oak, there were now regular bulletins on TV, radio and the internet, and the state of the tree's health was updated hourly by reporters affiliated with podcasts, newscasts and newspapers around the world. Stoneford's most famous tree had been symbolically adopted by one of the former Spice Girls. In South Korea, someone had created a Dancing Tree video, and it had received more than 250,000 hits in its first hour on YouTube. And in Alaska, a woman had reportedly given birth to a son she was determined to call Stoneford Oak, something Nick was convinced she would later regret, as the surname she and her husband shared was Barrall.

Meanwhile, at the top end of Poorhouse Lane, an impromptu barricade had sprung up, populated by Jack and Kirsty Parker, Edward and Mrs. Oldbutter, three of the eight McDonald children and half a dozen others Nick was sure he recognized, although he wasn't altogether certain that they actually lived in Stoneford. They were working their way through the soundtrack to *Les Mis* for the cameras, while Jack tweeted their solidarity to 3,000 followers and Kirsty provided regular updates to her Stoneford Facebook page.

And as day had given way to evening, the green had erupted with lanterns and fairy lights, burning torches on long sticks, spotlights and floodlights. It had taken on the air of a carnival. There were now dozens of tents. Food carts selling baked potatoes, ice cream, candy floss, hot roasted chestnuts, doughnuts, crepes and health drinks. And kiosks offering soaps and oils whose fragrant scents wafted over the open space and mingled quite interestingly with the commerce of hot dogs, popcorn and kebabs.

Nick perched on his accustomed place atop the stone wall, feeling slightly claustrophobic as there were now twice as many hippies, travellers, musicians, hawkers, tourists, politicians and reporters jostling for space with the villagers on the green. Under normal circumstances the little patch of ground was able to accommodate the occasional fete and travelling fair. But now it seemed indeterminably small and overcrowded.

He was joined, in short order, by Sam and Mrs. Collins, who'd been having a drink in The Dog's Watch.

"Reg Ferryman," Sam reported, "has decided to hold a Bottle Auction. Tomorrow night. The bottle will remain sealed. The winner has the privilege of opening it once they take possession. They're putting up signs over the bar as we speak."

"Shall we entertain a bid?" Nick mused.

"I'd rather not line the Ferrymans' pockets and contribute to free publicity for their illicit property developments, if it's all the same to you. And Reg's plans for renovating the pub are reprehensible."

"Although his fireplace is quite impressive," Mrs. Collins remarked, removing the plastic wrap from a chocolate brownie. "Imagine how many legs of mutton could be roasted there on a spit on a winter's eve."

"Don't bloody give the man any more moneymaking ideas," Sam said. "He'll be hosting Medieval Banquets next, with serving wenches and too much mead. Where did you get that brownie?"

"I was earlier walking past a tent which had a most peculiar scent. Several bearded gentlemen bade me sample a paper-wrapped cylinder which was lit at one end, and contained, upon closer inspection, some sort of pungent dried leaf. I declined, of course, as it seemed a very disagreeable pastime. But they were very taken with me nonetheless, and presented me with this, instead."

She bit into the brownie, then offered what remained to Sam and Nick.

"It is tolerably good. An interesting combination of tastes."

Sam removed the brownie from Mrs. Collins' custody, and tucked it away into her bag.

Nick switched on his mobile, and checked for messages from Charlie. There she was.

But he frowned as he read what his cousin had written.

"What's up?" Sam asked.

"A friend," Nick said, "needs your professional opinion."

"What, medical?"

"Yes. She's ill. She's got stabbing pains in her right side. They began yesterday and they're getting worse."

"Could be anything," Sam shrugged. "Kidney stone. Ovarian cyst. Appendix. She ought to see her doctor about it."

She turned to Mrs. Collins, who was investigating her bag.

"What do you want now?"

"I am possessed of an uncommonly strange hunger," Mrs. Collins replied. "Is there nothing else to eat?"

Sam gave her a handful of coins.

"Go and buy yourself some of those crisps you liked in the pub. And don't walk past that tent again."

"I don't think she can see a doctor," Nick replied. "She's not actually anywhere…accessible."

"Where is she?" Sam laughed. "The Outer Hebrides?"

Nick put his mobile down.

Moment of truth time.

How to explain?

How to begin to explain?

He'd promised himself he wouldn't…unless it was vitally necessary.

But what was more vitally necessary than Charlie's life?

"It's Charlie," he said. "She's here. In Stoneford. But not now. She's here…in the past."

"In the past?" Sam said, as a man dressed as a fool, on a unicycle, rode past, juggling shiny blue and red balls.

"1825," Nick replied, also watching the juggler. "Something happened with her computer. Some kind of malware. Lightning struck the old oak tree. Sprites and tachyons ran amok. Nanobits exploded. And she was…relocated."

The juggler dropped one of the balls, and it bounced across the grass, rolling into the stone wall.

"Simple. Really."

Nick reached down and tossed the ball back to the juggler, who carried on wheeling, barely missing a beat.

Sam looked at Nick.

"This is a joke, right? And if Charlie's in 1825…who is Mrs. Collins?"

"I wish it was a joke. I've spent the better part of today trying to work out how to bring Charlie back. And that is actually Mrs. Catherine Collins. Our distant cousin from the past. She and Charlie seem to have switched places."

Sam shook her head. "I can't believe I'm hearing this."

"Believe it," Nick suggested.

"Charlie's in 1825 and Mrs. Collins is here and they're two completely different people."

"Yes and Charlie's stuck in 1825 with a kidney stone. Or an ovarian cyst."

Sam took a few moments to digest it all.

"And you're in touch with her. On your phone."

"I am," Nick confirmed.

"What the hell," Sam decided. "I'm married to someone who spends his weekends re-enacting 19th century battles with otherwise sane men in full Napoleonic gear. Anything's possible. Ask Charlie if she has rebound tenderness, or if the pain lessens if she lies on her side with her knees up."

Quickly, Nick keyed Sam's questions into his mobile, and touched Send.

Across the centuries, as darkness fell, Charlie lay on her left side on the grass beneath the oak, reading Nick's message.

She pressed in on her right side, then let go.

"Ow!"

Typing quickly on the little keyboard, she transmitted her answer: *Yes to rebound. Yes to lying on my side—what is it?*

Only a few yards away, but separated by the tyranny of time and distance, Nick held his mobile up so that Sam could read Charlie's answer.

Sam frowned.

In 1825, hugging her side, Charlie read Sam's diagnosis.

Appendicitis.

The worst possible news.

She'd once had a conversation with Sam about burst appendixes. There was no cure. They had to operate. And in 1825, there was no such thing as a routine operation. Internal surgery had yet to be successfully attempted.

And even if she could convince the village surgeon to try, he had neither the knowledge nor the skills, nor the implements and access to sterilizing techniques. And there was no anesthetic. Ether and chloroform wouldn't be usefully recognized for another twenty years.

Much as she wanted, needed, to stay…she would have to return to the 21st century. Her life depended on it.

I don't want to die, Nick, she typed. *Do your best to bring me back. Thunderbirds are Go.*

Two hundred years into the future, Nick read Charlie's reply aloud to Sam.

"And she'll be coming here," Sam checked, nodding at the festivities on the green. "In the middle of all of this."

"Hopefully," Nick said.

"She's just going to…materialize. Without splashing everyone with cosmic ectoplasm, and completely unnoticed."

"That's the general idea," Nick said. "As soon as I can sort out exactly how to do it."

Sam considered the oak tree. And then their chronologically deposed cousin, who had returned at last with three bags of Smoked Monterrey Chili with Goats Cheese crisps, and was hungrily dipping into the first.

"And Mrs. Collins…?"

"With any luck they'll switch places again—and she'll go back. In Charlie's place."

"Jolly good," Sam said, just as some sort of commotion erupted behind them, from the general direction of Poorhouse Lane, where a car could be heard racing away at great speed, and a lot of people were beginning to shout.

"Excuse me, Mrs. Palmer!"

It was Gina, the barmaid from The Dog's Watch, out of breath from running.

"I'm so sorry, Mrs. Palmer, but there's a bit of an emergency over the way. Emmy Cooper's been knocked down. PC Smith has rung for an ambulance. Can you come?"

Nobody in the village, including Nick, could remember Emmy Cooper joining in on anything. She kept her own company. When she ventured out, it was to Paddy McDonald's down the road, to buy three apples, two potatoes and a cucumber. And then she'd wander off, and could most often be found sitting on the old wooden bench at the top end of the green, holding animated conversations with the pigeons as she tossed them yesterday's crumbs.

Which was why it was such a profound shock for Nick to discover that 89-year-old Emmy Cooper had put on her best lavender petal hat and emerged from her flat to join the barricade at the top end of Poorhouse Lane.

And even more of a shock to see poor old Emmy Cooper now, crumpled and unconscious on the cobblestones, her lavender petal hat spattered with blood, being attended to by Sam while they waited for the ambulance to arrive.

Nearby, PC Kevin Smith was taking statements.

"We all saw him!" Kirsty Parker said. "It was Ron Ferryman."

"Black BMW," her brother, Jack, volunteered. "Convertible."

"He'd sent one of his trucks round to try and drive through to the vacant lot at the back and we weren't having any of it," said Susan McDonald. "So he came round himself in his car and was trying to intimidate us."

"He was revving his engine," Jack added. "We thought he was going to drive over us."

"That's when we dared him," Susan said. "We all sat down."

"Thinks he owns the road," said Jack.

"I mean, we know he owns everything on either side of the road. But not the right of passage."

"He put his engine into reverse," said Kirsty Parker, "and it was like he was going to drive off…but then he came at us, full out."

"And we all managed to scramble out of the way except for poor old Mrs. Cooper," Susan said, her voice beginning to shake. "And the corner of his front fender caught her as she was trying to get up…and her head hit the pavement."

"And then he reversed out and sped off," said Mrs. Oldbutter, who had hated Ron Ferryman ever since he'd bought the house next door to hers and planted giant leylandii along their shared property line in the back. "Didn't even stop to see if she was all right."

PC Smith paused in his note-taking, and glanced down at Sam, who was kneeling over Emmy, looking very concerned. "Still unconscious?"

"I think she's got a broken hip," Sam replied, "but I can't tell what else. Her breathing's very shallow and her pulse is a bit dodgy. Can someone fetch me a blanket? I don't want to move her in case anything else is broken."

CHAPTER 28

Charlie was sleeping. And dreaming.

It was a very peculiar sort of dream, because in it, Jeff had come to visit her. And while she was quite used to Jeff invading her dreams in her future—two centuries hence—it seemed most odd that he should have followed her all the way back to now, and the past.

But then, dreams and memories were not really confined to space and time, were they? Dreams and memories travelled with you, contained in their own transparent spheres, attached, but detached, orbiting like moons and planets.

In her sleep, Charlie tried to make sense of Jeff, dressed in the simple trousers and shirt of a farm labourer, swathing hay in a field on the other side of the rise, not far from where a flock of sheep were grazing.

As she watched him wield the sickle, he paused, and looked up. And then he raised his hand, as if to wave. And he said her name, very clearly:

"Catherine."

This confused Charlie. Because she was not Catherine, she was herself, and it was odd, and then downright completely annoying, that he should not recognize her as such.

But then he said it again, this time with a sense of urgency, and the "Catherine" was accompanied by someone standing behind her, lightly touching her shoulder.

The third time did it, and Charlie woke up.

It was not Jeff calling her name, but Sarah, just as it was Sarah's hand that had been touching her shoulder, gently at first, but now with persistence.

"Catherine," she said, bending down so that her voice did not wake the children in the next room. "The Dog's Watch is on fire."

• • •

Smoke from the flames had cloaked the entire village by the time Charlie and Sarah had dressed, and run from the cottage to the top end of the green where the inn stood. The smoke billowed up into the night sky, blotting out the moon and the stars. It drifted between the houses and along the roads and lanes, pungent and insidious.

It was the single-storied drinking establishment which was burning, not the two-storey hostel adjacent. Smoke poured from its broken windows and open door. Sparks danced into the night sky.

It seemed the first to respond to the fire were Lemuel and Clara, who, roused from their sleep, had run into the burning building in order to try and save what they could. But the smoke had proven to be too thick, and Lemuel had staggered out, followed closely by Clara, who had collapsed on the ground and could not now be revived.

"Let me help," Charlie said. "I know what to do."

It was true. She had taken an advanced lifesaving course in Southampton. She knew about rescue breathing and CPR.

She quickly removed Clara, limp and unresponsive, from Lemuel's cradling arms, and arranged her on her back. She felt for a pulse, and determined that her heart was still beating, though faintly. She made sure Clara's airway was clear. She pinched Clara's nose and began to blow into her mouth to re-inflate her lungs.

And then, she paused.

They didn't know much about artificial resuscitation in 1825. If you stopped breathing, you generally died—as Clara most likely would, if she did not start supplying oxygen to her brain again soon.

And if Clara died, she would not give birth to Marcus Ferryman, and there would be no descendants.

There would be no Reg Ferryman to inherit The Dog's Watch, and no Ron Ferryman to go digging through archived records to claim ownership of the disputed ground.

There would be no Ferryman Bros. (Property) Ltd.

No poisoning of the Village Oak, no threat to the Village Green or Poorhouse Lane. No office to break into, no laptop to smash.

Charlie looked at Lemuel Ferryman. He was weeping.

And then she looked down at Clara.

If she did nothing, history would unwind differently. Unimpeded. Uninterfered-with. Un-nudged.

Stoneford, two centuries on, without the Ferryman brothers, would be a very different village.

But if she interfered…and took action…all would unfold as she knew it.

Charlie thought for a few precious moments more.

She could not let someone die when she had, within her, the means by which to save their life. It went against everything she stood for, everything she valued, everything she knew.

She could not. And would not.

And so, she began to breathe for Clara again. She forced the air into her lungs, watching her chest rise and fall, until she coughed, and was sick, and was breathing on her own again.

"There you are," Charlie said, to Lemuel Ferryman.

She got to her feet. Hard work. But worth it.

"What sorcery is this?" Lemuel replied, confused.

"There has been no sorcery, sir. Make sure she has plenty of fresh air. She will recover."

Charlie left Clara to Mr. Ferryman, and walked back to Sarah.

Nearby, the villagers had organized themselves into two snaking lines and were passing buckets of water hand-to-hand from the communal pump at the confluence of roads near the green. They appeared to be gaining ground on the flames. But smoke and steam still rolled from every opening, and Charlie could see the inside of the inn was charred black.

"You appear to have learned things in London which in Stoneford are uncommon knowledge," Sarah remarked. "I was once told of experiments upon dogs who had ceased to breathe. I was not of a mind to believe what I had heard, yet you have proven it true. You have my admiration, dear Catherine, for your bravery as well as your skills. I fear I should not be nearly so courageous as you."

"I may yet live to regret it," Charlie answered.

She spotted Mr. Deeley's friends, Mr. Wallis and Mr. Cole, in one of the bucket lines, and then Mr. Rankin, from the manor. And then Mr. Deeley himself, grimy with sweat and soot as he helped to swing the water forward.

"Hello," Charlie said, thinking she might take the place of a young boy behind him whose energy was flagging.

"Good morning," Mr. Deeley replied, with a smile.

Charlie grasped a full wooden bucket with both hands, meaning to pass it along to Mr. Deeley. But the bucket's progress was interrupted by Lemuel Ferryman and a stout gentleman that Charlie wouldn't have wanted to run into on a dark night on her own.

"There is your man," Mr. Ferryman said. "You may seize him, Mr. Reader."

To Charlie's horror, the stout gentleman fixed his thick fingers around Mr. Deeley's arms, and dragged him from the bucket line.

"What have I done?" Mr. Deeley protested.

"As you may know, sir," Mr. Ferryman replied, "arson is a heinous crime. In fact, I believe it is a hanging offence."

"Arson! I know nothing about arson!"

Mr. Ferryman waved a partially burned red handkerchief at him.

"I discovered this upon the floor, inside the door. It belongs to you, sir. You cannot deny it—I have seen it knotted around your neck many a day."

Mr. Deeley struggled—unsuccessfully—to free himself from Mr. Reader's strong hands.

"But as you may recall, sir," he said, with patience, "that particular article was not knotted around my neck yesterday. And this night, you will have discovered me asleep on John Wallis's floor."

It suddenly dawned on Charlie what the lesser Monsieur Duran had been doing in Mr. Deeley's bedroom.

"I think you should ask Monsieur Duran where that handkerchief came from," she said, boldly. "I believe he removed it from Mr. Deeley's wardrobe and placed it there so that Mr. Deeley would be blamed for the fire."

The two bucket lines fell silent.

Mr. Ferryman considered Charlie with a less-than-generous look.

"You are accusing Monsieur Louis Duran of theft? As well as a conspiracy? And arson?"

"I am," Charlie replied.

Mr. Ferryman laughed. "Your imagination does you credit, Mrs. Collins. But I fear your earlier exertions must have addled your delicate constitution. It would be better for you to confine your opinions to those more befitting your sensibilities, such as embroidery and household accounts. And leave the more consequential subjects to the gentlemen, who are better equipped to debate them."

"Excuse me?" Charlie replied. "Embroidery and household accounts? I *saw* Monsieur Duran go into Mr. Deeley's bedroom."

"And there, you beheld him removing this handkerchief?"

"No," Charlie had to admit. "I didn't see that."

"Well then," said Mr. Ferryman. "I rest my case."

He addressed his constable.

"It is clear that Mr. Deeley broke a window glass to gain entry, and then deliberately set the inn alight. He dropped his handkerchief in haste. You may remove him to the lockup, sir."

Mr. Wallis had, by this time, shouldered his way through the gathered crowd. He presented himself before Mr. Ferryman and Mr. Reader.

"I shall swear on the Bible, sir," he said. "Mr. Deeley was in my house all night."

But again, Mr. Ferryman interrupted.

"There were plenty of witnesses to Mr. Deeley's unpleasantness at the inn yesterday, sir. And you are Mr. Deeley's ally, not his alibi. If you were asleep in your bed, then you could hardly know when Mr. Deeley was in your house, and when he was not in your house. In the end, sir, Mr. Deeley's distemper appears to have got the better of him."

"Why won't you listen to Mrs. Collins?" Mr. Deeley said. "There is some weight to her argument. Monsieur Duran is unhappy with me, and would stop at nothing to see me removed from the village."

"Is my testimony required?" the lesser Monsieur Duran himself replied, as the crowd of villagers parted once more, allowing him to come forward. "This night I have watched Monsieur Deeley with my own eyes, running from the inn. And then from the inn, I have watched the smoke. And then, the fire."

"Then you are surely mistaken, sir!" Mr. Deeley shouted, his good-natured patience exhausted at last. "I was nowhere near the inn this night!"

"I know what an unpleasant person you are," Charlie said, to the lesser Monsieur Duran. "And I wouldn't have credited you with this before, but I saw how nasty you could be with your own father. And I heard you talking to yourself as you wandered in between the cabbage rows, plotting how you would send Jack and Tom to a boarding school and Mary to France to look after your invalid cousin."

The lesser Monsieur Duran stared at Charlie, his expression unmoved.

"You mock me," he said, at last. "And where were you concealed that you witnessed my speakings? Underneath the lettuce? Curled up like a hedgehog?"

He laughed at his own joke, and was joined by Lemuel Ferryman, who had also evidently decided to find his friend's comment humorous.

"And what is my reason for burning the inn? I have no quarrel with Monsieur Ferryman."

"No," said Charlie, "but you certainly have a quarrel with Mr. Deeley. And what better way to be rid of him than to have him arrested for arson? As for my concealment, I went to the manor to see Mr. Rankin. I was outside the garden gate when you were addressing the cabbages. And I was standing in the scullery when I saw you go into Mr. Deeley's room."

"So you did not see me remove any artefacts from the room? And you did not see me go into the inn and set the fire?"

"I did not. But I will swear to everything else."

"So," said the lesser Monsieur Duran, to Mr. Ferryman and Mr. Reader. "I entered Monsieur Deeley's room to survey his belongings. Monsieur Deeley was no longer in my employ, and I wished for his artefacts to be taken away. I observed what was there, nothing the more. I am outraged to be accused of these criminalities."

"Indeed, Monsieur Duran," Mr. Ferryman replied. "Perhaps this young woman suffers from some sort of hysterical affliction, which I have heard is common among widows and maids who want for a husband."

"I do not suffer from a hysterical affliction!" Charlie shouted.

But it was no good.

"Come, Mr. Deeley," said Mr. Ferryman. "We have new lodgings for you. Less comfortable than the manor, perhaps, but you will find this door is equipped with a sturdy lock."

"How is it you were awake and here, at this late hour, Monsieur Duran?" Mr. Deeley shouted, over his shoulder, as Mr. Reader manhandled him towards the village lockup in the cellar of the inn.

"I was very much vexed," his former employer replied, narrowing his eyes at Mr. Deeley, "by the events of yesterday. I was not able to sleep. And so I came upon the walk, down the hill, to here. It is a night habit I have often indulged."

Charlie turned to Sarah in desperation. "Are we not able to appeal to the village magistrate? This is ridiculous!"

"It is of no use, Catherine," Sarah replied. "The magistrate is Mr. Ferryman himself, elected by the villagers."

"What about the principle of innocent unless proven guilty? What about Mr. Deeley's legal rights?"

"He shall hang," the lesser Monsieur Duran replied, with a shrug. "And there is an end to it. I bid you good night, Madame Collins, Madame Foster. Sleep well."

CHAPTER 29

It was very early in the morning, almost sunrise, and the smoke from the fire was still creeping over the village, settling over ponds and streams, lurking in dips and gulleys and drifting over the green like a foul-smelling fog.

Charlie had followed Mr. Reader and Mr. Ferryman as they had taken Mr. Deeley down to the dark cellar underneath The Dog's Watch Inn, where Mr. Ferryman kept his barrels of ale and whatever else he was smuggling in from abroad.

And she had said goodbye to Mr. Deeley with a silent, desperate look. Which Mr. Deeley had returned as they'd pushed him through the darkened doorway.

And then, she'd walked back to the cottage with Sarah. And after Sarah had gone back to bed, Charlie had returned to the Village Oak.

The pain from her inflamed appendix was causing her to struggle for breath. This wasn't good. In fact, it was very very bad.

She switched on her mobile. 56%.

She used up precious battery power to send another urgent message to Nick.

He was probably still asleep. He wouldn't be awake for hours.

Charlie switched off her phone, and closed her eyes, to wait.

Nick was, in fact, very much wide awake. He'd been awake all night, existing on mugs of strong coffee he'd brewed one after the other, with lashings of cream and entirely too much sugar.

He'd isolated the virus. The clever piece of programming had attached itself to Sarah Foster's family tree entry.

He'd removed it. Studied it. Dissected it. Had noted and identified all of the coded commands. Except one, which he'd never seen before. Was that it? The binary blip? The elusive tachyon particle?

For the hundredth time that night, Nick clicked on Sarah Foster's square. For the hundredth time that night, the space just in front of him reacted with the same uncertain and incomplete flicker and shimmer.

It was there. It existed. And yet, the reaction was incomplete.

There had to be something else. A catalyst. Something that triggered the binary tachyon particle to do its work. Something that could provide a massive nanosecond of electricity, an energy field strong enough to propel Charlie backwards in time.

Something like a sprite.

Nick considered his cat, George, who he'd named after one of the Beatles, and who always liked to help him with his research by sitting on his papers and purring.

"Where would you look if you wanted to find a sprite, but there wasn't a sprite nearby?"

George responded with a flick of his tail. He was, in fact, quite interested in Particle Physics. He sometimes presented research of his own, mostly to do with small rodents which he'd discovered in the garden, and which he liked to bring to Nick, in his mouth and usually mostly dead, for a second opinion.

"Or, alternately, where would you look if you wanted to find the energy that a sprite was responsible for generating?"

George flicked his tail again. He found this sort of dialogue fascinating. His favourite TV program was that one about The Doctor who went everywhere in a blue police box. This was precisely what Charlie needed. A blue police box sort of thing that went backwards and forwards in time. Preferably with a man who wore a hat and a long striped scarf at the controls. But he would let Nick work that out for himself.

It was time to go into the garden to seek out breakfast.

George jumped down from the desk, which freed up Nick's papers, so that he could scribble some additional calculations onto them.

Nick shook his head in despair. He was only going to have one chance to get it right. And he was running out of time.

He needed to walk. A walk was always good for clearing his mind. And he could check to see if Charlie had left any more messages.

He went downstairs and, taking his cane, trudged the several village blocks over to the green, and the oak, which, at this very early hour was attended by the remains of the night shift: a group of tree protectors who were playing games, completing crosswords, updating their Facebook pages, knitting.

And that juggler. The one he'd seen earlier, dressed as a fool, tossing shiny blue and red balls up into the air and catching them as he'd ridden by on his unicycle.

The unicycle was now propped up against Ron Ferryman's flat-tired bulldozer. And the juggler was playing with a set of clackers. Fascinated, Nick watched as he adeptly swung the little red plastic balls together with one hand, so that they banged together underneath, and then over the top of, his fingers. He hadn't seen clackers since his childhood. And this fellow was very good.

Still watching, he switched on his phone.

There was indeed another missive from Charlie. Telling him that she only had 56% battery power left, and was worried about using it up. And something else.

The Dog's Watch has caught fire. Shaun Deeley's been arrested for arson. Is he hanged? Is he transported to Australia? What happens to him? Please find out!

Nick closed his eyes and let his breath out. This was a complication he certainly didn't need.

He dialled Sam's number, waking her up.

"What is it now?" she complained, into her phone. "Have you any idea what time it is?"

"Sorry, Sam. I need a favour. Charlie needs a favour. A fellow named Shaun Deeley. Can you look him up, see if there's anything about him online?"

"Why?" Sam answered, suspiciously. "What's he done?"

"Tried to burn down The Dog's Watch, apparently."

"What, now? Today? I didn't hear any sirens…"

"Not today. In 1825. I think there's a website. I'll text you the URL. It has all the historical data on capital punishment in England. Perpetrators and victims, accusers and witnesses, courts and judges, names and dates and verdicts. Ring me back as soon as you find out anything."

"And what are you doing in the meantime that prevents you from looking all of this up yourself?"

Nick looked at the juggler, and his clackers.

And had a thought.

Yes.

Brilliant.

Why hadn't be considered that before?

"I'm going back to take another look at Charlie's laptop. I think I might have figured out where all that energy came from to send her back in time."

There.

He'd found it.

Not one rogue virus, but two.

A second string of coding had attached itself to another of Charlie's family tree entries, this one belonging to Lucas Adams. Both entries had been open on her laptop when Nick had discovered it on her desk. He'd located the first virus easily. And had assumed it was the only one, because the second virus had been masked.

But now he'd unmasked it.

And there it was, complete with its own binary tachyon particle.

Tentatively, not quite knowing what to expect, he clicked on the square belonging to Lucas Adams.

He was rewarded with a familiar flash of brilliant mauve.

And that subtle ripple, that tiny uncertain crease in time and space he'd seen when he'd clicked on Sarah Foster's entry.

What Charlie had done was open both virus-infected pages

concurrently, which had caused their binary tachyons to slam together, like the juggler's shiny red clacker balls. The resulting explosion of energy, lasting mere nanoseconds, was the mechanism that had shot Charlie back in time.

Nick didn't dare put his theory to the test.

The best he could hope to do was recreate the right conditions on Charlie's laptop. And then what? There hadn't been any virus—or any laptop, for that matter—in 1825, to bring Mrs. Collins forward. There had just been Charlie, propelled backwards.

Perhaps Mrs. Collins' journey had simply been a case of being in the right place at the right time. A variation on the Pauli exclusion principle: no two identical bodies may occupy the same quantum state simultaneously.

So if that was the case, all he needed to do for the reverse to occur, was once again ensure that Mrs. Collins was in the same place, at the same time, as Charlie. And then activate the two strings of code, slam the tachyon particles together…and it would be done.

Simple.

And midnight tonight would be the optimal time for the transfer to take place. If he delayed any longer, he wouldn't be able to give Charlie her instructions.

Well.

The first step in the process was to take Charlie's laptop back to the theoretical launch pad: her cottage.

Letting himself in through Charlie's kitchen door, Nick was struck by the emptiness. And the quietness. When Charlie was here, there was noise. She had music playing, or had left the telly on upstairs. Or she was busy on her laptop, keys clicking as she looked something up on Google, or typed the details of one more nearly-forgotten aunt into her family tree.

But Charlie was not here now. Nick could actually feel her absence, made all the more poignant as he caught sight of her bike, leaning up against the milk can umbrella stand, and her helmet, plunked into the wicker basket on its handlebars.

He wandered into the sitting room, past her clutter. Charlie's home could never be neat and tidy. It just wasn't in her nature. She thrived on chaos.

He smiled. What better person to find herself tumbled back two centuries into the past. The ultimate in chaotic particle juggling.

He placed Charlie's laptop on her desk, next to the Wi-Fi hub, the printer and scanner and wireless mouse. And that clock. Nick stopped to admire it, to pick it up and turn it over in his hands. Time really had become something malleable and mutable, just like the images in the clever Dali painting.

His phone was ringing.

Sam.

"What did you find out?" he asked.

He could hear pages being flipped. Sam had a notebook where she kept jottings about her patients, reminders about prescriptions, the names of songs she'd heard on the radio. Things she thought Roger might like for his tea, on those occasions when he hadn't forgotten their wedding anniversary.

"Listen," she said, into her phone. "Shaun Deeley. I found a mention of him working at the manor. In a list of all of the employees that someone made in 1823. And someone else discovered in 2009, and put on a website about working conditions in early 19th century rural England. And he's even on the Stoneford Village History site. One of the kids at the Youth Club did a page about famous local criminals. Shaun Deeley, arrested for setting fire to The Dog's Watch Inn. Charlie must have forgotten. Or never saw it."

"What happened to him?" Nick asked.

Sam paused.

"What?" Nick said.

"The fire at The Dog's Watch was deliberately set. But Shaun Deeley apparently never went to trial. He was declared insane and sent to live out his days at the Bethlem Hospital in London."

"You mean Bedlam?"

"Yes, Bedlam, its nickname. In the building that's now the Imperial War Museum, Southwark. I found his name in a list of the inmates…one of the 'unfortunates.'"

"That's a shame," Nick said, meaning it.

"Yes, I thought so too. Will you tell Charlie?"

"I'll have to," Nick said. "She wanted to know. Thanks, Sam."

Walking back to the green, he composed, in his mind, what he was going to say.

Bad news about Mr. Deeley, Charlie…but at least he doesn't hang…

And now for some good news. I'm bringing you back. Wait in your cottage at midnight. In your sitting room. In the same place you were when you arrived, beside the desk. And we'll hope for the best.

He imagined Charlie reading that, and decided to change the wording.

In the same place you were when you arrived, beside the desk. I'll check with you at six tonight to make sure you've got this message. See you when you get here.

He arrived at the tree, and took out his phone.

CHAPTER 30

The sun was rising. Smoke from the night's fire coloured the pale morning sky with a pink-grey smudge. All of the village smelled of burned wood.

Charlie had not returned to her little bedroom in the cottage. She'd fallen asleep beneath the Village Oak. And it was a fretful sleep, not a restful one. The pain from her inflamed appendix had lessened a little, but it had not stopped, and several times during what remained of the night it had woken her up, a nagging, prodding reminder of the urgent decision she was very soon going to have to make.

After each of these times, she'd tumbled back into unconsciousness, sleeping on fitfully.

And now, a hand was gently touching her fingers.

Charlie staggered awake. It took a moment for her brain to make sense of her surroundings. The hard ground she was lying on, the smell of the smoke, the dew-soaked grass and that terrible, terrible ache inside that would not go away.

It took another moment to make sense of the gentleman who was kneeling beside her, his kind face lined with concern.

"What on earth are you doing here?" she asked, hazily.

"I had thought," Augustus Duran ventured, "of asking you a very similar question."

Charlie sat up properly. "Why are you not in France?"

Augustus joined her on the grass, settling his back against the broad trunk of the oak.

"In the first instance," he said, "I had no doubt whatsoever that the letter my son produced yesterday was a forgery. And his explanation was lamentable. Gaston is able to spell. Louis has been deficient in the subject since boyhood. The first letter of 'Urgent' has been a 'U' for as long as I can recall. Not an 'E'. Not even in French."

Charlie smiled.

"I departed believing I might spare you and Mrs. Foster from further disagreement with my son. But I realized, as I rode towards Southampton, that this was folly, and that my removal would likely result in more harm than good. And so I stopped for the night in the New Forest, and resolved to return this day."

"More harm than good has resulted," Charlie answered, unhappily, "although none of it is your fault, Monsieur Duran. Your son is despicable."

"My disappointment in Louis," Augustus replied, "far exceeds any sense of paternal loyalty I may once have harboured. Last night, I learned even more about his duplicity. You know of the Gypsies who live in the New Forest?"

"I do," Charlie said. "They make their camp in the woods and come into the village to mend pots and pans, and to buy and sell horses."

"I am well acquainted with one of the families," Augustus provided. "I have shared their fire, enjoyed their food and their singing and dancing. Last night I discovered them in the midst of a celebration. A marriage, in fact. Fenella, who is the eldest daughter of the patriarch, Stefan, has agreed at last to a suitor."

"A worthy celebration," Charlie said.

"More so due to the fact that Stefan has fathered five daughters, ranging in age from sixteen to twenty-four, including a pair of nineteen-year-old twins, and all have been happily married but Fenella."

"Then the celebration must have been a long time in the making," Charlie remarked. "Was there a feast?"

"Roasted hedgehog," Augustus confirmed.

Charlie made a face.

"It would have been rude of me to refuse. Although I found the stewed rabbit much more to my liking."

"I commend you on your gastronomical bravery."

It was Augustus' turn to smile.

"There was also boiled cabbage and cauliflower. And dumplings.

And beer. Along with a very fine brandy. With which I drank a toast to Stefan, all five of his daughters, and Jobey, his son."

"Jobey," Charlie said. "Jobey Cooper?"

"Yes, the same. You know of him?"

"I have seen him in the village," Charlie said. She stopped. She had given Eliza Robinson her word.

"He will be taking a wife soon himself," Augustus said. "He has not spoken of it to his father, but Esmerelda, who is his grandmother, has the skill of foretelling. She confided to me that he loves a woman who is not of the Gypsy life."

"I know who she is," Charlie said. "She has a son."

She stopped herself again. Too much.

But Augustus seemed unsurprised.

"She has indeed given birth to a son," he said. "And if Jobey marries this woman, there is every chance he will not be welcomed back by his father. Not because of her son, but because she is a *gadji*, not of their world. So, to mark her joy at his forthcoming wedding, Esmerelda gave Jobey a gift. A deck of cards, the Tarot. But missing one of its number. To mark also her sadness at his leaving."

The Tarot, Charlie thought. The incomplete deck in the Travellers Room at the museum. Missing just one of its cards...

"As the night drew on," Augustus continued, "Jobey approached me. He told me of his plans to work with leather, to make saddles and harnesses."

He paused.

"The woman who will become Jobey's wife was lately employed at the manor by my son. And here is the duplicity of which I spoke earlier. The child, Daniel, is his. But Louis will not accept paternity. I fear this is not the first time, and it dismays me more than any of the transgressions he has committed in the past. I have ensured Daniel receives a sum of money, each year on this day, to make amends for the wrongdoing."

"That is very generous of you," Charlie said. "And you have a good deal more generosity and kindness in you than your son. Who this night has committed a further outrage."

"This comes as no great revelation," Augustus said, wearily. "What has he done?"

"The Dog's Watch has been burned in a fire," Charlie said. "And Mr. Deeley has been accused of causing it. But your son is the guilty one, Monsieur Duran. He hates Mr. Deeley. And me. He set the fire to rid himself of both of us."

She stopped again, and bent over, holding her middle.

"You are in pain," Augustus observed, with concern.

"I am not well," Charlie whispered. "And I fear I must return home. Very soon."

She could not hold the tears back.

"I care very much for Mr. Deeley, Monsieur Duran, and I am certain he entertains the same feelings for me."

She shook her head, hopelessly.

"But I cannot bear the thought of leaving him. He will almost certainly be found guilty…and then he will hang."

"Why must you return home?" Augustus asked. "The journey back to London is certainly arduous, and the city air is foul and not at all conducive to healing. Would you rather not convalesce in the country, surrounded by your cousins? And you will be near to Mr. Deeley…who may yet be granted a reprieve."

Charlie looked at the gentleman who was destined to become her ancestor, searching his face for a way to tell him the truth.

"I cannot think of any way for him to prove his innocence, Monsieur Duran. The magistrate is Mr. Ferryman, whose loyalty is to your son, and whose dishonest word he will believe above all else."

Augustus thought upon this, and then withdrew something from the pocket of his coat.

"I have discovered," he said, "after many years of being, that in some instances, it may be better to put your trust in the fates, than to try to argue with them. This is the card that Esmerelda removed from the deck that she gave to Jobey Cooper."

Charlie looked at the faded picture of a trouserless man, his stockings fallen down about his knees, feathers in his disarrayed hair. He carried a long stick on his shoulder, and his face showed confusion.

"She told me it was the card of beginnings."

"It is the card of The Fool," Charlie said.

"I will overlook that unfortunate detail. So you know the Tarot?"

"I have a passing familiarity."

"Esmerelda told me that this card may also represent a journey. Perhaps of the physical. Perhaps of the spirit. Perhaps a journey made up of unexpected events."

Augustus pressed the card into Charlie's hand.

"I will give it to you, with Esmerelda's words. 'Choose your direction wisely and quickly. Your answer may lie at the beginning, not at the end.'"

Charlie looked again at the card, and then at Augustus.

"You may pass this off as insanity," she said, slowly, selecting her words with care. "You may ascribe it to my delicate health, to a turning of the mind caused by the illness that is coursing through my body…"

She paused. Augustus was staring at her, intently. Would he understand? Could he understand?

"I live here. Here." She indicated the village, with her hand, sweeping her arm across the view of the green that was before them. "But not now. I live almost 200 years from now. Sarah's cottage is my cottage. Sarah is my great-grandmother. Six times into the past. And you…"

She looked again at Augustus, staring deeply into his blue eyes— the same blue eyes she had inherited, through the generations.

"You are my great grandfather."

Augustus' eyes were fixed on hers.

"Six times into the past," he said, clearly, slowly, and without a hint of doubt.

Charlie picked up her mobile, and switched it on. 49%.

She flipped to the portrait that Nick had sent her.

"Look," she said, showing Augustus the little screen. "That was painted in 1827. Two years from now."

Augustus took the mobile from Charlie's hand. He turned it over and over, curiously, delicately, like a geologist examining a rock that had been cracked open to reveal the glittering minerals inside.

He looked, then, at the picture on the little screen, which

showed Sarah and himself, side by side, not just a passing likeness, but a painting which had captured their faces exactly.

"If you believe this is insanity, I would not blame you for a moment," Charlie said.

Augustus' eyes were transfixed on the portrait. "And how does this likeness come to inhabit the device?"

"It was sent," Charlie replied. "Dispatched by my cousin. From the future. Through the air."

"Ah," he said, with a nod, although Charlie was quite certain he understood none of it.

He placed the mobile back in her hand.

"You have a message," he said.

CHAPTER 31

The cellar beneath the Dog's Watch Inn was an unaccommodating hole dug into the earth, lined with rough bricks, and more or less abandoned to whatever decay and pestilence might find a home in its depths. It was a foul, dark and damp place, Charlie thought, as Lemuel Ferryman led her down the stairs. There was water everywhere, and it smelled of burned, wet wood.

At the rear of the cellar, a small room had been constructed of more bricks and mortar. Mr. Ferryman selected a large iron key from his ring and inserted it in the lock of the heavy wooden door. Opening the door partway, he held his lantern up, so that Charlie could observe the prisoner.

Huddled on a wooden bench, which did double duty as a bed, Mr. Deeley slept without pillow or blanket. His face was unshaven and bruised, and bore the marks of a beating administered out of sight of witnesses.

Charlie set the bowl of porridge she had been carrying down on the muddy floor beside the bench. She had also brought a heel of bread, and a mug of water, all that Lemuel Ferryman would allow.

The smell of the porridge—or perhaps the noise of the door scraping open and squeaking on its hinges—awoke Mr. Deeley.

"Stay as you are," Mr. Ferryman advised, as his prisoner struggled to sit up. "Mrs. Collins has brought you breakfast. Make the most of it, as lunch is optional, and entirely dependent upon my disposition."

Mr. Deeley abandoned the idea of sitting up, and instead eased himself onto his back.

"Your kindness," he said, "is unparalleled."

"I daresay your temper has improved with the passage of night."

"Mr. Reader made an excellent argument with his fists. And his boots."

"I shall convey your compliments to him," Mr. Ferryman replied. "And leave you to your conscience. And your breakfast."

He turned to Charlie.

"You have seen he is safe and sound. Are you satisfied?"

"I am greatly dissatisfied, sir," Charlie replied. "But I will stay with Mr. Deeley a while, if you will agree to it."

"My disposition on this Monday morning has yet to be tested. I will agree to one hour."

"As you wish," Charlie said. "Thank you."

Lemuel Ferryman placed his lantern on the floor, then closed the door behind her, taking care to ensure that it was once again securely locked.

"Hello, Mr. Deeley," Charlie said.

"Hello, Mrs. Collins," Mr. Deeley answered, with a smile. "I am cheered greatly by your presence. Although the circumstances and surroundings leave a great deal to be desired."

"I would find happiness in your company," Charlie said, "anywhere. And under any circumstance."

She knelt beside him, and gently touched his bruised face.

"This is a terrible, horrible miscarriage of justice."

Mr. Deeley turned his head towards her.

"I know. But Mr. Ferryman will believe the lesser Monsieur Duran's words over mine. There is nothing to be done."

He shut his eyes.

"I will hang."

"You will not hang," Charlie said.

"So I shall be shipped off to Van Diemen's Land. Fifteen years hard labour for a crime I did not commit. If I survive the floggings."

"You will not hang and you will not be transported."

"How can you be so certain?" Mr. Deeley answered, sadly.

"Mr. Deeley…"

Charlie stopped. And then began again, with a great deal of hesitation.

"I am in this place by accident…"

"More so, me," Mr. Deeley replied, grimly, not entirely understanding. How could she explain it to him? Augustus had understood readily.

The thought of losing Mr. Deeley was devastating. As devastating as the fate that awaited him, that Nick had described in his last message.

"I cannot bear to think," she said, struggling to control her voice, so that he would not see her tears, "that we will be apart."

She touched his face again, and he grasped her hand. He kissed her fingers, her wrist, the delicate skin on the inside of her arm.

"Mr. Deeley…Shaun…"

He stopped. "Forgive me. I have taken too much of a liberty."

"You have not," Charlie said. "And I would be happy for you to take much, much more."

Still on her knees on the floor, she leaned over, and kissed him tenderly, on his lips. She loosened his shirt, and touched her lips to the smoothness of his chest…

Mr. Deeley's fingers brushed the plunging edge of her gown, caressed the curve of her breasts hidden by the fabric, felt her rising response…

He drew her close to him, and then kissed her lips, her neck… then slipped his fingers beneath her bodice and, emboldened, lifted her breast, exposing what lay beneath. He discovered the concealed rosebuds of her passion, touched them with his lips and tongue, then devoured them, greedily, and without restraint.

"I cannot imagine a life that is without you," he whispered.

"Nor I," Charlie said. "I ache for you."

He drew her close once more, found the fastenings that ensured her modesty, and quickly loosed them.

"If these are to be my last memories of you," he whispered, "then let them be my sweetest."

CHAPTER 32

From the top end of the Village Green, where the Dog's Watch Inn—and Mr. Deeley's prison cell—were situated, it was only a short walk back to Sarah's cottage.

Charlie stopped to observe the activity around the public house, which had been partially damaged by the flames, but was not, apparently, beyond repair. The windows could be re-glazed. The door, floor and ceiling were still intact. The walls inside were smoke-and-water stained, but in no danger of collapse.

Outside the building, Lemuel Ferryman sat perched upon an upended cask, compiling lists of what needed to be done for the local tradesmen. The last completed, and dispatched by way of a boy from the stables, Mr. Ferryman got to his feet to greet his old friend, the lesser Monsieur Duran.

"I have the honour of wishing you a good morning, sir. But alas, not the wherewithal to afford you a drink. You will have to patronize The Rose and Crown for some days, until my damage is made right."

The lesser Monsieur Duran surveyed the whitewashed exterior of the inn, which had been blackened where the smoke had rolled out of the broken windows and the open door.

"It is with regret that I take my custom to The Rose and Crown," he replied. "But I will welcome the restoration of your establishment. I feel a certain...responsibility."

You can say that again, Charlie thought, uncharitably, watching from a safe distance across the road.

"How is this, sir?" Mr. Ferryman laughed.

"Monsieur Deeley was lately employed by me. So. I will pay for your repairs."

"This is an unexpected offer," said Mr. Ferryman, "but it is welcomed. And accepted with much gratitude."

"May I ask after the contents of your insides? All has been lost?"

"Not all," Mr. Ferryman answered. "Less than I had at first believed. Regrettably, some libations. Several tables, and a number of chairs. The bar and the wall behind it, which must be restored."

"I suppose," said the lesser Monsieur Duran, "that the paper which you held most highly in your esteem, and most lately upon your wall, is now in cinders."

"You suppose correctly, sir. As I can find no trace of it within the vicinity of where it was last seen. It is a lamentable loss."

And there, Charlie thought, holding that place in her middle that would not cease to cause her pain, was the undisputable answer to what had happened to the deed to the Village Green, and the vacant square of land at the end of Poorhouse Lane.

Burned up in a deliberate fire.

That would likely never have happened at all, if she had not convinced Sarah to go the ball.

Cause and effect.

The lesser Monsieur Duran took his leave of Lemuel Ferryman.

And Charlie continued on her way. It was half past eleven, according to the clock in the steeple of St. Eligius Church. Sarah's lessons would soon be finishing at the vicarage—for she was still employed there, even if that employment was due to shortly cease.

She wondered where Augustus had gone. Back to the manor, to further incur the wrath of his son? Not likely. Not after what he'd revealed to her as they'd sat together under the Village Oak. Not likely the hostel attached to The Dog's Watch, either. Lemuel Ferryman would have wasted no time in informing his very good friend of the presence of his father.

The hostelry at the Rose and Crown, then?

Her pondering was answered the moment she unlatched the cottage's kitchen door, and let herself inside. For there sat Augustus, at the big wooden table. And there, also, sat Sarah, beside him, a pot of fresh tea steeping nearby.

"My dear cousin!" Sarah exclaimed. "Where have you been? Your bed was not slept in. I have been most concerned."

"I fell asleep under the Village Oak," Charlie said. "I apologize if I caused undue alarm. Monsieur Duran discovered me earlier, and we had a conversation. Has he not mentioned to you that we spoke?"

"It is my turn to offer apologies," Augustus replied. "For I was distracted by other things."

"Monsieur Duran has proposed that we might marry," Sarah said, her eyes bright. "He came to the vicarage, and sought me out. In the middle of the children's lesson in Algebra."

"I hope you said yes," Charlie replied, with humor.

"Mrs. Foster gave me the honor of a swift and positive reply," Augustus confirmed. "The inspiration for my impulsive request having come directly from you, Mrs. Collins. For you are easily the most gloriously impetuous woman I have ever encountered."

"Oh," Charlie said. And then again: "Oh."

"Of course, I gave my notice to Mrs. Hobson on the spot," Sarah said, with just a hint, Charlie thought, of self-satisfaction. "Her children are now no doubt attempting to burn down the lesson room. I am certain Reverend Hobson will be able to take charge. Sooner, if not later."

"May I be the first to offer my congratulations to you," Charlie said, meaning it. "I cannot begin to tell you how pleased this has made me."

"I believe I have an understanding of the depth of your feelings," Augustus replied, with a smile. "Your congratulations are welcomed. And very much appreciated."

"If it had not been for you, my dearest Catherine, Monsieur Duran and I might never have become acquainted. I owe a debt to you for my present, and future, happiness."

Charlie sank onto a chair. The throbbing, stabbing appendix pain was too much. She shut her eyes.

Sarah was on her feet immediately, and at Charlie's side. "Will you not allow me to fetch Mr. Tamworth, Catherine? He is the village surgeon. Surely there is a tonic he can prepare for you, or a poultice which may draw out the affliction?"

Charlie shook her head.

"No," she whispered. "I thank you, but no. What I suffer from cannot be cured by a poultice or a tonic. Although it would be good if you could find something that might take away the pain."

Augustus also stood. "I know where there is a dose or two of laudanum," he said. "If you will permit me…?"

"Yes," Charlie said. "Please."

Augustus departed, with haste.

"Surely you will lie down," Sarah coaxed. "It cannot have been good for you, sleeping on the ground outside. Let me help you upstairs, to your bed. And I will put some hot water into a bottle for you, to warm away your distress."

It seemed, to Charlie, that Augustus was gone only a matter of moments, before he was back. But then, she realized, she must have been asleep—or had lost consciousness.

Lying in Mary's little bed, hugging the clay container that Sarah had brought up, filled with hot water from the pot over the fire, she listened to Sarah, talking to Augustus, their voices echoing in the kitchen below.

And then she heard Sarah's footsteps as she made her way up the stairs. And her knock upon the bedroom door, followed by her entry, carrying a cup of hot tea.

"I have stirred a few drops of the tincture into this with a little sugar and milk," she advised, helping Charlie to sit up. "The sweetness will take away the bitter taste."

Charlie sipped from the cup.

"I hope Monsieur Duran did not meet with any disagreement from his son," she said. "Will you thank him for his kindness?"

"He was able to visit the manor undetected. I will convey your thanks."

Sarah paused.

"My dear, you are very pale."

"Perhaps if you opened the window a little, the fresh air would help revive me."

Sarah did so, admitting a warm afternoon breeze, and the trilling of a pair of robins in the apple tree below.

"I will come back in a little while to ensure that the laudanum has had the desired effect," she promised. "You must try to rest."

Charlie slid down beneath the covers again, to wait for the opium tincture to do its work.

And it seemed that this happened very quickly indeed.

Her mind lapsed into a kind of drifting consciousness, where she was neither here nor there, but she was aware, nonetheless, of the lessening of the grip that the pain had on her body.

She was aware, too, of a distant knocking, downstairs and far away. The kitchen door. And voices. Augustus...and who...?

He was familiar-sounding.

Mr. Rankin?

The voices continued through the house, and emerged in the back garden as the gentlemen stood beneath the open bedroom window.

"I thank you for agreeing to see me, Monsieur Duran. I have done something which you may judge me harshly for. But I must declare, in my defense, that I have acted only out of concern for Mr. Deeley, who is my friend. And who I believe now, more than ever, to have been wrongly accused of setting last night's fire at the inn."

There was a moment of silence.

And then: "This morning, before the sun was up, I was standing at the scullery sink, washing away the soot from the fire. The lesser Monsieur Duran entered the house from the kitchen garden. He did not see me. But I observed him, and watched as he opened the door to Mr. Deeley's room. What he did whilst inside the room, I cannot honestly say. Only that after he departed, some minutes later, I found the piece of paper you now hold in Mr. Deeley's wardrobe drawer, unconcealed, and placed in such a manner as to be easily discovered."

"What is it?" Augustus asked.

"It is a deed, sir. Concerning, firstly, a piece of property which now comprises the Village Green, and secondly, the property at the end of what is known as The Poorhouse. It was most lately in the possession of Mr. Ferryman, the proprietor of The Dog's Watch

Inn. He had posted it on his wall."

In the additional seconds of silence that followed, Charlie crawled from the bed and stood, unsteadily, at the open window. She was able, unseen, to look out and down, at the tops of the heads of the two gentlemen below, and at the bloodstained parchment that Augustus was holding in his hands.

"You were wise to remove it," he judged. "And you have shared this knowledge with no one else?"

"Not a soul," said Mr. Rankin.

"Then let this remain between us alone. Will you take this document back into your safekeeping?"

"I will not, sir. Your son's sense of rancor knows no bounds, and I would not wish it to be discovered upon my person. You may keep it. It is my fond hope that you may somehow use it to secure the freedom of Mr. Deeley. If I am called upon to give an account of what I have seen, I will step forward and speak with honesty."

"I will think on this," Augustus promised.

He folded the paper, and tucked it inside his shirt.

"Although given the politics I have thus far observed, I suspect I may be required to invoke a more immediate solution to Mr. Deeley's unfortunate circumstances. Will you gather together two or three of his most trusted friends, and meet me shortly at a location which is mutually acceptable and discrete?"

"I know of such a place," said Mr. Rankin. "A hayfield, in the corner of Beckford Farm, not far from this village. It is surrounded by hedges and affords a tolerable degree of privacy."

"Then we will adjourn there in one hour's time," Augustus decided. "Again, I thank you for your actions. Until then, Mr. Rankin."

CHAPTER 33

"My dear!" Sarah exclaimed, as Charlie appeared on the stairs. "You are improved?"

"A little," Charlie answered.

It was the truth. The pain was much less, but her words seemed very distant, as if she was speaking through a nearly transparent tissue. Some of it, she was certain, was due to the poison from her inflamed appendix. And much of the rest was because of the laudanum. But there was something else…an unworldliness that she was unfamiliar with, a feeling of not being quite present, not being quite there.

Most peculiar.

She looked at the clock. Three hours had passed. It was four o'clock. Eight hours until midnight, and the appointment she was meant to keep here, in the sitting room, with Nick.

In the chair beside the fireplace, Augustus was sewing a button onto Jack's shirt.

"Do keep still, sir," he said, "or my needle may land most inopportunely upon your person."

He looked up at Charlie, who lingered on the staircase.

"Your sleep has benefited you," he judged. "Will you join us? There is a little honey cake left over in the kitchen."

He cut his sewing thread with a pair of scissors borrowed from Sarah's hussif.

"There you are, sir. I recommend you master this skill as soon as you are able. I myself have sewn all of the buttons on all of my waistcoats twice over."

Jack, who appeared to be rather more aware than Augustus of the inopportune places upon his body where the needle had landed, removed himself without comment.

Augustus tucked the needle, thread and scissors back into Sarah's carrying case.

"Monsieur Duran," Charlie said. "Will you come into the garden with me? There is a matter I wish to discuss with you."

The patch of grass in the shade of the obliging apple tree, beneath Mary's bedroom window, was the most comfortable spot for a conversation, and so it was there that Charlie and her great ancestor repaired.

"Monsieur Duran," she began. "I spoke to you earlier about my origins. Where I have come from."

"Indeed," Augustus agreed. "And although the knowledge you imparted was both surprising and, I confess, not a little confusing, I have no trouble whatsoever believing what you say."

"Thank you," Charlie said. "This gives me great relief. But there is something more. In my future, two pieces of land are under threat of redevelopment. The Village Green. And a property at the end of Poorhouse Lane."

"Ah," Augustus said. "These very same subjects have recently been discussed by Mr. Rankin and myself."

"I confess," said Charlie. "I overheard your discussion. And that is why I am speaking with you now. If, in the future, the plans for development succeed, they will tear out the heart and soul of this village."

She paused.

"Mr. Rankin gave you a piece of paper which he had removed from Mr. Deeley's room."

Augustus reached inside his shirt, withdrew the folded deed.

"This piece of paper?" he inquired, offering it to her, so that she could see it properly.

Charlie unfolded it, carefully, as it was very old and fragile.

"This is the same document I saw posted on the wall at The Dog's Watch," she confirmed. "And I do not believe it was Mr.

Deeley who removed it. I believe it was your son. Who took it from the wall, then set the fire which implicated Mr. Deeley. And then he placed the deed in Mr. Deeley's wardrobe to cast further guilt upon him, to ensure a conviction of theft as well as arson."

"This goes without saying," Augustus agreed. "Although whether Mr. Rankin's testimony would be enough to save Mr. Deeley's neck is debatable."

"He will not hang," Charlie replied. "I know what is written in our historical documents. There will be no trial."

She paused again. The laudanum was making it very difficult for her not to cry.

"The village surgeon will declare him insane," she said, sadly, "and he will be sent away to an asylum. For the remainder of his life."

"And this outcome cannot be changed?" Augustus asked, his face clearly troubled.

"I wish it could be so," Charlie said. "But if, in the future, the outcome has been recorded, then I believe these events in the past which have caused it to happen cannot be altered at all. Unless we wish for chaos to ensue."

Augustus pondered this for a moment.

"I must admit," he said, "this supposition plays havoc with my simple understanding. It is indeed a conundrum. However, I will think further upon it. I have already set a plan in place which will, if all goes well, release Mr. Deeley from his prison this night. I will have a horse waiting. And he will have safe and swift passage to France."

Charlie looked at him.

"Then our history books will be wrong."

"It would not be the first time, surely."

"It would not," Charlie said, slowly. "For what is the consequence otherwise? Mr. Deeley is delivered to Bedlam and forgotten for all of time."

"Yet whether he spends the remainder of his days in Bedlam, or in France, he will not alter the future of Stoneford."

"He will not," Charlie agreed.

It did make sense to her.

She very badly wanted Nick to weigh in on the argument. What would he likely say? *What would happen if Mr. Deeley went to France and ended up leading another revolution. What would the history books have to say about that, then?*

Charlie shook the thought away. It was too complicated for her mind to work out.

She would have to put her trust in The Fool from the Tarot card, which she had tucked into her bodice, next to her phone.

"And what of this deed?" Augustus inquired. "In your future, who owns the land it describes?"

"Ron and Reg Ferryman. Two brothers who are direct descendants of Lemuel Ferryman. But their ownership has always been in question. The two properties originally belonged to an ancestor of Mrs. Foster. Here, you can see. John Harding."

She showed him the name.

"When Mrs. Foster married Mr. Foster, her land became his. But he lost the deed to pay off a gambling debt. Mr. Ferryman came by this paper illicitly, but he will never admit to the circumstances. And in my future, this deed was believed destroyed by the fire at The Dog's Watch Inn. So there has never been any proof of ownership. For anyone."

"Then here," Augustus concluded, "must be one more instance of the past and future standing at odds with one another. For as you can plainly see, this deed is not destroyed."

"But if my future is to remain unchanged," Charlie said, slowly, "then this deed must not exist. Because the end result must always be that Ron and Reg Ferryman believe the properties belong to them."

She looked at Augustus, hopelessly.

"I don't know what to do."

"You have told me," said Augustus, "that you must return home, very soon, to seek a cure for your physical ailment. Might you not take this paper with you? No history will be changed. The document was merely misplaced over the centuries, not lost. And now it will be found. And the wrong will be made right. By you."

Charlie didn't say anything.

"You are perhaps having some second thoughts?" Augustus guessed.

"I cannot bear the thought of abandoning Mr. Deeley," Charlie said. "I had halfway made up my mind to stay with him, here, until he was taken to London. And whatever was to become of me, and my illness…"

Her voice trailed off. She would die. The pain of a burst appendix would be lessened by the tincture of opium that Augustus had provided. But the poison would still take over her body, and she would be dead before Mr. Deeley was ever removed to Bedlam.

It was a detail she would spare Augustus from hearing.

"But just now, Monsieur Duran, you have offered me a new hope. If your plan is successful, and Mr. Deeley is able to escape to France…then I would wish only to go with him, and spend the rest of my life in his company. Will you help?"

"There is nothing more majestic than the constancy of true love," Augustus replied. "Of course I will help. But what of the Village Green and this other property? Do you not wish to ensure their security for the future?"

Charlie glanced back at the cottage. The sitting room window sill, which overlooked the garden, had been decorated by Mary with a collection of glass bottles, all handmade and all quite exquisitely beautiful. Some held bunches of dried flowers. Others were filled with tiny shells and pebbles from the beach. One was empty, awaiting its treasure.

There was a way.

Of course.

"There," Charlie said.

Carefully, she folded the deed, then bent it down through the narrow neck of the glass bottle. She stoppered the bottle, tightly, then sealed the opening with a dribble of wax from the lit candle she had thought, at the last minute, to bring with her.

"That's got to last two hundred years."

She placed the bottle in the hiding spot Augustus had dug out between two gnarled roots of the old Village Oak, using the spade from the kitchen fire that was more usually employed to remove ashes and embers.

"The deed is done," Augustus pronounced, filling in the hole again. He stepped the mound of earth down with his boot, and replaced the bits of turf, so that it was indistinguishable from the ground around the remaining roots.

"Thank you," Charlie said.

She took out her cell phone, and switched it on. 34%.

Enough to let Nick know that she'd got his message. And where to look for the buried bottle, and to tell him what it contained. The wrong, at last, made right.

Proof that the properties belonged to her family. Instructions for him to sort it all out.

A message of thanks. For finding a way to bring her back. For everything. And to advise him that she would not, after all, be waiting in Sarah's sitting room at midnight. She had decided to stay here, in 1825.

Try and remember to put a fresh flowering geranium on Jeff's grave every few weeks…

And goodbye, Nick. Goodbye. God bless. And goodbye.

She touched Send, and watched as it went.

"Mrs. Collins," Augustus said. "I find I am now in need of your assistance. Will you explain your device's workings to me, in preparation for tonight's events?"

CHAPTER 34

It was nearly six o'clock and the early evening protests around the Village Oak had taken on a brand new cause.

Nick detected a rising anger, a backlash aimed directly at Ron Ferryman, for the criminal act of striking down old Emmy Cooper with his car.

Just inside the low stone wall on the green's west side, Jack and Kirsty Parker were raising money to help Emmy with her rent, inviting people to drop coins and notes into a jar with a slotted lid. When she was released from the hospital, they planned on presenting her with the takings, and then, petitioning the Parish Council to house her somewhere so she would have help in her day-to-day living. Regardless of what her own views were on the matter.

Nearby, the McDonald family had hung a large white bedsheet over the wall, and were encouraging everyone to add their Get Well Soon wishes to it with coloured marking pens.

Nobody seemed to have any idea where Ron Ferryman had disappeared to. Least of all PC Smith from the Stoneford Constabulary, who was signing his name to the bedsheet as Nick arrived.

"Most likely in hiding with his lawyer," Nick supposed. "If he hasn't already relocated to the Canary Islands."

"I suspect we'll find him somewhere closer to home," Kevin replied. "We're just waiting for an update from the hospital before we officially lay charges."

"You said that with a certain amount of satisfaction, Kev."

"Did I...?" Kevin replaced the cap on the marker, and handed it back to Susan McDonald. "Dear me. I must try to be more circumspect in the future."

Nick wandered across to the oak, where someone, presumably Reg Ferryman, had posted a notice on a large stand-up board about The Dog's Watch Bottle Auction at 9 pm that night. And someone else, presumably one of the tree protectors, had crossed out "Watch" and written "Breakfast" in its place. And someone else had written *All proceeds to benefit the Teach Hedgehogs to Eat Ron Ferryman Foundation.*

Nick smiled.

His sense of humour needed a boost.

He'd spent far too many hours in front of his computer, trying to second guess everything that could possibly go wrong with his plan to bring Charlie home at midnight.

For instance, what if he activated the two viruses, and what he thought would be the correct sequence of events turned out to be horribly wrong? And nothing happened. Or worse…Charlie and Mrs. Collins were transported somewhere else? Or to a netherworld between then and now, and never completely returned, but rendered into ghosts of themselves, lost and forever-wandering disambiguations?

Horrendous thought.

He switched on his mobile.

Final instructions for Charlie.

There was an incoming text.

Nick read the message.

Twice.

Three times.

"Bloody hell, Charlie," he said, shaking his head, his heart beginning to pound. "Bloody hell."

Situated at the top end of the green, The Dog's Watch was close enough to the Village Oak that if Nick stood in the open doorway of the pub, he found he was still able to send messages to 1825.

He'd arrived at this realization by accident. He'd needed to reassure himself that the glass bottle Mike Tidman had coaxed out of the earth between the roots of the tree was still there.

On top of the bar.

Unopened.

Undisturbed.

Yes, there it was.

Cork still sealed with wax, paper inside still intact.

He'd needed also to try and contact Charlie.

To implore her to reconsider, using the most persuasive words he knew.

He'd sent his plea and re-sent it, every fifteen minutes.

And was still sending, as twilight gave way to night, and as the hour of the Bottle Auction drew closer.

He had received no reply.

He had, however, received an answer from Sam. Who was in the middle of a conversation with Roger and Mrs. Collins about Roger's up-and-coming re-enactor weekend. As well as supper, which this evening was a very fine roasted chicken with rosemary, and a goat's cheese, butter lettuce and cranberry salad.

A farewell feast for Mrs. Collins, Sam wrote. *I thought you weren't remotely interested in the Bottle Auction.*

I am remotely interested now, Nick texted back.

He copied what Charlie had written, and sent it on to Sam.

Sam's response was immediate.

We'll be there in two ticks.

Two ticks were more like half an hour.

But there they were. Sam and Mrs. Collins. And Roger, in his red wool 33rd Regiment of Foot re-enactor jacket.

Sam parked the Civic in the paved lot beside the inn.

"No joy from Charlie, I suppose," she said, joining Nick in the open doorway.

"None," Nick said, worriedly. "Evening, Rog. Getting the drinks in for Napoleon?"

"Hopefully he'll get the drinks in for us," Roger replied, humorously. "Bill Allen. Already inside at a table loaded with best British beer."

He escorted his two female companions into the pub.

Nick stayed where he was.

The Dog's Watch was busier than usual. Not only because of the Bottle Auction. But also because of the journalists who had descended on Stoneford to provide ongoing updates on the plight of the Village Oak. And now, additionally, the fragile state of Emmy Cooper's health.

The inn had turned into the reporters' base of operations.

"Ladies and gents!" Reg Ferryman announced, in his best publican's voice. "Ten minutes' notice to make yourselves ready for the first and only Dog's Watch Bottle Auction. Register your names with our guest auctioneer, Mr. Dobbs, and take your places. Twenty-five percent of all proceeds to be given to charity."

Generous sod, Nick thought, unkindly. There was a tax dodge for him in it somewhere.

He checked his phone again.

Nothing.

Keeping his eyes on the bar, and Charlie's glass bottle, he listened in unabashedly while Reg discussed his planned renovations with Mr. Dobbs.

"A bank of slot machines over there," Reg said, indicating the passage that led to the toilets. "And two of those big flat screen tellies up on the wall."

"Ah," said Mr. Dobbs. "Then you're thinking of Sports Nights."

"Sports, karaoke, quizzes, live cabaret…"

"Whatever happened to a nice friendly game of darts?"

"Rose and Crown," Reg replied. "Down the road. Though you'll see it's boarded up. Lack of custom."

He nodded at the big stone fireplace in the corner.

"If we cover that up," he said, "we can put in a stage. Wire in a sound system. Multicolored lights. And a pair of dancer's poles."

"You'd think owning a pub dating from 1790 would give him a feeling for history, wouldn't you," Nick remarked, to Sam, Roger and Mrs. Collins, whose faux-antique table was situated within talking distance of the door. "You'd think having it in his family for 200 years would give him some pride in preservation."

"Is it a pair of maypoles that he wishes to install?" Mrs. Collins inquired, confused.

There was laughter from the bar. Reg pulled out an iPad and called up a set of plans, to show to Mr. Dobbs. Plans not previously heard about in Stoneford. Plans for a hotel, Nick realized. An entirely new structure, adjoining the existing buildings, and incorporating the listed Grade II red brick barn.

Charlie would have been aghast.

"We'll leave the barn virtually untouched," Reg said. "Keep the Parish Council happy. It becomes our very special function room. Weddings, conventions…And we can build the new hotel around it."

Disgusted, Nick watched as the project was erected on Reg Ferryman's iPad. An adventure inn. With a smugglers theme. Bedrooms named after assorted colorful characters from Stoneford's sea-roving past. Cheap antiques sourced from an overseas factory that specialized in good resin copies. Front desk staff in period costume. A gigantic water feature in the back garden with a replica pirate ship.

"For the kiddies," Reg added, as the mobile belonging to one of the London reporters rang.

"You're joking," Nick heard him say.

And then the reporter snapped his fingers at a colleague, and the two of them rushed outside, past Nick, to the parking lot.

Other phones were beginning to go off. There were hurried and hushed conversations, followed in quick succession by a mass exodus of the journalists.

"Emmy Cooper's just died," Gina said, at the far end of the bar, to Reg. "That'll be your Ron in a serious spot of bother, then."

Nick looked in alarm at Sam, who already had her own phone out, and was ringing one of the nurses she knew at the Royal Memorial Hospital.

"What's going on with Emmy Cooper, Fliss?"

As Sam waited for Fliss to go and check, Reg Ferryman hurriedly commanded the attention of his customers.

"Ladies and gents, due to unforeseen circumstances, tonight's Bottle Auction must regrettably be cancelled. Thank you for your interest. Gina!"

CHAPTER 35

Next to The Dog's Watch Inn was the hostelry that shared its name, but hardly any of its custom. It had been constructed, Charlie knew, as a late addition to the 1790 tavern, fuelled by a rumour that Stoneford was on the verge of becoming a destination for visitors desirous of bracing sea air and an escape from the unhealthy environs of London.

The rumour proved to be unfounded, and there had been no great influx of travellers. The accommodations which were attached to the inn did a middling trade, as they were convenient for wayfarers who had ridden in the mail coach from London. But the rooms were usually less than half occupied, and Charlie was of the opinion the hostel would have gone out of business altogether if it hadn't been for the thriving custom at the drinking establishment next door.

The accommodations were handy, however, for Lemuel Ferryman, as they happened to contain his lodgings. And on this particular Monday night, candlelight could be seen flickering through his upstairs bedroom window.

It was 11.30 pm.

Outside Mr. Ferryman's window—one floor below and on the ground—a certain amount of furtive activity was taking place.

While Charlie kept watch, four gentlemen—Augustus, Mr. Rankin, Mr. Wallis and Mr. Cole—silently crept up to the building.

Once there, Augustus quickly located the empty wooden cask that Mr. Ferryman had been sitting on earlier, toppled it, and rolled it against the exterior wall.

Upending it once more, he climbed onto its top, exhibiting, Charlie thought, a surprising amount of agility for a gentleman of his accumulated years.

"Mr. Rankin," he said, quietly and cordially, extending his hand, and the manor's gardener followed him up, aided by Mr. Wallis and Mr. Cole.

Mr. Rankin was not nearly as agile as Augustus. It took some careful manoeuvring and several unsuccessful attempts before he was able to clamber onto the older gentleman's shoulders, and raise himself—rather precariously—so that he could see directly through the window.

Feeling the gardener's full weight pressing down upon his shoulders, Augustus braced himself against the whitewashed wall of the hostelry.

"Make haste, Mr. Rankin," he suggested, in a loud whisper, "else I fear you may cause my internal workings an irreversible mischief. What do you see?"

"Mr. Ferryman," the gardener replied. "Snoring in a chair."

"And his keyring?"

"Attached to his waistcoat by way of a substantial chain."

"You have my permission to proceed, sir. At your earliest convenience."

Still balancing precariously atop Augustus' shoulders, Mr. Rankin reached into his pocket, and withdrew Charlie's mobile. He switched it on—having practised it several times earlier, under the greater Monsieur Duran's close tutelage—and expertly cued the tune he had personally chosen from Charlie's collection.

Mr. Rankin did not understand Charlie's phone. He hadn't pretended to know what caused it to light up, or how its internal workings were able to summon music at the simple touch of his finger. But he had accepted what the greater Monsieur Duran had shown him without question.

And now, holding the device up to the open window, Mr. Rankin touched Play. And the not unfamiliar twangs of Hank Marvin's lead guitar on *F.B.I.* loudly infiltrated Mr. Ferryman's bedroom, and, by default, his dreams.

There was a loud *thump*.

"Awake?" Augustus checked.

"Decidedly," Mr. Rankin confirmed. "And on the floor."

With swift precision, Mr. Wallis and Mr. Cole assisted him down from Augustus' shoulders and onto the ground.

The music continued to play as the four gentlemen repaired to the back of the building, concealing themselves from Mr. Ferryman, who, red-faced and befuddled, poked his head out through the open window.

Charlie remained where she was, hidden behind an obliging shrub.

Mr. Ferryman withdrew his head, and moments later, burst through the downstairs door, seeking the source of the strange sound that was assaulting his ears.

Charlie swigged from the bottle of laudanum that Augustus had entrusted to her care. The pain was just there, *there*, trying to break through.

She was running a fever. She was hot, so hot.

And now shivering.

Clutching the bottle, she watched as Lemuel Ferryman ran towards the vegetation that grew wild at the rear of the inn, tripping through the brambles and the grasses, the bushes and the thistles. Until, by the light of the moon, he spotted the device which was responsible for the strange musical noise. Propped against the woody trunk of an obliging rhododendron was Charlie's mobile, its little screen filled with colourful patterns that danced in time to the resounding guitars.

Bending down to examine the device further, his fear and unfamiliarity overcome by reckless curiosity, Mr. Ferryman extended a tentative finger. He was about to actually touch the screen when a sack was thrown over his head from behind, and he was hurled, unceremoniously, into the middle of the brambles.

Mr. Wallis held Mr. Ferryman to the ground, and Mr. Cole tightened his grip around the sack. Quickly, Mr. Rankin relieved the publican of his key ring, tossing it to Augustus, who caught it neatly and made an efficient departure towards the Dog's Watch's cellar.

Most of Reg Ferryman's customers had finished up and gone home.

Gina had rung the bell for last call, and was preparing to lock up for the night.

Only a few scattered diehards remained, downing their beers according to their own schedule, unmoved by the legal necessity of their removal from the pub in twenty minutes' time.

Nick slumped in the doorway, staring at his mobile, unable to convince himself that he was never going to see Charlie again. He'd brought her this far. He'd worked everything out. And now, he was going to lose her.

Why?

He shook his head.

"What do you want us to do?" Sam checked.

Nick glanced at the bar, where the stoppered glass bottle still stood, unopened, beneath the portrait of Reg's ancestor, Lemuel.

Regardless of Charlie's decision to stay in 1825, there was no way he was going to let the Ferryman brothers win. She'd buried that deed for a reason. It was her legacy.

The wrong, at last, made right.

"I need Mrs. Collins in Charlie's sitting room at midnight," Nick said, checking his watch.

"I thought Charlie told you she wasn't coming back."

"I refuse to believe that. And I can't risk not doing it. We only have one chance. We'll go ahead as planned. And whatever happens... happens."

"What about the bottle?"

"Bring it with you," Nick said.

"What," Sam said. "Just...take it?"

"It was never Reg's to begin with, Sam. Ron grabbed it out of my hands. And if that's really the deed inside, he doesn't have any claim to the land it was found in at all. Just take it."

Nick looked at his watch again.

Seventeen minutes.

"I'll just make sure there's room in the car for all four of us," Roger said, good-naturedly, downing the last of his best bitter.

And it was while Roger was rearranging things in the back seat of Sam's Civic that the Stoneford Constabulary arrived.

Screeching to a stop, PC Kevin Smith and PC Oswald Brown leaped out of their own car and raced into the pub, disappearing into Reg Ferryman's private room behind the bar.

Two minutes later, they emerged with Ron Ferryman between

them, followed by Reg.

"Blimey," said Gina. "Hiding in plain sight all along. Who'd have guessed it, Reg? Where were you keeping him all this time? Down the cellar inside a barrel?"

"Lock up, Gina," Reg replied, curtly, collecting the glass bottle from the top of the bar. "Everyone out. Pub's closed."

Alarmed, Sam looked at Nick, and silently mouthed: *What now?*

Nick was trying to work out just exactly what needed to be done next, when several details became obvious.

The first was that PC Smith and PC Brown had arrived without handcuffs, and were therefore only able to escort Ron Ferryman as far as the door before he dug in his heels and refused to go any further.

The second was that Roger Palmer, in his red wool 33rd Regiment of Foot jacket, was actually blocking the way out.

And the third was that, wielding Mrs. Collins' 1796 British Cavalry officer's sword before him with all the skill of a Battle of Waterloo veteran, Roger was now parrying his way across to the bar, and Reg Ferryman.

Aiming the point of the sword directly at Reg's chest, Roger deftly relieved him of the stoppered bottle.

"Many thanks," he said, tossing it across the room, where it was caught, neatly, by Mrs. Collins.

"Flee!" Mrs. Collins shouted, to Nick, Roger and Sam. "In haste!"

Shoving past Ron Ferryman and the two police constables, Nick, Roger, Sam and Mrs. Collins raced outside and dived into the Civic. Sam threw herself into the driver's seat and started the engine.

At that point, and almost simultaneously, Ron Ferryman decided that now would be an excellent time to make a run for it himself. Elbowing the two police constables aside, he darted out of the pub, and was caught in Sam's headlights as she jammed the Civic into reverse.

His eyes crazed with rage, Ron Ferryman glared at Mrs. Collins.

"You're not getting away this time!" he bellowed, as Sam's car screeched out of the parking lot. "If I'm going down, so are you!"

And he set out after them, running at top speed, chasing the car down the road that skirted the western edge of the Village Green, all the way to Charlie's cottage.

CHAPTER 36

There was a brisk wind blowing. Charlie could smell the sea.

As Mr. Cole and Mr. Wallis struggled to keep Lemuel Ferryman pinned to the ground, Mr. Rankin led three of the manor's quickest horses out into the open.

He smiled broadly as he spotted Augustus, accompanied by Mr. Deeley.

"Shaun," he said. "Here is your freedom. Monsieur Duran will ride with you to Southampton, and from there, you are guaranteed a safe passage across the channel to France."

"Three horses?" Mr. Deeley replied, rubbing the sleep from his eyes.

Charlie stepped out of the shadows, pale and shivering.

There was no need for words. She lost herself in Mr. Deeley's ready embrace. Regency manners be damned.

"And here we have a further conundrum," Augustus said, "and a regrettably insufficient amount of time in which to resolve it. For I fear, Mrs. Collins, that if you do not return from whence you came, you will almost certainly die."

"I will not return," Charlie answered, surprised by her ancestor's sudden change of heart. "I would rather flee to France with Mr. Deeley, and leave this world in his arms, than forsake him now. He is my everything. And there is nothing for me in the future."

"Wait," said Mr. Deeley, now fully awake. "You will die?"

Their attention was momentarily diverted to the rear of the inn, where there was a series of grunts, followed by a solid *thud*, and a far-too-satisfied and entirely inappropriate chuckle from Mr. Wallis.

"Yes," Charlie answered, bravely, gazing into Mr. Deeley's eyes.

"I will die. But I will do so willingly and without fear, for I will not abandon you…"

"But Monsieur Duran has told you that you may live," said Mr. Deeley, "if you return to your home."

"I do not wish it," Charlie replied simply, resting her head against his chest.

"But—what if I should wish it?" Mr. Deeley asked.

Charlie looked at him, her eyes filling with tears. "You should wish it…?"

"I love you," Mr. Deeley answered. "And it is my desire that you may live. For the knowledge that you are somewhere safe, and remembering me, would guarantee me the far greater joy. Even if we must forever afterwards be apart…"

And here his voice trailed away, and he was given to silence, as he again wrapped his arms around the woman he adored, and Charlie hid her face, and they stood for long moments, enveloped in sorrow.

"Might Mr. Deeley not travel with you, Mrs. Collins?" Augustus interrupted, gently, with a glance at the clock in the St. Eligius steeple.

11.55. Charlie turned her head, and looked at Augustus. "How?"

"I do not know how," he admitted. "I know only that I have pondered an endless stream of urgent messages from someone called Nick, on your device. He implores you to return, and speaks of you waiting in Mrs. Foster's sitting room at midnight. When you will be assisted back to your time. Why must Mr. Deeley be excluded from this journey?"

Augustus glanced again at the St. Eligius clock.

"I confess to a further interference," he said. "But I have thought upon it, and I believe this meddling will have no ill effect upon the present. Yet it will mean everything to your future, and to the future of Mr. Deeley. By this night's actions we have already altered the history books, as Mr. Deeley is clearly not destined to spend the rest of his life in an insane asylum. Unless we are very much more delayed and suffer the misfortune of being apprehended by Mr. Reader as the clock strikes twelve."

Charlie's mind was a muddle. It was becoming more and more

difficult to understand what she knew ought to have made logical sense. She took Mr. Deeley's hands into her own.

"Will you come with me, Mr. Deeley?"

"For you, Mrs. Collins," Mr. Deeley replied, "I will go anywhere."

"Then let us make haste," Augustus suggested. "There is very little time."

As Charlie, Mr. Deeley and Augustus ran along the western edge of the Village Green, Charlie faltered.

"I cannot," she whispered, overcome at last by the poison coursing through her body. "I cannot—"

And she fell, unconscious, onto the cobblestones just beyond the wooden garden gate.

"Tell me what I must do!" Mr. Deeley, shouted, panicking.

"You must wait in the sitting room," Augustus replied. "Beside the desk. That is all I that I know."

Gently, Mr. Deeley lifted Charlie's limp body into his arms. And then, racing against time, he staggered through the garden gate and kicked open the cottage door. He carried her through the kitchen and into the sitting room.

He watched, terrified, as her breaths grew short and laboured.

He knelt on the floor with her, cradling her head, holding her close.

Struggling back to awareness, Charlie grasped Mr. Deeley's shirt.

Something horrible was going on inside her.

Something had ruptured.

The pain was all-encompassing and beyond anything the laudanum could touch. She could feel its poison coursing through her veins, sapping away her life.

"Please don't leave me," she whispered.

"I will never leave you," Mr. Deeley promised, as the hands of the steeple clock at St. Eligius Church ticked over to midnight.

• • •

In the middle of Charlie's sitting room, grasping her cavalry sword, Mrs. Collins took her place next to the big wooden desk.

On the other side of the Village Green, the St. Eligius clock began to chime the strokes of midnight.

Five...six...

Nick opened the family tree program on Charlie's laptop.

There.

He clicked on Lucas Adams' entry.

Saw the square turn brilliant pink.

Saw the smallest of ripples in the room.

Seven...

"Stay in the garden!" Nick warned, waving Sam and Roger outside.

Eight...nine...

There was a commotion in the front garden. A scuffle.

Ten...

Eleven...

He clicked on Sarah Foster's square.

Brilliant mauve.

Ripples.

Small.

Then growing...

...washing forward like a surging tide...

Yes!

Nick bolted out of the sitting room, nearly colliding with Ron Ferryman as he crashed through the open kitchen door and made a bee-line for the sitting room.

"Don't go in there!" Nick shouted.

"Wait!" Mrs. Collins called, with urgency. "The bottle!"

As the St. Eligius clock chimed twelve, she hurled the glass bottle in the general direction of the kitchen, missing Ron Ferryman's ear by fractions of inches.

It crashed to the floor, shattering into pieces, as Ron Ferryman lunged at Mrs. Collins.

But it really didn't matter.

Because something else was beginning to happen. The furniture, carpets and curtains were starting to change, to dissolve…

The transparent wall of ripples pulsed forward, eddying like the surface of a vertical whirlpool.

And as Nick watched from the safety of the kitchen, it swallowed the sitting room.

And Mrs. Collins.

And Ron Ferryman.

Kneeling beside the wooden desk in Mrs. Foster's sitting room, Mr. Deeley wrapped his arms around Charlie, and listened as the last bell in the St. Eligius tower chimed twelve.

The sitting room was beginning to change. A raging waterfall was surging forward, cascading and tumbling, a deluge of thundering spray.

Swallowing hard, Mr. Deeley shut his eyes.

He hugged Charlie close.

And waited.

CHAPTER 37

The room in the Intensive Care wing of the Royal Memorial Hospital was crowded with monitors. Each of them flashed and beeped as it recorded a vital function of the patient who lay, unconscious and unresponsive, on a nearby bed.

Beside the bed, Fliss, the Acute Care nurse who had been assigned to Charlie, checked her blood pressure and respiration, her heart rate and oxygen levels, the various drips and drains, noting them all in her hour-by-hour logbook.

"How is she?" Nick asked, his face lined with worry. He'd been at her bedside since she'd been brought in. He'd notified her family. Her sister and brother in London had asked for regular updates. Her parents were on their way from Portugal.

"She's stable," Fliss replied. "No better…but no worse."

"Patients in deep coma have been known to recover completely," Sam added, quietly. "Mind you, patients in mild coma have died without ever regaining consciousness."

"I love your optimism," Nick said, testily.

"Just being realistic. Part of my training, I'm afraid."

"This world could sometimes do with a bit less of that realism," Nick said, taking Charlie's hand and holding it gently in his own. "Come on, Charlie. We need you. The hedgehogs need you. The Village Oak needs you."

Fliss finished the last of her hourly notations.

"Sometimes," she said, "it helps if you play a favourite song. Music seems to touch a different part of the brain than the spoken word."

Nick pulled his mobile out of his jacket pocket, and switched it on. He searched his music library, found what he wanted, and then placed his phone on the pillow next to Charlie's head.

It was a song that The Shadows had recorded decades earlier. One of their earliest compositions, credited to their manager but later revealed to have been written by Hank Marvin, with help from his band-mates.

"My favourite," Charlie'd once told him. "Jeff's too."

The pounding introduction on guitar and drums filled the hospital room. The twanging lead line on Hank's red Fender Strat seemed to synchronize with the illuminated peaks and valleys and blips on the monitors.

F.B.I.

As Nick and Sam watched, Charlie stirred. There was a flicker of something behind her eyelids, a fleeting glimpse of a small awareness, so brief and so tiny that it might almost have been imagined.

The music filled Charlie's mind.

She was sitting on a white linen picnic cloth on the grassy hillside, surrounded by wildflowers and butterflies and misty trees. She could see a herd of sheep grazing nearby, and, in the distance, Stoneford Manor.

She was sitting alone. But she could see Tom and Jack, with their home-made kites, and Mary, picking buttercups with Sarah.

It didn't seem real to her. It was more like a dream.

It was as if she wasn't quite there.

And that music...that lingering familiar tune...where was it coming from?

Not from her phone. She hadn't even brought it with her. She'd left it...where had she left it? She couldn't remember.

Her gaze shifted, and she saw Mr. Deeley, lovely Mr. Deeley, strolling across the face of the hill, on the footpath that had been worn into the turf by generations of travellers.

She waved.

But Mr. Deeley didn't see her.

Surprised, then frustrated, she tried to get to her feet…but was held back by a deep pain in her abdomen. Not the same pain as before. Something different.

She struggled to stand…but succeeded only in getting to her knees. She waved again.

Surely he could see her now.

Surely.

Mr. Deeley stopped walking. He looked at Charlie.

But as he stood looking, Charlie collapsed back to the ground, struggling to breathe.

She fought to stay conscious as Mr. Deeley ran towards her.

Reaching her at last, he dropped to his knees, and as she lost her battle with consciousness, he leaned over her, kissing her, tenderly, on her lips…

In the hospital room, Charlie lay on her back, her eyes closed.

Mr. Deeley was kissing her, and she wished the kiss never to end.

The monitors beside her bed registered a skip in her heartbeat, an increase in her respiration…

Her eyelids flickered.

"Fetch the nurse," Sam said urgently, to Nick.

Charlie opened her eyes, and was momentarily confused. She could see him…and yet…

"Mr. Deeley," she whispered, uncertainly. "Are you here? Or are you there…?"

CHAPTER 38

It had been a month.

And while Charlie had been recovering in hospital, the Village Oak had staged a small recuperation of its own.

According to Mike Tidman, who had visited his favourite patient daily, its condition was beginning to stabilize.

Meticulously excavating the contaminated soil from the roots on the north, east and south sides of the tree seemed to have halted the progress of the poison. Mike's workers had layered the roots with a mixture of charcoal and microbes, to help break down the herbicide that still coursed through the oak's vascular system. Then, they had brought in truckloads of fresh, clean topsoil to replace what had been removed.

It was only the west side of the tree that still needed attention. The ground had not been broken in order to maintain the oak's stability. A scaffold was being built to support the roots in the new soft soil. And once the props were in place, Mike's crew were going to finish the job.

In the meantime, there had been no more showers of dead leaves from the spreading branches. And the beginnings of tiny buds could now be seen, the promise of new and sustained life.

Charlie walked the short distance from the museum to the Village Green, where Nick was waiting by the low stone wall.

The reporters and politicians were long gone. The Tree Protectors had wandered home. The triangular patch of grass at the heart of Stoneford had returned to its quiet contemplation.

The green was not, however, deserted.

In the corner closest to Poorhouse Lane, Reg Ferryman, in a bright blue hard hat, was consulting with his brother's contracted workmen. Ron Ferryman himself had not been seen, or heard from, since the night of July the fourth, when he'd been witnessed running into Charlie's cottage.

A bulletin had been issued for his immediate arrest. The ports and airports had been alerted.

Next to Reg, two bulldozers stood by in readiness, all tires mended and re-inflated, ready for duty. The battle for the Village Green might temporarily have been put on hold by the tree's near-miraculous recovery, but there was nothing to stop the development of the land at the end of Poorhouse Lane.

"Have you brought it?" Nick asked.

"Indeed I have," Charlie replied.

"Then let's do this. It's about time."

They walked together, to the little gathering at the edge of the green.

"Good morning," Charlie said, to Reg. "I don't actually believe you have the legal right to proceed on this project, Mr. Ferryman. So I think it best that you cease your operations, in order to avoid a lengthy, and costly, court case challenging your purported ownership."

"Mrs. Lowe," Reg replied, in an amused voice. "And upon whose authority might you be acting?"

"Upon my own authority, Mr. Ferryman," Charlie replied, unfolding the fragile piece of paper she was carrying, and allowing him to read it. "See the name on the deed?"

Reg squinted at the ink-quilled signature.

"And who's John Harding when he's at home, then?"

"He's my great grandfather," Charlie said. "Nine generations back. I have the documents that establish the line of descendancy. And this piece of paper proves the Village Green and that land at the end of Poorhouse Lane belong to my family. Not to yours."

Reg Ferryman roared with laughter. "It's a forgery!" he exclaimed. "The deed was destroyed in a fire in 1825! We all know that, Mrs. Lowe. Even you!"

"There was indeed a fire in 1825," Charlie said. "But it did not destroy the deed. That's a piece of misinformation which I intend to correct."

"And how do you know that? Were you there?"

Charlie, wisely, said nothing.

"Bit suspicious, that," Reg said, turning to address the contractors. "All of a sudden, this mysterious piece of paper comes to light? You can make anything these days on a computer."

"You're welcome to look it up at the Land Registry office," Charlie suggested. "You'll find the other half of this deed—the official registration—in their historical archives. It took a lot of hunting, especially as it seems to have been deliberately misfiled, and would never have been found at all but for Nick's persistence. The two sides match up exactly. We've had them verified."

"As I said," Reg repeated. "You can make anything these days on a computer."

"But not," Nick said, "a DNA match."

"Eh?"

Nick took back the piece of paper. A precautionary act.

"See this?" he said, pointing out the rusty brown stains at the paper's top edge. "Blood. Belonging, we think, to my ancestor, Artemus Weller, a notorious smuggler in 19th century Hampshire. Mysteriously disappeared in 1825. Most believe he was murdered. We've had the blood analyzed, and it's a definite match back to me."

"What's that got to do with anything?" Reg said, suspiciously.

"Why don't you tell us, Mr. Ferryman? You've already acknowledged that Charlie's family once owned the land. We think you've known all along that Charlie's ancestor gave the deed to Artemus as payment for an outstanding gambling debt. And that your ancestor, Lemuel Ferryman, murdered Artemus in cold blood in order to steal the deed and claim it as his own. This small patch of blood here—"

Nick paused, to point out one further stain, at the bottom of the paper.

"—is not related to me. However I propose that if we were to extract a vial of your blood, Mr. Ferryman, and have it analyzed, we might find a very good DNA match to you."

"Proves nothing," Reg maintained, although he was clearly unsettled by Nick's accusations. "And where's that piece of paper been all this time, then, eh?"

"Here," Charlie said. "Under your very nose."

One of the workmen—perhaps he was a foreman—stepped forward. His name was Aldous Reader, and his ancestors had lived in Stoneford for generations.

"I think," he said, "that you ought to reconsider your plans, Mr. Ferryman. I think that you ought to at least seek legal counsel before going any further. I'm not prepared to order my men to undertake work on what could be an illegal jobsite."

"Now is probably not the most opportune time," Charlie added, "for you to make a grave error in judgement, Mr. Ferryman. Especially as your brother is currently a wanted man. And the tabloids are only a phone call away. They like a good scandal."

"I'll see you in court," Reg promised angrily, whipping off his hard hat. "There's still the matter of you breaking into Ron's office and vandalizing his computer."

"Looking forward to it," Charlie replied. "Without your brother to testify, I don't believe there's any proof that was me. Since the fingerprints the vandal left behind were far too smudged to be of any use."

Reg Ferryman stormed off without looking back.

"It's amazing what comes to light when you start digging around in your past, isn't it, Mr. Ferryman?" Charlie called after him, with a satisfied smile.

A little later on, while Charlie was tossing scraps of her baguette lunch to the pigeons, Nick paused to watch the completion of the wooden scaffolding that was going to brace the Village Oak during its final stages of rehabilitation.

And as was his habit, he took out his mobile, and checked for messages.

Naomi's birthday had been an unqualified success. And the car she'd been hinting about had, of course, been delivered. Smiling, he downloaded a picture of his eldest daughter removing her L plates. She had passed her driving test. His life as a father was never going to be the same.

There was a second message.

Nick had to look twice at its sender, and at the date.

How could it be from Charlie? Charlie was just over there, sitting on old Emmy Cooper's favourite bench. The one that had been fashioned out of a limb severed from the Village Oak after the famous lightning strike of Wednesday, June 1, 1825.

Curiously, Nick opened the message.

It wasn't from Charlie at all.

It had, however, been sent from her phone.

"I've received something," Nick said, "from your past. Look."

Charlie stared at Nick's mobile.

It was a photo of the assembled members of a wedding party, standing on the steps of St. Eligius Church. There was Augustus. And beside him, Sarah. And there were Tom, and Jack, and Mary, in their best Sunday clothes, beaming. And there was Mr. Rankin. All were waving at the camera.

"Oh," Charlie said, as her heart fluttered, and then leaped. "But it was always going to happen, wasn't it, Nick. Because I'm here now. And I wouldn't be, if all this hadn't taken place."

"Also," Nick said, consulting his phone, "I'm to tell you that Jack has learned to sew buttons on his shirt. Tom has been apprenticed to the manor, as a stable boy. Mary has made friends with a young man named Richard Tamworth, the son of the village surgeon, and is teaching him to turn cartwheels. And Mrs. Collins, who apparently took the picture, has found herself enamored of Mr. Rankin, and, as the attraction is mutual, she has decided to remain in Stoneford as plans for their own marriage are now being made."

Charlie smiled. She contemplated the birdbath, perched atop its stone pedestal, which bore the inscription about Stoneford's first suffragette, Mrs. Mary Tamworth.

Mary Tamworth.

Of course.

"One more thing."

Charlie dragged her attention back to Nick.

He read the message aloud.

"I have been guided by the clever idea you devised to deliver the deed to your cousin. I have borrowed a tin box from Mary. She was using it to collect buttons, but assures me she will find another. If you will investigate the ground between the two largest roots of the oak tree, on the opposite side to where we buried your bottle, you will discover the box. It will contain the device I am using to send this message, as it tells me there is only 5% battery power left, and it will shortly cease to function. I will also include a letter, written by my hand on this day, which will provide some further news."

Nick switched off his phone.

"Shall we dig…?"

CHAPTER 39

The tin box was ancient and rusty, and its corners were crumbling. But it was where Augustus had promised it would be, and it was intact.

Charlie sat alone at her ancient desk, almost afraid to look inside. The box's retrieval had been something of an event, with the editor of the *Stoneford Village Post* wanting to write a story around the idea of buried treasure, and Natalie, from the museum, suggesting that if it contained anything of historical value, she'd be happy to put through a requisition to purchase it for a display.

Charlie had no intention of sharing any of it.

Taking a deep breath, she opened the lid.

There was her phone.

In very good shape, all things considered.

She switched it on.

Nothing.

She'd expected that. The battery had been dead for more than 200 years.

She attached it to its plug, and watched, amazed, as a graphic appeared on the little screen, indicating it was preparing to charge.

And, as promised, underneath the phone, there was a letter.

With great care, Charlie lifted it out, and unfolded the paper. There were several pages of script, handwritten with a quill and ink.

Captivated, she began to read.

> *My dear Mrs. Collins (though this seems to me to be a form of address which is no longer appropriate, as you have explained to me that you are in fact Charlotte Duran, my descendant, and therefore not Mrs. Collins at all),*

I bring you news that will allow me to close the chapter on what have been the most extraordinary days of my life time. And perhaps the facts as I describe them will allow you to gain some knowledge as to what happened once the midnight clock ceased its chime, and I ceased to disbelieve what my eyes had, at that most astonishing moment, beheld.

You will recall that, with the assistance of Mr. Wallis, Mr. Rankin and Mr. Cole, the keeper of the keys, Mr. Ferryman, was rendered incapable for some minutes leading up to the aforementioned events.

I am sorry to say that this indisposition was only temporary.

Understanding that they might be accused of causing grievous harm to Mr. Ferryman's person, Mr. Wallis, Mr. Rankin and Mr. Cole thought it best to repair elsewhere, quickly and with my blessing. They had spoken no words during the execution of their duties. They left nothing behind which might allow Mr. Ferryman to recognize them.

For my part, I remained in the kitchen of the cottage belonging to Mrs. Foster (who is now my dear wife, and may call herself, entirely without regret, Mrs. Duran).

As I first observed the sitting room, I feared that nothing whatsoever had happened, other than a peculiar effect on my sight which had lasted mere moments, and which had ceased as quickly as it had begun.

There was Mr. Deeley. And there you were. Although your circumstances were very much altered. Both of you wore clothing which to me was unfamiliar. Additionally, you were armed with a sword, which I did not recall at all.

It was Mr. Deeley who convinced me that a great change had, indeed, taken place. His eyes grew wild as he beheld his surroundings. He looked at you (although it was not you, as I now know), and then at me. And then, with a roar, he fled from the room, and ran through the kitchen, into the night.

And there, my dearest granddaughter, I am sorry to say, he was discovered by Mr. Ferryman and Mr. Reader, wandering without aim, the victim of a windblown tree branch landing squarely upon his head.

Dementia has now ensued.

He speaks nonsense, and insists he does not belong to this time. He demands to be addressed as Mr. Ferryman. He denies all knowledge of the circumstances of the fire, does not recognize any of his friends, and is a most disobliging individual to all he encounters.

He has been returned to the gaol, where he has been examined by the surgeon, Mr. Tamworth. There will be no trial, as it is Mr. Tamworth's learned opinion that this unfortunate soul should be sent to London, there to be housed in the asylum for the insane, for the rest of his days.

Charlie put down the letter.

The historical documents weren't wrong, after all.

She smiled at her Dali clock, which was ticking round to midnight.

She turned the paper over.

And lastly, I will tell you about my son. I have excellent knowledge of this event, as I was present when it took place.

You will recall that Lemuel Ferryman's establishment is so far damaged by the fire that it requires restoration. This continues apace.

In the meantime, Mr. Ferryman's regular custom has repaired to The Rose and Crown.

It was there, some days ago, that you might have observed my son, Louis, seated at a table, addressing a tankard of ale.

His mood was, I would judge, foul. I had arranged for a gentleman of my acquaintance to meet with him, to discuss his sanitary invention, and the gentleman was, alas, proving to be exceedingly late in arriving.

Rising from my chair, I offered to look outside, to observe whether our friend could be seen upon the road.

Once outside, I did not encounter my friend. However, there were four other gentlemen riding into view upon some very fine horses.

One of the villagers—Algernon Oldbutter, who I have been told arranges funerals—was standing beside me as we observed these four horsemen. He took his leave very quickly, and went inside The Rose and Crown, and with apparently well-understood remarks, let it be known that Conquest, War, Famine and Death were about to descend.

Therefore, by the time the four gentlemen themselves had reached the front door of the inn, most of those inside had exited by way of the door at the back. The exceptions were the elderly, the lame, a consumptive, the publican himself, and my son.

I did not acknowledge the four, although in truth I will tell you that I have had a longstanding acquaintance with the first, Mr. Samuel Brown. And I will admit to you, for I know my words will go no further, that I had engaged him in a close conversation a few hours earlier.

"Good evening, sirs!" the publican said, greeting them honestly.

"Good evening," said Mr. Brown. "You are unlucky this night, Mr. Marsden. Your custom is diminished."

"No thanks to you," Mr. Marsden replied, without any hint of disrespect. "What will you drink?"

"Four of your best," the second horseman replied. "And one more for the gentleman at the table beside the window. He seems lacking in social congress."

"With the greatest of pleasure," Mr. Marsden answered, pouring and delivering the tankards, as the four gentlemen invited themselves to my son's table.

"Good evening to you, sir," Mr. Brown said, by way of a friendly introduction.

"Is it," my son answered, unhappily, as he had descended into quite a foul mood, which the consumption of alcohol had only enhanced.

I sat in my chair again, and inquired after the nature of their business in Stoneford.

"I am acquainted with your son," said Mr. Brown, revealing no hint that he knew me as well. And then, to Louis: "You must remember me, sir. We were introduced at your Grand Summer Ball. I am a friend of Mr. and Mrs. Montagu, from Bournemouth. You invited me to share a drink with you should our paths ever have occasion to cross in the village. I am Samuel Brown."

My son, who had by then consumed the better part of four ales, was confounded, as he did not recall an introduction to Mr. Brown at all.

"No matter," said Mr. Brown. "I see you have brought drawings with you. Are these the plans for your sanitary device?"

"You know of my invention?" Louis inquired, with a good deal of surprise.

"But of course!" Mr. Brown said, with assurance. "Word of your invention has spread as far as Southampton in one direction and Bournemouth in the other. I might venture to say the Duran Cistern and Water Closet will be a permanent fixture in households well into the next century. Come, sir—show me the drawings!"

It was while my son was explaining his sketches to Mr. Brown, and engaging him in the most engrossing details concerning pipage and effluent, that the second horseman, whose name was Lucas Adams, went to the bar. There, he requested another round of drinks. And as the drinks were carried from the bar by Mr. Marsden, Mr. Adams dropped a coin into the tankard meant for Louis.

This action, witnessed by me, did not go unnoticed by Mr. Marsden, nor by the several elderly gentlemen sitting nearby, nor by the consumptive in the corner. For their part, the other three horsemen barely looked, and if they did see what he had done, they showed no sign of recognition or acknowledgement.

Mr. Marsden placed the cups upon the table.

"Drink up, my fine friends," Mr. Brown suggested. "The long day is ending, and the merry night is before us."

I drank from my tankard.

And my son drank from his.

I will end this letter now, my dear granddaughter, as I believe you will surmise what fate had in store for Louis. I entertain the hope that you will not think any the less of me for my interferences. Indeed, where you are now, you may have more knowledge than I concerning my lamentable son's adventures. It will do him, and the village of Stoneford, some tolerable good if he sees more of the world in the years to come.

I remain, with affection and respect, Monsieur Louis Augustus Duran (the Greater).

CHAPTER 40

Dressed in her 19th century frock, Charlie was once again immersed in her role as the museum's Historical Guide and Interpreter. Although, since the successful sale of her now-complete deck of antique Tarot cards by Sotheby's in London, she had no real need to keep working. Her job description had reverted to that of enthusiastic volunteer.

She had shared some of her windfall with the museum, which had allowed them to create a new Nautical Display that explored Stoneford's links to its seafaring past. And she had donated a substantial sum to the Village of Stoneford, so that the square of unoccupied land at the end of Poorhouse Lane could be turned into a garden, with trees and grass, meandering paths, flowering shrubs, a playground for children and seats in the shade for the elderly. It was going to be called Emmy Cooper Park, and the grand ribbon cutting was tomorrow afternoon.

This morning, however, she was explaining the new Nautical Display to a group of curious seven-year-olds on a day excursion from school.

"Two hundred years ago, when your great great great great—"

Here Charlie paused, and drew in a deep breath.

"—great great…how many greats is that?"

"Six!" the children shouted, in clever unison.

"…great grandparents were alive…life was very hard for the sailors. They had to deal with terrible food and really brutal working conditions. So it wasn't surprising that nobody ever volunteered to join up."

Charlie picked up a pewter tankard from the plank board display table.

"But the Royal Navy needed able-bodied men to crew its warships, and so they resorted to press gangs."

She held out the tankard so that the children could observe its see-through bottom.

"Now—what do you think you might drink out of this cup?"

"I know what my granddad would drink!" a small boy with red hair and a face older than his years piped up from the back, to much giggling.

"These press gangs went into the pubs," Charlie continued. "They were especially well known in one of Stoneford's inns, the old Rose and Crown. There, they plied their targets with ale until they were drunk."

Charlie feigned falling to the floor in a hazy stupor, to more gleeful giggling.

"And the next thing they knew," she said, in a loud whisper, peering up over the edge of the table, "they were guests aboard one of His Majesty's warships."

"But why's the cup got a see-through bottom?" the small boy with the red hair persisted.

Charlie got to her feet.

"Well," she said, confidentially. "I'll tell you, shall I? While our poor would-be sailor was distracted, someone from the press gang would drop a coin into his cup."

Charlie picked up a big brown 1d coin the museum had saved from the 1960s and plinked it into the mug.

"He'd drink his ale—and by doing that, unknowingly, he'd signal that he was accepting the King's Shilling. And whether he was aware of it or not, he'd now officially volunteered for service."

Charlie held the mug up so that the children could see the coin inside.

"Publicans everywhere became so concerned about losing their customers that they introduced glass-bottomed tankards. That way, people could discover what else was in their ale before they drank it down."

"Wouldn't help my granddad!" the red-haired boy from the

back piped up. "He'd be so rubbered he'd forget to look!"

Charlie smiled, and led the children to the second part of the display, The Smugglers and Pirates Den, in what had once been Reverend and Mrs. Hobson's bedroom.

"Here you can see," she said, "some of the caskets the smugglers used to bring illicit liquor ashore. One of their favorite landing spots was just down the beach, at Stoneford Bunny. And this is what the living quarters were really like if you were an ordinary sailor aboard a pirate ship. Pretty grim, really."

Charlie waited while the children explored the below-decks mockup. She then took them to a collection of posters she'd researched and sourced online. Not the originals, but very good reproductions.

"And this is a poster, printed about 1830, warning villagers all along the south coast about a particularly troublesome pirate, Louis Duran."

"Never heard of him," said the red-haired boy, who, Charlie was convinced, likely knew the names of every raider and rover in Hampshire. And was likely descended from one.

"He wasn't very well known to historians," she replied. "Although he was, in his life before going to sea, quite well known here in the village. He once lived in the manor on the hill, which you'll be visiting later."

She perched on one of the upended casks to continue the tale.

"He was one of those unfortunate gentlemen who ended up being press-ganged into the King's Navy," she said. "And his protests that he was a citizen of France were completely ignored, as he'd chosen England as his home. But, after some years of service, Louis Duran decided he'd acquired all of the knowledge he'd need in order to mark his place in history. So, on a sunny morning in June, 1830, this sailor, who was destined to become known as the slightly dreaded *Petit Pirate Barbu*—he was quite short, and had by then grown a rather unruly beard—grasped a stout rope in his hands and swung to the main deck of one of the King's ships, off the coast of Jamaica. He seized the vessel, spearheaded a mutiny, and cast the Captain and several obstinate but loyal crew members adrift in a small boat."

"What happened to him?" the red-haired boy asked, his eyes wide with a renewed spirit of adventure.

"We don't know," Charlie said, darkly. "He terrorized the seas for some years, caused a good deal of alarm in Stoneford when it was rumoured he might return to avenge a perceived, but long forgotten, wrong…and then…he disappeared. Although there was a possible reported sighting of him in Australia, where a gentleman answering his description was observed trying to interest the locals in something he'd invented…a variation on what you now know as the flushing loo."

Charlie stood up. The red-haired boy was giving her a sceptical look. She smiled.

"Come along outside," she said. "And we'll continue the tour."

The other project Charlie had financed was the one she'd dreamed about since she'd first discovered the ancient wagon in the ramshackle shed at the back of The Old Vicarage.

The wagon had been restored. It was truly magnificent now, painted in the colours of the Royal Mail. The upper part of its box was a beautiful glossy black, its wheels and underneath bits were a brilliant scarlet, and its lower half was a chocolate brown. And with the help of a local farmer, Horace Inkersby, the museum had launched a horse-drawn tour that took children around the village, to all the historical sites, and then up Manor Rise, for a picnic.

The wagon, and its driver—wearing clothing that would not have been out of place in 1825, including a bright red handkerchief knotted around his neck—awaited.

"Hello, Mr. Deeley," Charlie said, with great fondness.

"Hello, Mrs. Collins," Mr. Deeley replied, with equal affection.

He helped her aboard. And then assisted the children. And finally, Nick, who had decided to join them, as he had a free afternoon and was as nosy as an old woman when it came to Charlie's love life.

After ensuring that all of the children, and Nick, were safely accounted for, Mr. Deeley took his place beside Charlie on the seat, and jiggled the reins.

"Our first stop," he announced, "is The Dog's Watch Inn. You are all too young to have seen the inside of this establishment, but I can tell you that it once did double duty as the village lock-up."

"I'm not too young," Nick said.

"And I've been in the village lock-up," Charlie added, sharing a secret smile with Mr. Deeley.

Mr. Deeley drove the wagon into the pub's parking lot, and stopped.

"Downstairs is a horrible dark cellar where the inhabitants of this village—guilty and innocent alike—were imprisoned until it was their turn to stand before the magistrate."

"Were there rats?" asked the red-headed boy.

"Rats," Mr. Deeley confirmed. "Spiders. Great creepy crawling things with six legs and enormous eyes."

The children peered over the sides of the wagon at the pub, studying its foundations with a renewed interest.

Charlie turned around, so that she was facing Nick.

"I'm perplexed," she said. "How is it that Ron Ferryman and Mrs. Collins switched places with me and Mr. Deeley, and Mrs. Collins arrived as herself in 1825, but Ron Ferryman was immediately mistaken for Mr. Deeley?"

"I don't know," Nick answered, truthfully.

"And how is it that I can arrive back here, and everyone knows it's me…but Mr. Deeley is not mistaken for Ron Ferryman at all, and is immediately accepted as himself, with no questions asked?"

"It's one of those mysteries," Nick replied, "that has yet to be solved. And the best I can do is theorize that when Ron Ferryman accidentally crossed into Mrs. Collins' spatial plane, her act of throwing the bottle past his head resulted in a spurious positive charge at one end of the space-time continuum. Which in turn caused a simultaneous delinquent discrepancy at the other end. And there was an anomaly in the persistence of memory."

Charlie looked at her cousin. And then at Mr. Deeley. And then at her cousin again.

"An anomaly in the persistence of memory…?"

"It's a term we use in physics," Nick said, "to account for anything to do with shifts in collective awareness which can't otherwise be scientifically explained. If you're active in the anomaly—if you're a catalyst, for instance—you cause a ripple, an incongruous plop, that can't be rationalized, although you can very definitely observe the result."

"That's all you are, then," Charlie said, nudging Mr. Deeley. "An incongruous plop."

Mr. Deeley considered this suggestion for some moments.

"He really doesn't know, does he?" he concluded.

"He doesn't," Charlie said.

"Next," Mr. Deeley announced, to the children, "I am going to take you up the hillside, and show you what used to be a very grand manor, with servants and gardens, a stable, horses and a truly excellent groom."

"Will there be tea?" the red-headed boy inquired, mindful of the refreshments promised in the brochure that had advertised the tour.

"Tea," Mr. Deeley confirmed, "fizzy drinks, sandwiches, crisps and chocolate. Served in a very special picnic spot up on the hillside."

He nudged Charlie back.

"I anticipate no incongruous plops."

He jiggled the reins attached to the Clydesdale's harness.

"Come along, Marie-Claire…let us continue our adventure."

IN LOVING MEMORY

"Kent combines time travel, mystery, and romance
in a delightful sequel to *Persistence of Memory*
that's easily accessible for new readers."
—*Publishers Weekly* Starred Review

In this mesmerizing romance, a woman out of time falls in love with a man for whom time is running out.

In Winona Kent's novel *Persistence of Memory*, Charlie Lowe, a young widow in Stoneford, England, was accidentally transported back to 1825, where she fell in love with Shaun Deeley, a groom employed at Stoneford Manor. They are only back in the present for seemingly a breath before a piece of wartime shrapnel sends them tumbling back through time to 1940, the height of the Blitz. There, they discover pieces of Charlie's past that counter everything she thought she knew about herself.

Charlie and Shaun have decisions to make—do they interfere in time's progress to save a man? Do they put their own future at risk by doing nothing? And how much time do these two lovers have left?

SKYWATCHER

Robin Harris grew up watching the 60's spy show Spy Squad, starring his dad, Evan Harris. So when the police deem the mysterious death of a Russian woman with rainbow-colored hair a suicide, Robin knows better.

Robin soon finds himself in the middle of an awesome plot that seems to be lifted directly from one of his father's old Spy Squad episodes, and, as he discovers, his father really was a spy. Now Robin and his brothers have inadvertently walked onto the scene of a real life-

and-death spy drama, and as far as the free world is concerned, Robin's entrance into the family business comes not a moment too soon.

THE CILLA ROSE AFFAIR

A novel of espionage, intrigue, and mysterious sound waves underneath London.

Evan Harris's experiences as a spy helped make him a star playing one on TV. When Britain's best-loved breakfast show DJ dies, only Evan knows what it has to do with a pirate radio station, a long-lost diary, a suspected double agent, the London Underground, and mysterious sound waves underneath the Fitzroy Theatre.

So Evan recruits his three sons to help him unmask the traitor deep within the British spy community in a sting operation not unlike a storyline from his own cult 1960's TV show...

COLD PLAY

Jason Davey ran away to sea after the death of his wife, finding work as a contract entertainer aboard a cruise ship, the Star Sapphire. But when faces from his past come aboard as passengers, Jason's routine week-long trip to Alaska becomes anything but relaxing.

Jason's wife once worked for Diana Wyndham, a beautiful and eccentric actress. And hard-drinking ex-rocker, Rick Redding, once toured with a band Jason has strong ties to. Now Diana occupies one of the ship's luxury suites, and Rick dwells in the stateroom next door. Between them, they may know more about Jason's secret past than anyone suspects.

Jason narrates his—and the Sapphire's—story with drama, humor, and a touch of the supernatural as he tries to survive a trial by fire and ice on the journey to Juneau, Skagway and Glacier Bay.

CPSIA information can be obtained at www.ICGtesting.com
Printed in the USA
BVOW08s0614160816

459169BV00004B/72/P